MOZART

The Protagonist

Copywright @ Jeff Murray

2024

All rights reserved

The rights of Jeff Murray, identified as the author of this work has been asserted in accordance with Sections 77 and 78 of the Copywrights, Designs and Patents Act 1988.

This is a work of fiction. Characters, Corporations, Institutions and Organizations in this novel are either the product of the author's imagination or, if real, used fictitiously without any intent to describe their actual conduct.

Acknowledgements

This novel is intended to be the first of two which are prequels to my debut crime novel, **THE FAMILY BUSINESS – OPERATION FORSYTH.**

It is intended to show the history and adventures of the Mozart Family, from their origins in pre-World War 2 Austria, through the war, until this branch of the family morphed into becoming British. The story spans the period, pre-world war 2, to modern times, and uncovers the history and dark family secrets of the Mozart family along the way.

I have to thank many people for encouraging me to continue writing, especially my wife Sonia, for her support as I isolated myself in hours of research and composition.

I would also like to express my gratitude to my friend David and his wife Sue for their support, editing skills, and plot suggestions, which kept me focused and on message.

There are many other people, too many to mention, who have also helped with their encouragement, especially those who read my first novel and wanted more. This book is dedicated to my family and them.

I hope you enjoy the journey of the Mozart family through, what was for them, very trying and dark times.

There is more to come…….

Jeff Murray

June 2024.

Luftwaffe Ranks

GERMAN	BRITISH
SCHUTZE	PRIVATE
GEFREITER	LANCE CORPORAL
OBERGEFREITER	CORPORAL
HAUPGEFREITER	SENIOR CORPORAL
UNTEROFFIZIER	SERGEANT
UNTERFELDWEBEL	STAFF SERGEANT
FELDWEBEL	SERGEANT 1st CLASS
OBERFELDWEBEL	MASTER SERGEANT
STABSFELDWEBEL	SERGEANT MAJOR
LEUTNANT	2nd LIEUTENANT
OBERLEUTNANT	1st LIEUTENANT
HAUPTMANN	CAPTAIN
MAJOR	MAJOR

OBERSTLEUTNANT	LIEUTENANT COLONEL
OBERST	COLONEL
GENERALMAJOR	BRIGADIER GENERAL
GENERALLEUTNANT	MAJOR GENERAL
GENERAL	LIEUTENANT GENERAL
GENERALOBERST	GENERAL
GENERALFELDMARSHALL	FIELD MARSHALL

Schedule of Characters
(In order of appearance in story)

Name	History
Dr. Maximillian Mozart	Joseph Mozart's father
Joseph Eckart Mozart	Student- ME 109 pilot
Dr Frederick Von Schmidt	Joseph's headmaster
Walter Baumgarten	Joseph's school friend
Ernest Bruen	Older student – Bully – SA member
William Camden	1st Headmaster – Westminster school. England
Robert Kronfeld	Champion Gilder pilot Escaped to England
Fabien Von Weiser (Baron)	Glider instructor & Luftwaffe pilot.

John Christie	Headmaster – Westminster School
Hon. James Cavendish	Headboy – Westminster school
Jonas Pilkinton-Ward	Anti-Nazi pupil. Westminster school
McKenzie	Pupil. Son of Canadian Ambassador
Menzies	Pupil. Son of Scottish Laird
Munroe	Pupil. American
Wilhemina Stone	Matron – Westminster school
Cliff Wyatt	Housemaster. Westminster School
Thomas Webb	Sports Master
Jacob Picozzi	Maths teacher
Heinz Bruen	Father of Ernst Bruen
Jurgen Engels	Stammfurhrer – Vienna Hitler Youth
Johann Fischer	Innsbruck University

Rudolph Leitner	Innsbruck Hitler Youth
Tomas Jager	Student – Innsbruck University
Ernst Mayer	Colonel – Innsbruck Hitler Youth
Dr Boris Schaffer	German Armed Forces Medical Unit
Leutnant Muller	Adjutant to Dr. Schaffer
Hauptmann Hans Reiter	Luftwaffe recruiting officer
Col. Heinz Wagner	Commandant – Flight training school
Oberstleutnant Boris Konig	Chief Instructor – Flying school
Major Horst Leitner	Flying Instructor. Brother of Rudolph
Hauptmann Erik Schaffer	Orly Flying School
Leutnant Petr Muller	Flying trainee - Orly
Gen. Major Otto Schwarbe	Commandant – Orly flying school

Major Heinrich Von Graf	Chief Instructor - Orly
Hauptmann Erik Jager	Mozart's flying instructor
Oberst Karl Von Kaufmann	Commandant Alakurtii Air Base
Baroness Ursula Von Ritter	Wife of Baron Von Ritter
Marta Von Hase	Friend of above
Louis Aldon	Owner – Aldon Hotel, Berlin
Gen. Eberhart Von Ritter	Commandant Orly Air Base
Major Reinhart Wagner	Staffel leader – Orly airbase
Shutze Freidrich Koch	Orderly to Mozart
Hauptmann Matthias Brockner	Intelligence officer - Orly
Annaliese Von Weisner	Major Von Weisner's sister
Baroness Sophia Von Weiser	Mother of above
Bauer	Manservant of above

Emma Mozart	Mozart's mother
Prof. Joachim Kaufmann	Surgeon – friend of Mozazrt family
Dr Edgar Wheatley	RAMC – Shoebury Barracks
Wing Commander Hugo Randall	Commandant – Flixton POW camp
Gen. Darius Ahren	New Commander – Orly Air Base
Dr. Maurice Key	Flixton POW Camp
Leutnant Paul Schaffer	POW Flixton Camp
George Ward	Flixton Farmer
Martha Ward	Daughter of above
Margaret Judd	Landgirl – Farm worker
Sqdrn Leader Duncan McKenzie	Commandant POW Camp - Luce
Bombadier Willaim Stone	Royal Artillery – Shoebury Barracks
Captain Bernard Camp	Army Intelligence Corps

Margaret Judd	Land Girl – Maylands Farm
Squadron Leader Duncan McKay	Commandant – Luce POW camp

THE RELUCTANT PROTAGONIST

Prologue

It was the 2nd December 1937. There was four inches of snow on the ground and more was falling, deadening the sounds of the city. Despite the season of supposed good will, a deep and depressive atmosphere of gloom permeated the city of Vienna, which was gradually spreading to the remainder of Austria. The atmosphere originated from its dominant neighbour, Germany, now under the leadership of the National Socialist Chancellor, Adolf Hitler.

Hitler, an Austrian by birth with revolutionary ideas, was finding an increasing following and empathy with German speaking peoples, but in so doing was creating a tidal wave of distrust, hate and persecution encouraged by militant elements formed and encouraged by him. This false patriotism, with its persecutory dogma, was spilling over into more sectors of Austrian society with increasing effect, as it recovered from what they considered the shame of defeat in the first world war.

Hitler particularly turned his hatred towards the Jews and other non aryan sections of the population, who became his scapegoats for all ills. This hatred and false blame enabled him to further his own and his party's ambitions. Spreading the ideology of his Nazi party through political rallies, swaying the mob with his unhinged rhetoric, duping the people which allowed him to increase his power and hold over the people. He began by ruling Germany with growing autonomy, and at the same time consolidating his leadership as Fuhrer. By increasing state control, and crushing opposition, often by violent means, he became a hero to a large part of the German and Austrian populations, especially as his methods seemed to be bringing his country out of post war depression.

Hitler could not do this alone, of course. He had a cadre of like minded disciples, and with the formation of organizations such as the Schutzstaffel (SS) which had been formed originally as his personal bodyguard, but which over time became a powerful organization under the command of his friend and fellow party member, Heinrich Himmler, and the Sturmabteillung (S.A) who wore a uniform of brown shirts, and used violent methods to enforce Nazi rule. Hitler's rule solidified as his hold over the German people increased.

Later, Hitler disbanded youth organizations such as the Boy Scouts, forming instead the Hitler Youth, which became a training ground later for recruitment to the SS, SA and Germany's armed forces. Part of the youth ethos, was to provide activities which would appeal to young people, and vicariously instill a code of discipline, patriotism and blind obedience to the Fuhrer. He also prevented entry to higher education unless through the Hitler Youth, thus ensuring only those adhering to party principles gained access to higher education.

It was in this atmosphere that fourteen year old Joseph Eckart Mozart found himself standing in the headmaster's office of his school, the Akademisches Gymnasium of Vienna with his Father, Doctor Maximillian Mozart, a practicing surgeon in the city, and an old boy of the school. They were in the presence of the headmaster, Doctor Fredrich Von Schmidt who was the great grandson of the famous Austrian architect and previous professor at the school, whom he was named for. They were all standing, adding a solemnity to the occasion, causing Joseph some anxiety to be present in such august company.

"Your father and I have discussed your future at great length Joseph," said the Headmaster. " I understand that you wish to study to become an architect. I commend you for your ambition, but would suggest that it is a bit early to define a career at such an early age. We both feel that your education at this point needs to be more rounded."

Joseph's head went down. His trepidation showing in a noticeable tremble of his left knee. What is coming next he wondered. What have I done wrong? He was near to tears.

The Headmaster continued. "How is your English Joseph?" Are you able to converse freely in that language?" He looked down questioningly at Joseph with arched bushy eyebrows.

"I can speak some English Headmaster. I am learning all the time."

The headmaster then asked in English, "Tell me how your studies are going. Reply in English."

Joseph, haltingly said, "I study English since I was eleven. I enjoy languages."

"Good," said the headmaster, with some satisfaction.

"Now, to the point of this meeting. Your father and I have talked about your future, and we feel that you would benefit from an exchange with an English school, where you would be able to study English and further your interest in architecture."

Joseph's mortified expression, and the beginning of tears showed how he took the news. He didn't want to leave his home, his friends, particularly his gliding squad, which he started in the scouts before they were usurped by the Hitler Youth. It was a hobby which took a lot of his spare time, and in which he harboured an ultimate ambition to fly. He looked appealingly at his father.

Joseph's father said, "Cheer up my boy. The Headmaster and I have discussed your future. As you know at this time there is much unrest in our country. The political situation is getting worse by the day, and your mother and I, and the headmaster, believe that it would be good for you to open your horizons, and see how things are done in other countries. We have chosen an exchange for a year at Westminster School, in London. This will broaden your education. Broaden your view of the world. You will be able to make new friends, and improve your language skills and you will still be able to return to your gliding squad. There is time."

Joseph, with trembling lip said, "I don't want to go to England. I don't want to leave home and leave you and mother. I would like to stay. I don't want to leave my friends, and I don't want a year out from my glider training."

"The headmaster and I are worried about the future of Austria and of course your future," said his father with a concerned expression.

"With the rise of the National Socialists in Germany and the rise to power of Herr Hitler, we feel the unrest in Germany he and his party are creating, has already started to spill over into Austria. There is much political unrest. You are too young to appreciate the dangers which might be coming, so for your own good we wish you to have a year out at a well known English Public School. Particularly this one which has an architectural history behind it, and particularly since the headmaster there is a friend of your headmaster. It is all arranged. Next January you and I will travel to England to the new school."

Joseph started to sob. His father looked distraught and put a comforting arm around his son.

"Joseph, after a year, you will come back here. You should know however, that you are not the only one to go on this exchange. Two pupils have been chosen to go. One of them is your special friend Walter." Said the headmaster, with a kindly expression.

"There are two of the Westminster School pupils coming here in exchange. I have arranged this with my good friend William Camden, who is the headmaster of the school in England."

"Walter?" said Joseph. "He's going as well?" His expression changing quickly from grief to hope.

"I have spoken to Herr Baumgarten and we will travel to England with him and Walter and help you settle in. Ernst Bruen was due to go, but his father is heavily involved with the Nazi's and has refused to let his boy go."

"Not Ernst Bruen. I don't like him. He bullies people," said Joseph. "He's never liked me, or Walter. He is older and he and his friends pick on us"

" Like father like son. But he is now not going. Never the less, " said his father, "The arrangements are made and next month we travel to London to settle you in. It is for your benefit, and I am sure that you will enjoy the experience. It will take you away from the present unrest in our country for a time. Now, wait outside while I talk to Dr Schmidt."

Once Joseph had left the room Joseph's father said, "As you know Germany has been involved in the Civil War in Spain, supporting General Franco's Nationalists. There are rumours, supported by the foreign press, that Hitler is using the involvement of German forces as a training and testing program to ultimately achieve his ambition to rearm his forces, particularly to reform the Luftwaffe, which is strictly against the principals laid down in the Treaty of Versailles, It makes me very worried about Joseph's future ambitions, as he wants to fly, and how rearming might affect our country. I have my suspicions that Germany is preparing for another war and the way Hitler is doing away with youth organizations and replacing them with the Hitler Youth worries me. It is a form of brainwashing, and I don't like it. How that leaves Austria remains to be seen, but I can't help feeling our future looks uncertain as a country, and that is one of the reasons I would like my son to have this exchange. I do not want him politicized at his age."

Herr Schmidt said, "I have been watching the situation carefully, and I agree with you. It looks likely that the unrest in German since Hitler took power, has the potential to move the country toward another war, and I can only foresee Germany's involvement in Spain, may be a prelude to what is coming. I feel there is every likelihood Austria will become embroiled in the situation. In my view, Germany using its air power in Spain clearly breaches the terms of the Treaty, and I share your pessimism that Hitler is preparing for war. I wouldn't want to share my views outside this room at this time, of course. I hope you understand my friend."

"Completely. It will remain between us."

Dr. Mozart called his son back into the room. "Thank Doctor Schmidt and we will go home. Until January Dr. Schmidt."

Dr. Mozart shook the headmaster's hand and urged Joseph to do the same.

Outside, it was a cold December day, people were muffled against the chill. Traffic moved freely and everyone went about their business as normal.

Although it seemed to Joseph his world had collapsed, life on the outside appeared as normal.

Joseph said to his father. "I don't want to go, but if I have to, it will be better with Walter."

"This is a rare privilege, " said Dr Mozart. "You and Walter have been chosen out of your whole year to represent your school in London. I hope you won't let our family or the school down. The best is that Christopher Wren the famous architect, who built St Paul's Cathedral in London and other famous buildings was a pupil at the school, so their architectural heritage is strong, and if that is the path you wish to follow, you couldn't go to a better school."

Joseph's heart sank. It was a fait accompli. He had to accept the situation, much as he didn't like the idea.

Two days later Joseph was walking into his school with his friend Walter. They were talking about their coming adventure and did not notice a gang of four older youths, led by Ernst Bruen following. As they entered the school grounds, the Bruen gang surrounded them, pushing them to the side of the building, where they pinned them against the wall.

"Teachers pets," said Bruen, thumping his fist in the chest of the two boys, and pushing his face into Joseph's so that the stench of his fetid breath caused Joseph to turn his head in disgust.

"I hear that you are going to England, taking my place, because my father refused to let me go. Not that I wanted to anyway. I am sure we will be fighting the English soon enough and they will be our enemies. You are a traitor leaving our country at such a time, and we know how to deal with traitors."

Both boys were grabbed by the gang, their arms pinned to their sides. Bruen then sank his fist into Joseph's stomach and as he doubled over, brought his knee up into Joseph's eye, leaving him prostrate and bloody. The other youths dealt similar punishment to Walter, leaving him bleeding and gasping for air on the ground.

"That's how we deal with traitors," shouted Bruen. He kicked both boys in the stomach as they lay prostrate, and swaggered away laughing.

Joseph and Walter helped each other to their feet and painfully made their way into the school building, where they cleaned themselves up in the toilets, before entering their first class of the day.

" You are both late for class. What happened?" said their teacher, noticing their injuries, and the dirt on their clothes.

"We took a shortcut and fell in a ditch, said Joseph. "We will be alright. We are only scratched." He then shot a warning glance to Walter, who nodded and said, "That's right. We will be fine in a minute."

Bruen and his friends at the back of the class smirked in self-satisfaction. They had got away with it.

The teacher gave each of them a knowing look, "Well in that case. Sit down and let's get on with the lesson."

He then glared at Bruen and his friends. "Bruen take that smirk off your face and get on with your work."

Chapter One

"Joseph, tell me about your gliding in the scouts." Joseph had been summoned, with some trepidation, to his father's study at his home

"It is what I most enjoyed about the scouts. To soar above the clouds, free as a bird. It's wonderful. I want most of all to fly. It's thrilling."

"Well, I have a treat for you. I know how disappointed you are about going to England and with the demise of the scout movement, but I hope now you know Walter is going with you, you will look forward to it and enjoy the experience. What you may not know is that I have a friend who is a fellow Doctor who also writes books. His name is Adolf Kronfeld and his nephew is Robert Kronfeld."

"Not **THE** Robert Kronfeld, the famous gliding champion we have all heard about in gliding circles," gasped Joseph, awed by the mention of his hero's name.

"Yes, the very same. He fled Austria in 1933 because he is Jewish and has gone to England to avoid the growing hatred towards members of his faith, by the Nazi regime. He foresaw this hatred would overspill into Austria, and he was quite right, it is growing. Not only does he hold the gliding distance trophy, but he has recently won another trophy for crossing the English Channel. However, that is not what I wanted to speak about. Through his uncle I have secured a training flight for you with Kronfeld's successor Fabien von Weiser, and if you do well, I have been promised that when you get to England the great man himself, will take you up for a training flight. What do you think of that?"

Joseph stood, his eyes alight in anticipation, a tremor running through his body. His hero Robert Kronfeld, and his Austria successor Von Weiser. It was beyond his wildest dreams.

"Papa. It would be wonderful," he gasped. Overcome with excitement by the turn of events.

"How did you manage to get them to agree?"

"I worked with Kronfeld's uncle and he is still in contact with him in England, and Kronfeld's father was my dentist until he retired. Here in Vienna." I have known the family for years. They are very proud of Robert, but believe, because of the current climate in Germany which is certainly overspilling into Austria, he has made the right decision to escape to England. That way he will avoid all the prejudice and hatred growing against those of his faith. It's appalling the way that Hitler and his Nazi party have stirred up the population in Germany against the Jews and this is already affecting our beloved Austria. I see nothing but troubled times ahead. This is another reason I believe it is necessary for you to go to England."

Four days later, in the light of early dawn, Joseph and Walter, defiantly in their scouts uniform, stood on the grass runway at his gliding club on the outskirts of Vienna. Beside them were their fathers, Doctor Mozart, and Herr Baumgarten. They were standing beside the club's dual seated glider, watching it being hitched to the bungee apparatus ready for the first flight of the day and both were filled with the anticipation of a thrilling day to come. There was no sign of Fabien Von Weiser, and they were worried. Would he be there, would they fly with him? Time dragged and still he did not appear. It looked like the day would be wasted.

They watched as other youths climbed into the club glider to take off with their local instructor, helping with the bungee apparatus, and jealous of the take offs and landings taking place, whilst they still stood there waiting.

"Is he coming Papa," asked an anxious Joseph.

"He said he would be here. I am sure he will turn up. We just have to be patient."

Suddenly another glider entered the circuit. It circled the perimeter of the airfield, swooped and soared in an exhibition of perfect flight. Joseph, who had studied gliders over the last year identified it as a British made Falcon III, side by side, dual glider. These were one of the most expensive and maneuverable flying machines on the current market. Constructed of wood and cloth treated with clear dope, to stretch the cloth over the frame. The group watched as the glider came down to perform a perfect landing. The canopy opened and out stepped Von Weiser pulling off his flying helmet as he walked toward them, sporting a wide smile.

"Doctor Mozart, and Herr Baumgarten I presume?" He said, smiling. He shook hands with both parents and introduced himself. "I am Von Weiser. Are these two young men the ones I am to fly with?"

"This Is my son Joseph, " said Dr Mozart and this other young man is his friend, Walter." Indicating the two boys. "They are both excited to be given the opportunity to fly with you. You are one of their gliding heroes, don't you know. You might know who the other is."

Von Weiser raised his eyebrows and smiled., "Let me guess – Kronfeld?"

Both boys gaped at their hero, their eyes alight as they studied the lines of the most modern glider they had ever seen.

"Well," said Von Weiser, "Let's get started. If you will help me hitch up to the bungee I will take you up in turn. But first I have to ask the permission of the controller. Whilst I talk to him, perhaps you will get ready, and I will take you up one after the other."

"I am puzzled. Where did you take off from to get here. I don't recall another airfield close by?" Said Dr Mozart.

My father is Baron Fredrick Von Weiser. We live at the Schloss Weiser about 10 kilometers outside Vienna. The Schloss overlooks the Danube and I am lucky enough to have my own glider set up in the grounds. It saves coming through the city to get here and saves much travel time Now, let me show you the glider and run you through how it works. As you may have guessed it is British built, made mostly of wood, and will take two people sitting side by side. Robert Kronfeld sourced it for me from England. As you know he left Austria some time ago and now lives in England, and he arranged to have it shipped to me here. It is a sturdy craft, easy to fly and the controls are the same as you have been used to, so once you have looked over the machine, and familiarized yourselves with the controls, we will get started."

Joseph was secured to his seat alongside Von Weiser, the bungee was attached and the ground crew awaited the signal from the pilot to release. Joseph was trembling with excitement and anticipation. To receive instruction from Fabien Von Weiser, who was mentored and friendly with his all time hero Robert Kronfeld, was thrill enough, but to actually fly with him as instructor was beyond his wildest dreams. He was overcome, impatient to be off, and in such awe of Von Weiser he could hardly respond to what he was saying.

"As I just said," Von Weiser repeated, but louder. "Before we take off, there are certain checks we must always carry out. We have walked around the machine, and already tested the flaps, the tow hitch and the tail. What else is required?"

"The controls, the instruments, the safety harness, and that the canopy is secured."

"Correct. And this has to be a routine every time before we take off. Never forget," said Von Weiser with a stern face to emphasize his point. " Now we are ready to take off."

Von Weiser waved to the ground crew. Joseph looked at his friend Walter and his father standing nearby and smiled a nervous smile. Suddenly the bungee sprang into life, pulled them on the wheel dolly across the grass, with Von Weiser on the control column to bring the wings level. Joseph felt the usual juddering as the craft gathered speed across the grass, and suddenly the sound and shuddering ceased, all he heard was the sound of rushing wind as the glider gathered speed and lift. They were airborn, rising quickly to 100 metres, soaring in a mini thermal coming off the edge of the raised ground on which the airfield was situated.

"I will pass the controls to you Joseph, "said Von Weiser, "Look for the birds. As they circle you will see that they are gaining altitude. Use them to find the thermals. Now look at the compass, we want to head away from the city. Plan a course for roughly North West, that will take us over open country."

Joseph, his face puckered in concentration, with perspiration beading his forehead, took the joystick, and move it to the left. The nose dipped alarmingly as the left wing went down, and the craft started to spiral downwards.

"Don't jerk the controls, " said Von Weiser, "Use the stick gently. Now bring the wings up level, gently now, and try to feel at one with the glider. Look there are birds spiraling over to the left, head for them and we will gain height. Always be gentle with your control movements. There is no hurry. Now relax."

Joseph's efforts brought them into a thermal, where they joined the circling birds. He identified two buzzards, and a stork, as well as some smaller birds, sharing the air with them, and at this point he started to enjoy the experience and notice the view. Way to his right he saw the city of Vienna laid out in all its majesty. He was able to identify some of the larger landmarks, and the Danube in the distance, but his path was taking him away from the city, further north towards a loop in the river.

The altImeter showed them now at 2000 metres, and the countryside expanded in his view. He soared and banked, dived to gain speed and climb even further until the speed worked off the machine. He was thoroughly enjoying himself.

"That's better, " said Von Weiser. "We are here to enjoy ourselves. Now head further north west, and cross the river."

Joseph did what he was asked to do, and they quickly passed over the mirrored Danube, flying over open countryside. He was now relaxed enough to enjoy the view, thrilled at what he saw. As they headed further north, in a heavily forested area Joseph saw a large baroque style schloss appear. As they drew closer, he saw at the back of the building there were formal gardens, and beyond that a field, with a glider resting on the grass."

"That's my home, " said Von Weiser, "and that is my competition glider. That is where I took off from."

Joseph gasped in amazement. "You live there? It's beautiful. So big."

"Our family have owned it for generations. It's too big. We only use part of the building to live in. My father is Baron Von Weiser. He was an Oberst in a cavalry regiment, during the first world war. He was wounded in battle at what the British call the Somme, and invalided out, He still walks with a stiff leg, but otherwise he is fit and healthy for his age.

He manages the estate. But that's enough of my family, now concentrate. We need to turn and go back, it's Walter's turn."

Joseph gently turned the machine, feathering the controls as he had been shown, getting a nod of approval from his instructor, and once across the Danube again they were soon in sight of the airfield.

Joseph looked down, identifying the field, seeing two other gliders on the ground, and groups of people standing watching the sky, and pointing as they saw the glider come into view.

"Now, are you ready to land."

"Me, land?"

"Yes. Remember what you have been taught, We will approach the field from the east. See which way the windsock is indicating. We need to land into the wind. So bring her round gradually and descend slowly. Remember, only minor and gentle adjustments are needed,"

Joseph's face showed a rictus of concentration, as he approached, making careful minor adjustments to the trim of the craft as he neared the ground.

"Now, flare slightly up, then gently put us down, " advised Von Weiser in a calm and steady voice. "We are 2 metres up, gently does it."

Joseph caressed the joystick, until he felt the rumble of the wheel dolly touch the ground, and taking his hands from the controls, he allowed the glider to come to rest, until it stopped and the left wing tilted slightly towards the ground. He then let out an audible sigh of relief.

"That was good. Well done," said Von Weiser as he undid the canopy, to reveal Walter, his father and Dr Mozart standing beside the glider beaming smiles shown on their faces.

"Did you enjoy that?" said his father.

The return beaming smile, told him all he needed to know.

It was now Walter's turn so Joseph helped with the bungee connection, and stood with his father and Herr Baumgarten, whilst the glider took off once again, heading north west away from the city centre until it went out of sight. It was gone for 45 minutes and then suddenly it appeared over the field, and swooped down for a landing. Walter got out with a broad smile on his face.

"That was fantastic. What a ride. I was allowed to fly it. It was wonderful. Thank you Herr Von Weiser. Thank you for your patience and instruction. I had a great time."

"I did too. I am also very grateful to you Herr Von Weiser,"said Joseph.

Their father's joined in the thanks and shook hands with Von Weiser.

"You can repay me by assisting in hitching the machine to the bungee. I have to get home you know. I hope you see you all again, but I hear you are off to England on a school exchange, so it will not be for some time. However I will follow your progress." Von Weiser shook hands with the boys and their father's, waving farewell as he stepped aboard his glider once again.

Little did the boys realize how prophetic those words would be in the coming years.

The party then watched as the bungee released with a savage jerk, and the glider climbed to the heavens once again, fading into the distance north west.

Chapter Two

On 6th January 1938, Joseph, Walter and their parents met at the Westbahnhof station in Vienna, suitcases in hand, to start their overland journey to England. Tearful farewells were taken from their mothers as they climbed aboard the train, each accompanied by their father. Joseph, with moist eyes, clung to his mother, who hugged him with all her strength. Walter was affected the same way as his friend.

The train jetted steam from its boiler. Its whistle sounded twice, and with a roar and loud hiss of steam, it crept away from the station, gathering speed, as the boys and their fathers hung out of the window and waved to their mothers until they disappeared from view. The boys settled into their seats for the long journey to England.

The train made its way from a snow bound Vienna, across country to the German border, where there were checks made by officious uniformed border guards. Once in Munich they change trains for their onward journey through Germany. The boys noticed an odd militarization. There were large numbers of the population in uniform. Some in black uniforms and others in brown. There was a palpable atmosphere of tension, and everyone appeared serious and humourless. An air of suspicion prevailed, which was noticeable and worrying to the boys even in their excited state. The train slowed down considerably when it entered the outskirts of various cities en route. They passed slowly through Stuttgart, Frankfurt and Cologne, passing over the Dutch border into Maastricht, where the train stopped and officers of the Dutch Koninlijke Marechausee boarded the train to check their documentation whilst the train journeyed on via Rotterdam to the Hoek van Holland. The journey, whilst tedious, had fascinated and excited Joseph, he had never before left his beloved Austria. This was a grand adventure, and there was more to come.

Arriving at the Hoek Van Holland, it was now evening. The party walked from the train station to the adjacent dock, where Joseph saw two large ships tied to the quayside. One appeared to be a cargo ship, with cranes operating under floodlights and the other was the SS Amsterdam, their ferry to England. It was now late in the evening and the ship was a blaze of light both from quayside lighting and lighting onboard. Joseph was excited to find that he was sharing a first class cabin with his father and he would be sleeping on board. After settling into their cabins, he and Walter were allowed the freedom of the ship to explore.

Joseph and Walter took in the sights, and once they got over the shock of leaving their homes and families, they became more animated and excited as the journey progressed. They were on deck to see the departure from Holland, keenly watching as tugs pulled them off the quayside, and they remained on deck until the lights on land faded from view. They were too excited to contemplate seasickness.

The two families met for a very pleasant evening meal in the first class dining room, after which both families were allowed to visit with the Captain on the bridge, where the boys were allowed a turn each at steering the ship. Both boys were then taken to their respective cabins to bed down for the night.

The following morning the boys were up just after dawn and after a quick breakfast, were allowed on deck to watch the approach to the coast of England. They remained to witness the ship's arrival to the port of Harwich.

Tugs met the ship and nudged it gently against the quayside, where the stevedores secured the ships hawsers to quayside bollards, and the ship finally came to rest. It was time to go ashore. The boat train, smoke billowing from its funnel, awaited its passengers, it would take them directly to London from the quayside platform. The boys sat window gazing, viewing the countryside and the towns through which the train passed, until an hour and a half later, it slowed to enter Liverpool Street station, in a cloud of fog-like smoke and steam.

In the street outside Liverpool Street Station, the party walked into a grey drizzle. It was cold, but not as cold as Vienna and there was no snow. The roads of the city were busy with traffic of all sorts. Horse drawn drays carrying barrels of beer to public houses, mixed with omnibuses. Lorries belched smoke into the grey atmosphere, cars rattled along cobbled and paved streets, and taxicabs plied their trade. Despite the weather Joseph felt the atmosphere in London was much less hostile than he had felt in Germany. The only uniforms he could see were on Policemen walking the streets and railway workers in the station.

Doctor Mozart hailed a taxi and the boys watched through its steamy windows as it slowly progressed through the busy streets, to the Thames embankment until the Houses of Parliament came into view, where they were deposited at Liddell's Arch, the main entrance to Little Dean's Yard and Westminster School.

Doctor Mozart, Herr Baumgarten, Joseph and Walter soon stood before the Headmaster, in his imposing office. He wore a black gown over a sober suit of dark grey, with a high winged collar and bow tie.

"Welcome to Westminster School," he said his voice deep and confident.

"You are here as part of the exchange scheme which your headmaster and I have devised and encouraged. Two pupils from our school have gone to the Akadaemisches Gymnasium in Vienna. Your alma mater in exchange and now you are here. Let me therefore welcome you to our school, and hopefully within a short period of time you will look upon our school as yours as well."

He then solemnly shook hands firstly with the parents and then with Joseph and Walter in turn, as if sealing a deal between the parties.

" My Name is John Christie, I am the headmaster, and a particular friend of your own headmaster. Now, let me give you a glossary of our history. The school is what we call a public school, and was established by the Benedictine Monks of Westminster prior to the Norman conquest, in 1066. The earliest written records of the school date to 1340 and we are located as you probably know in the precincts of Westminster Abbey. It is therefore a much older educational establishment that even your school which I believe was established in 1553. Most boys join at 7 years of age and after passing an examination at 13 they go on to senior school. Many from there go on to university, especially Oxford and Cambridge. Our school motto – **DAT DEUS INCREMENTUM** – translates to " **I planted the seed…. But God made it grow"** is a direct quote from the Bible, 1st Corinthians 3:6. In your case, Joseph and Walter, we want to plant the seed of international fraternity, by that I mean to further friendship between our two countries. I am well aware that the timing is tricky because your neighbour Germany, under the leadership of Herr Hitler, is making waves by internal agitation and re-arming. Even now, I understand, he is forming an airforce which is contrary to the terms of the treaty of Versailles, but we have every hope that his machinations will not spill over to your beautiful country, which Austria, as I well know from my many visits, is. Now, let us settle you into your accommodation."

The headmaster opened the door and directed the pupil standing outside his office to enter.

"This is the Honorable James Cavendish. His father is the Earl of Luce and he is our head boy. He shares an interest with you two lads. He is a member of our Air Defence Cadet Corps and a member of a gliding club which is his hobby and yours I believe, so you have a mutual interest.

Cavendish held out his hand to the two boys and said, "Welcome to Westminster School. My name is James."

"Cavendish, will you take the boys to your dormitory, they are bunking there and settle them in while I talk to their fathers. Once they settle in and unpack, take them to supper and look after them. Bring them to me after supper."

"Yes, sir." He turned to the boys with a smile saying," Please follow me."

Once the boys had settled in their dormitory they were taken on a brief tour of the school building and then to the dining room. There was a high table on a raise platform, with long tables, laid with pristine white table cloths the length of the room. The room filled with boys of various ages, the more senior boys towards the high table. The room went silent when about 20 gowned teachers paraded into the room, led by the headmaster, accompanied by Doctor Mozart and Herr Baumgarten. All the pupils stood in silence. The headmaster positioned his guests either side of him.

"Be silent for grace," said the headmaster, nodding at James Cavendish. Who then repeated the formal words of thanks to The Almighty.

Then "Be seated."

At this instruction the masters sat, followed by the pupils and a general hub bub started as the boys passed bread rolls and filled water glasses at their tables. A team of catering staff then entered the room from a side door, serving the meal to the masters in order of seniority and then the boys in the same format. Joseph and Walter, sitting next to the head boy were among the first of the pupils to be served, with a dish they had never experienced before. Roast Beef, and Yorkshire pudding, followed by spotted dick and custard.

Joseph looked at his companion with a quizzical look on his face. "Vas ist Das? He whispered to Walter.

Cavendish overheard the comment and said, "Roast Beef and Yorkshire Pudding, a very traditional and tasty English dish, with gravy, a kind of savory sauce, followed by spotted dick and custard. Another traditional English dish. We have it once a week or on special occasions. I guess this might be in honor of your arrival."

Both boys tried it. They were hungry and their expressions turned from hesitant to delight as they ate. They liked it and it sated their hunger. They would have much to tell when they returned home, in this strange new land with strange new customs.

Cavendish took time to introduce the two visitors to fellow pupils, and in the main they felt welcome, especially when Cavendish told them that both the Austrian boys had been members of the scouting movement and had been training to fly gliders. It seemed many of their companions were members of the Air Defence Cadet Corps. They were lucky that Cavendish appeared to be an amenable character, and he carried the role of head boy with an easy grace and inbred authority. He made them feel at home.

After the meal, the boys stood in silence as the master's marched from the high table and left the room. Then, and only then, were the pupils allowed to leave but strictly in order of seniority, head boy and his charges first.

Later in the Headmasters office, the boys were urged to say farewell to their Fathers.

"Joseph, we have both booked into a hotel nearby for the night and will be returning to Vienna at lunchtime tomorrow. We will come to see you before we depart. We have left funds with Doctor Christie. So please do your best, remember you are representing Austria, our family and your school. Learn the language and customs, and make sure you attend to your studies. Please write every week and let us know how you are getting on. Make me proud my boy!"

They hugged. The two parents then shook hands with Doctor Christie and departed, leaving their sons misty eyed and apprehensive.

Cavendish took the two boys to the senior Common Room, where he introduced them to some of the more senior pupils. Mostly they were accepted with politeness and courtesy, however there was a small group of the senior boys that grudgingly and rudely acknowledged Joseph and Walter, and after the introductions were seen and overheard whispering about housing Nazis.

Later in their dormitory Joseph spoke to Cavendish about what he had overheard.

"We are true Austrians, Walter and I, not Nazis. We have nothing to do with what is going on in Germany. There are some, I must admit, in my country and even at my school, who do sympathize with the Nazis, but so far they are in the minority and Walter and I do not share their views. We are Austrian and proud of our country. We fear what is happing in Germany at present, and our greatest fear is that it might spill over into our country. These are troubled and worrying times. I hope you can understand our worries."

"I understand and sympathize," said Cavendish. "These sort of things are not under your control. Take no notice of Jonas Pilkinton-Ward and his cronies. They are bullies and should be avoided at all costs. They are always in trouble. If you get trouble from them, see me. I will sort them out."

There as a soft knock on the door, and at invitation from Cavendish, a middle aged woman entered the dormitory. She was medium height with dark but greying hair, and was dressed in a dark blue nurses uniform.

"Ah, Matron. May I introduce Joseph Mozart, of famous name and Walter Baumgarten. They are exchange pupils, here for a year, from Austria. Joseph, Walter, this is our Matron, Mrs. Wilhemenia Stone. She looks after our welfare."

Matron smiled a benevolent smile at the boys, shook their hands and said, "Welcome to Westminster school. Austria's a lovely country. I have often holidayed there. I especially love the Tyrol, and Salzburg."

"We come from Vienna," said Joseph. "We are pleased to meet you."

" I have been there too. Lovely city," she smiled, " I am here to look after your welfare. I am a qualified nurse. If there is anything I can do, please let me know. James Cavendish will tell you where to find me. Now it's time for bed, so please prepare. The bathroom is through that door." Indicating a door near the corner of the room.

Three other youths entered the room.

"These," said Cavendish, "share our dormitory. McKenzie is Canadian. The son of the Ambassador,

Menzies is Scottish, the son of a laird, and Munroe is American, the son of an industrialist, who is also with us for a year on exchange. We call them the three Ems."

They boys all shook hands and made the new visitors welcome. They then started to ready themselves for bed.

Joseph looked at his assigned bed. It was made up of sheets, blankets and an eiderdown. He looked nonplussed. He was used to continental duvets and had not seen sheets and blankets before. McKenzie, the Canadian, saw his hesitation.

"Yes, they are what we call sheets and blankets. It's not what we are used to. They are comfortable once you get in, but of course it's more difficult to make your bed in the morning."

Both Austrians started to climb into their beds. They pulled back the covers to get in only to find that instead of their feet sliding to the bottom of the bed, their feet stopped halfway. No matter how hard they pushed, their feet would go no further. Embarrassed, they got out of bed and pulled the covers fully back, to find that the sheet had been folded halfway down, had formed a shortened envelope which stopped them from lying full stretch.

Cavendish and the rest of those in the room were laughing, "Ah, an apple –pie bed. It's our way of welcoming you to Westminster. A joke and a kind of initiation."

Joseph and Walter joined in the general laughter at the joke played on them and their standing with their room- mates rose in appreciation of joke perpetrated and joke accepted in good spirit.

"However," said Cavendish becoming serious, "Watch out for Pilkinton-Ward and his friends. They are not nice people. They are known bullies and will use any excuse to create trouble. Now you are here, I suspect they will concentrate their efforts on you. If they give you any trouble, let me know."

He gave them a hard stare as he said these words. "I mean it. I know things are in upheaval in Austria at the moment, and that some of the population have welcomed the Nazis, and have adopted their slogans, and bullying tactics."

"I don't understand all the implications of what is going on in my country at the moment, but I have heard my parents talking so I do know that The

National Socialist Movement in Austria, is agitating in support of the Germany National Socialists, which unfortunately is being led by Adolf Hitler, himself an Austrian by birth, and there appears to be a growing anti-Jewish feeling coming from them. In the Scouts I met Robert Kronfeld some time ago. He was a champion glider pilot, and he is Jewish. He left Austria with his family some time ago and came to England because he felt unsafe, and I later read that he took on the challenge of crossing the English Channel by glider. The first time this has been done. He was our chief scout and I met him at a jamboree and was taken up by him over the Tyrol for a lesson. He was a wonderful teacher and a great man. The situation now in Austria has not made my parents happy at all, especially as they have Jewish friends," said Joseph with a sigh of nostalgia and resignation.

"I have heard of Kronfeld," said Cavendish, "I read about him in the papers. It was the first time, as you said, anyone had crossed the channel by glider. As far as I know he is still gliding in this country, and I thought I read somewhere that he had joined the RAF. Now let's all get some sleep"

The two boys remade their beds and climbed in. It was their first time sleeping in a shared room and the first time they had slept under sheets and blankets. Never the less, they slept well, having been very weary after their journeying.

The next day the boys were issued with a uniform. A dark grey suit, with waistcoat, and high collared shirts with a house tie.

"You are lucky," said the storeman. "Not long ago you would have had to wear a top hat as well."

The boys looked at each other in their new clothes and burst out laughing at the strange image they were portraying.

The next few days passed in a blur of visits to Westminster Abbey, a walking tour of the school premises, and introductions to school staff, masters and fellow pupils. They discovered they were not the only pupils from foreign countries. There were several sons of diplomatic staff from various countries across the world. The school, whilst an English Public School, with foreigners in the minority, had an international feel about it.

The boys had their voices checked by the choir master, and Joseph, who had a fine voice was encouraged to join the choir of Westminster Abbey, which meant he would have to attend choir practice at least twice each week in his own time.

They also found school did not finish in the late afternoon for borders, they had what was known as "prep" to complete school related assignments each weekday evening, and they were expected to participate in some sporting activities at weekends. Both boys chose boxing as their preferred activity, but this meant a commitment to training two evenings every week, and every Saturday afternoon. Church was compulsory on Sundays, and as Joseph had been chosen for the choir, his commitment was greater that his companion, Walter. The plethora of activities meant that the boys had no time to be homesick.

Two weeks later, both boys were called to the headmaster's office.

"I have some news for you, " said the headmaster. It appears that your father," indicating Joseph, "Has been in touch with Robert Kronfeld the Champion glider pilot. As a result he is coming to the school next week to give the school a lecture. The theme of which will be the principles of gliding. He has particularly referred to you both, and would like to see you afterwards. This is a rare privilege and provides a lot of kudos for the school. It is of particular interest to those in our school who are members of the Air Defence Cadet Force. I also wanted to ask you if you had heard from your parents lately."

"I have had a letter from my father. He is worried about what is happening in Austria at this time. It appears that there is a lot of unrest particularly in Vienna, and he tells me that there is a move toward militarization, with a lot of influence coming from over the border with Germany," said Joseph with a worried expression.

"Well, I am sure that your father's are monitoring the situation back home, and will do what is best for you. Just get on with your studies and try not to worry. I am sure it will be alright in the end, " comforted the headmaster. "I will be posting the details of Kronfeld's visit on the bulletin boards, and the whole school with be present to hear what he has to say. You may go and spread the news."

The boys departed, bursting with pride, and they quickly spread the news to their companions, and through the school. An air of excitement and anticipation prevailed over the next few days until the big day arrived.

Chapter three

On 28th January 1938 Robert Kronfeld, dressed in the uniform of a Royal Air Force Squadron Leader, walked on to the stage in the main assembly hall of Westminster School and shook hands with the headmaster who cut an imposing figure, bedecked in gown and mortar board. A hush fell over the crowded room as the headmaster raised his hands to silence the ensemble.

"Masters, and pupils of Westminster School," he exhorted in stentorious tone "Let me introduce you to Squadron Leader Robert Kronfeld. He is here to give the school a talk on the art of gliding. You should know that Squadron Leader Kronfeld is Austrian by birth, fleeing that country because of Nazi persecution. He is a famous world champion glider pilot, who holds records for long flight both in his home country and England, where he crossed the English Channel in his glider. He is also a renowned glider designer, and we invited him here originally to talk to our school Air Cadets, but I felt his story would be of great interest to the rest of the school, so I asked him to address you all. Please be attentive and listen with care to what he has to say. Masters and pupils, I present to you Robert Kronfeld, RAF!"

Kronfeld stood before a lectern on stage, looking slightly embarrassed at the fulsome praise he had received. He took a moment to look around the hall. He saw the aged oak paneled walls, viewed the honour boards of the fallen from World War 1, names picked out in gold, and the pillars holding up the gallery which was as packed with pupils as was the space in the main auditorium. The gold pipes of the organ above his head glowed in the light giving him an ethereal aura as he nervously viewed the row of gowned masters in the front of the ensemble. He cleared his throat.

"Gentlemen. As you have heard I am an Austrian by birth, proud of my country and I became interested in flight in my early teens. The prospect of being able to soar with the birds seemed an ambition which I could not shake and which I still retain to this day. You will have heard that after the First World War, Germany, who controlled Austria at the time, signed the Treaty of Versailles in 1919, which prohibited Germany from forming an airforce. When Herr Hitler came to power in Germany earlier in this decade, with his Nationalist Socialist movement, things started to change. His party started to blame those of the Jewish faith and others, for the ills that Germany suffered after the war, and this feeling spilled over to Austria.

I am of the Jewish faith, and I and my family felt so uncomfortable in our own country that I came to England recently, and have now settled here. I applied to join the Royal Air Force and as you see they have accepted me. I wish now to be a British citizen, I could never return to Austria whilst Hitler is in power. I am working to get my father to follow me out of Austria before it is too late.

However, enough of my personal circumstances, and back to gliding. I became a member of the first Austrian gliding school, where I learned the principles of soaring. In this I was lucky because I had a friend who was a meteorologist at Darmstadt University who was studying air movement and he discovered and studied the principles of thermals. Anyone who knows gliding today, understands how important thermals are to a glider pilot, because in certain circumstances air rises, and this allows gliders to gain height. You will often see birds in flight circling in the air as they gain height. They use the thermals to their advantage, and my friend passed this knowledge on to me.

I applied the principle to my gliding, and as a result I learned to fly for longer periods. On one occasion

I flew for five hours and travelled just over 102 km. As a result I won a prize which allowed me the funding to build a larger sailplane, which I named "Austria". It had a wingspan of 30 metres and with this glider I was able to eventually fly 164km and soar to over 2500 metres, using the knowledge I had gained from my friend about thermals. Efforts for which I was awarded the Hindenburg Cup.

I joined the Austrian Air Scouts, known as the Osterreichischer Pfadfinderbund and eventually became its Commissioner and was made an honorary member of the Scout Association where in 1933 I took part in a Scout Jamboree in Hungary where we treated the crowd to an airshow. By this time I was living and working in Germany, but the Nazi Government banned those of the Jewish faith from flying. I therefore started to fly more in England. I am now Chief Instructor for the Oxford University and City Gliding Club, as well as a commissioned RAF officer, and try to teach my pupils the principles I have learned over time. I aim to improve the skills of those pilots who have experience, and to instill an enthusiasm for the sport in novices. I am lucky in that I have access, through my experience to several gliding clubs in this country, and I have arranged with your Head

Master to host a small number of the members of your own Air Cadet Force next week, at the London Gliding Club for a training session. Now, are there any questions?"

Several pupils stood and raised their hands. Kronfeld pointed at Cavendish, sitting in the second row behind the masters.

"Your question?"

"The Treaty of Versailles banned Germany from forming or having an air force. Yet Herr Hitler seems to have ignored the treaty. Aircraft made in Germany are operating, as I understand it, with German pilots in Spain, on the side of Franco's forces. Is this correct?"

"As far as I am able to understand it is correct. Hitler has adopted two policies. The first one is that he has increased the formation of gliding clubs all over the country, and has encouraged would be pilots to join and learn to fly. It my view they will provide the personnel for a newly formed airforce. Secondly, totally ignoring the terms of the treaty he has secretly at first, and now quite openly, had German industry design and manufacture airplanes of various types, bombers and fighters, which he has sent to Spain, using their conflict to work out tactics and test the capability of these aircraft. He has totally defied the Treaty and none of the allied countries who drew up the treaty have seriously challenged him."

Jacob Piccosi, the master of mathematics stood, "Do you mean that Hitler will be able to form an airforce and that the allies will allow him to do so."

"It would appear so. He appears to be able to tread roughshod over what he deems as an unfair treaty, holding the German people back. Defying other countries to challenge him, which so far they haven't done. I have no doubt, that as we speak, Herr Hitler is arming for war, and an essential part of his ethos is to rearm his ground forces, and reform an airforce with the latest machines. It is an open secret in Germany that aircraft manufacturers have been given the go ahead to go into full production once again, and hang the consequences." This statement caused the hall to erupt into noisy disbelief.

The headmaster stood, "Gentlemen, he shouted. Peace and quiet please." He held his hands to the sky for silence. When the sounds subsided he said, "Herr Kronfeld. You are saying that Germany under the leadership of Herr Hitler are making ready for war. Are there other factors which make you believe this?"

"Yes, there are. " He hesitated gathering himself. "Germany today is not a good place to live. The National Socialists, the Nazi's, have started by making life uncomfortable for Jewish people and others they have blamed for Germany's ills. They have formed organizations with loyalty to the Fuhrer, which are militaristic in their outlook and bullying in their concept. These organizations are spreading fear and causing disruption to normal life throughout Germany. I fear this will quickly spread in Austria, where Hitler is viewed by some as the savior of the German speaking people. Not by everyone I hasten to add, but he has a large number of supporters who are responding to his Nationalist rhetoric. Times in Germany are dangerous and unfortunately this unrest seems to be spreading to my country, Austria. This saddens me greatly."

Walter stood, with his hands raised. Kronfeld nodded to him.

"What can you tell us of the Hitler Youth Organization?"

"Well," said Kronfeld, "It began with the rise of the Nazi's in the 1920's, and from small beginnings, has grown to replace all other youth organizations in Germany. These days it is almost compulsory for the Aryan youth of Germany aged between 14 and 18, to join the Hitler Youth. Boys are prevented from further education unless they join up. There is a similar organization for girls. It seems to me it is a training ground, a kind of political militaristic brainwashing, to provide an army who are obedient to the principles of the Nazi party, and loyal to their leader, Adolf Hitler, whom they call their Fuhrer. Unfortunately, there is no doubt that the organization is spreading quickly throughout Germany and will undoubtedly spread to other German speaking nations such as Austria. They have a military style uniform, on which are displayed Nazi emblems. They hold rallies and camps and are encouraged to toe the political line. It looks to me as if the organization is a breeding ground to supply manpower for the growing German armed forces."

Walter sat down, a look of horror and disbelief on his face. Would this spread to his beloved Austria. He had much to think about, most of it depressing. Joseph looked similarly distraught. It was his ambition to attend university to study architecture. Would he have to join the Hitler Youth to achieve his ambition?

The headmaster stood, raising his arms again for silence. Once the gathering had quietened, he said, "That must be the last question. Herr Kronfeld has given us much to think about. I wish to thank him, on behalf of everyone here, for his time and timely warnings. His words have left us all with much to contemplate." The whole audience rose and gave Kronfeld a standing ovation, who, embarrassed, quietly walked off the stage.

Three days later a fume ridden and leaky charabanc stopped outside the headquarters of the London Gliding Club on high ground overlooking Dunstable Downs in Bedfordshire. Six members of the Westminster School Air Cadets disembarked together with housemaster Mr Clifford Wyatt MA, and their sports master Mr. Thomas Webb BSc. The air cadets were led by James Cavendish and the party included Joseph and Walter. Standing outside the main entrance to the clubhouse, to greet them was Robert Kronfeld, together with another man clad in white overalls, clutching a flying helmet, he introduced as Mr. Keith Wheatcroft the club's chief flying instructor.

"Welcome everyone, to the London Flying Club," said Kronfeld. "This is my friend and the club's Chief flying Instructor Mr. Wheacroft. He and I will be taking you up today, but first come and have a tour of the clubhouse and some refreshment. We will carry out a briefing and then introduce you to the flying machines."

The party entered the clubhouse, and after a short tour of the building, and refreshments, they were taken to a small room, where Wheatcroft ran them through safety procedures.

The party were then taken out to the field.

"This is Hanger Ridge," said Wheatcroft. It leads out over Dunstable Downs, and provides a good up draught to assist the gliders to take to the air. We will be using two Slingsby Falcon III gliders, which are configured for two pilots, sitting side by side. There have been very few of these made and this club is lucky enough to have the two. I will be taking one up and Herr Kronfeld the other. That way you will all have at least 30 minutes in the air, maybe a little longer. Who has flown before?"

Four of the party of six pupils raised their hands, including Cavendish, Joseph and Walter.

Mr. Wheatcroft pointed at Cavendish. "You will come with me. You," pointing at Joseph, " will go with Herr Kronfeld. You have all been issued with white overalls, and flying helmets, so please prepare yourselves and let's get started."

Joseph sat beside his hero, listening intently to his pre-flight briefing, and he took a little time to strap himself in and familiarize himself with the controls. The bungee was attached. All was ready.

Suddenly there was a push Joseph felt in his back, and the glider gathered speed, bumping on wheels over the rough grass, until suddenly the ground fell away and the machine dipped into Hanger Ridge. It caught the air and rose majestically, soaring on a powerful updraft to quickly rise to 200 feet above the ground.

"Look to your right," said Kronfeld. "See those birds circling in the air. They are using a thermal. Although it's overcast, air still rises in certain places, and you must read the signs. We will join them."

He banked the machine, to the right and joined the birds circling. Joseph felt the rising air in the open cockpit, and enjoyed the feeling of uplift as the machine slowly turned within the thermal. They quickly rose to 2000 feet and the view became panoramic. They broke out of the clutches of the thermal and headed slightly across the countryside of Bedfordshire.

Kronfeld pointed to his left and banked in that direction. "Down there is Whipsnade Zoo, part of the London Zoological Society, but more like open plan parkland. We would not like to crash land there in the lion or tiger compound. They have large teeth," and he laughed.

Joseph smiled nervously, and was relieved when Kronfeld steered a more northerly course away from the zoo.

"Now you take the controls Joseph. Look for a thermal."

Joseph look around and saw further north, birds were again circling. He banked in that direction, the wind whistling around his ears, and was relieved to find he was joining them in uplift. He had found his very own thermal and they rose another 1000 feet.

Kronfeld smiled encouragingly, "well done," he said, "You found one. Now you know the signs, let's have some fun."

Joseph used the controls lightly, as directed, and before too long, it seemed only minutes, they were heading back to the airfield.

"Have you landed a glider before Joseph?" asked Kronfeld.

"Only once. I've never been solo."

"Well now is your chance to carry out your second landing. I will talk you down all the way. Remember, light touch to the controls. Now start losing height."

Joseph turned the machine into slow circles, losing height as he did so, until Kronfeld was satisfied they were at the right height to approach the field.

"There's the landing field. Straight ahead of you, now bring her down slowly, **SLOWLY**," he emphasized.

The machine headed for the raised part of Hanger Ridge. Where the ground dropped away, it seemed to Joseph they were way too high but Kronfeld's reassuring voice held him steady until they cleared the ridge 10 feet above the ground.

"Now put her down gently," said Kronfeld calmly.

Joseph brought the machine down gently onto it's under carriage and they rumbled to a stop. The sound of the wind and the rumble of the wheels on the grass ceased as they sat there in silence, the gentle breeze fanning their faces.

Joseph let out a huge sigh of relief. It seemed he had been holding his breath since takeoff, and he then allowed a big grin to weave its way across his face. He was alive with elation. He looked over to the others in the party, and his wide smile told them all they wanted to know. He thanked Herr Kronfeld, so excited that he lapsed into German, formally shaking his hand.

"That was the most wonderful experience of my life. Thank you very much indeed. Your advice on following the thermals I will remember always."

As Joseph sat in the cockpit, undoing his strapping, the second glider landed nearby, and Cavendish got out of the machine with a broad smile on his face. He leaned over and vigorously shook the hand of his instructor, thanking him profusely.

Joseph and Cavendish help the instructors hitch both gliders to the bungees, and assisted the next two pupils, to strap in. Walter was excited to find he was also with his hero Herr Kronfeld.

The session seemed over in minutes, so excited were all the trainees, after which the party returned to the clubhouse where the instructors carried out a detailed debrief on each individual and on the whole day.

The return journey to school was noisy as the boys compared notes on their experiences. There was a party atmosphere in the charabanc. The babble of voices told of a wonderful day.

The party arrived at school as evening was drawing in. They were all in ebullient mood, cross talking on their experiences, and the discovery of the theory of Thermals, which until now, for all of them, had been one of the mysteries of flight.

The party entered the school dining room for their evening meal. They were unable to contain their boisterous behavior. They were so wrapped up in their euphoria, they failed to notice the dark mutterings of Jonas Pilkinton-Ward and a group of his bully boy cronies glaring in jealous envy. Their resentment growing like a cancer, as the delight of the flying party showed an obvious joy of the day.

Joseph found it hard to sleep, as did his friend Walter. The events of the day coursed through their minds, as they re-lived it, blow by blow. Joseph got up from his bed. He couldn't sleep. He made his way to the dormitory door in the dark, only to find Walter following him.

"Can't you sleep?" said Walter.

"No, " said Joseph. "I keep thinking of the day we have had. It was one of the best days of my life. It's made me even more determined to fly. But now, I need the toilet."

Joseph, followed by Walter made his way along the corridor to the toilet and bath room. They entered the room and as they started to leave the door burst open. Pilkinton-Ward and six of his cronies crowded around the two boys.

"Bloody Krauts," sneered Pilkinton-Ward. "Coming over here. Getting all the privileges. Taking our places, when we should have been the ones to go gliding with the Kraut instructor. We'll teach you!"

"We're not Krauts. We're Austrian. Different countries," said Joseph defiantly.

"No difference," growled Pilkinton-Ward, "You're all bloody Jerries. We beat you in World War 1, and we're going to teach you your place."

With that they surrounded the two boys, and started to beat them with belts, and fists, until bloody and bruised the two boys sunk to the floor, curling into the fetal position, as kicks and blows rained down on their bodies. Their objective achieved, the group then ran from the room.

Cavendish had heard the noise, he burst into the room. Seeing the two boys curled up and bloody on the floor demanded, "What's going on. Who did this to you?" He then helped boy boys to their feet.

Cavendish looked directly at Joseph.

"Who did this?" he demanded again.

Joseph muttered, "Please leave it. We don't want to cause further trouble."

"Was it Pilkinton-Ward? I am aware of how much he resents you for some reason. I know he is jealous, but he is a known bully boy. A nasty character."

Joseph said, "We will get cleaned up. It would do us a great favour if you would keep this to yourself. We will sort it out in our own way."

"I will be keeping an eye on him and his cronies from now on. If it happens again, I will make his life a misery. Despite his family being very well off. They own large tracts of land, and his elder brother is a Member of Parliament. The family have influence. Pilkinton-Ward is a spoiled brat but he has a following at the school, and because of his connections he thinks he can do as he wishes. He really has to learn the hard way. Watch out for him from now on."

In the following days, Joseph and Walter, had to stand the sniggering and glares of the Pilkinton-Ward group as they watched the two boys limp into class, showing obvious injuries. Several of their teachers looked askance at them, but only Mr Piccozi asked after their welfare, which they fobbed off with an excuse of horseplay at boxing training. These obvious lies about their injuries only increased Pilkinton-Ward's arrogance, causing him to snigger and glare more vehemently. Obviously nothing was going to be done about the assault, and he and his cronies had got away with it.

Over the next few days, Joseph and Walter threw themselves into their studies, but they went out of their way to increase their boxing training. They were lucky that the sports Master, Thomas Webb, had been a physical training instructor in the army after WW1 and he had specialized in boxing. As a result they both began to get fitter, and responded with enthusiasm to his encouragement. Within a few short weeks, they became fairly proficient in the noble art. They made a point of keeping their distances from Pilkinton-Ward and his group. If there was to be a next time, they wanted to be ready.

Over the next few weeks, both boys recovered well from their injuries, and they successfully avoided close contact with Pilkinton-Ward and his cronies, especially as Cavendish, in collusion with their room-mates, had devised a plan to keep an eye on the two boys. It seemed wherever they went, one of their room-mates was close by and watchful.

Joseph was more concerned about events in his beloved Austria, and he followed the British press reports, particularly an article which indicated that the Nazi party was gaining influence in his homeland. The article told of the oppression of the Jews in both Germany and Austria, and spoke of a growing exodus of Jews from both countries. It spoke of the growing influence of the right wing government which was suppressing free speech, and their alignment with the Nazi party of Germany. The article also indicated Hitler had invited the Austrian Chancellor to Germany, demanding the Austrian Nazi party be given a free hand.

Joseph showed the article to Walter, and they discussed the implications. In their absence, trouble was brewing in their home country, and letters from their parents confirmed all was not well in Austria at this time. However the letters urged the boys not to worry but to continue their studies and make the best of their time in England.

On 14th March 1938 the headmaster sent for Joseph and Walter. They waited in nervous anticipation outside his office until called in.

"Ah, Joseph and Walter. Sit." He indicated two chairs in front of his desk. "I have some news for you from your home. Your father's have been in touch and asked me to inform you that two days ago, on 12th March, Herr Hitler and his troops marched into Austria. There was no bloodshed, he was invited in and welcomed by the Nazi party of Austria, and he has taken power. The papers in Austria are calling it the "Anschluss". As a result there are changes being made in your country. Of course by annexing Austria, Herr Hitler has broken the terms of the Treaty of Versailles, and there may be repercussions. Your father's will be coming over in the next few days, to explain what is going on. However they stress nothing has changed at the moment, you are to remain here and carry on as normal, and not to worry. Your families are fine, and life goes on as normal, but it is clear Austria is now governed by Hitler and his Nazi party. It is early days and time will tell. Meantime, they instruct, you are not to worry. Remain calm, and carry on with your studies here."

Joseph and Walter were bursting with questions. Their beloved Austria was now governed by Germany and the Nazi's. A situation neither of them relished, or wanted.

Joseph, with a devastated expression said, "We are Austrian, not German and certainly not Nazis. We don't want be part of Germany. There is too much going on there from what we hear, and a lot of it is not good."

"We know you are Austrian Joseph. We know you are not Nazis. However, some of your countrymen are, and now we wait to see what will happen. I wish you both well. Now get on with your studies and I will make an announcement to the school about your predicament. The majority of the pupils and masters will understand and sympathize. Don't forget I have two English Exchange pupils in Vienna at this time taking your place in your school. How they will be effected, I don't know. Perhaps we will know more when your father's come."

Joseph and Walter returned to their class room, with much to contemplate, and that night they explained the situation to the others in their dormitory. They were pleasantly surprised at the amount of sympathy and understanding shown by their new friends, but they feared what the bully boys would say and spread around the school. It was sure to be to their detriment.

Chapter four

A few days after receiving the news about the Anschluss, the headmaster again called for Joseph and Walter to come to his office.

Standing in the room was their hero, Robert Kronfeld.

The headmaster said, "Squadron Leader Kronfeld came to me having heard the news from Austria. He has been in touch with both of your father's, who have updated him on the situation in Austria. He feels he should tell you what he has learned of the situation.

"Well, from what I understand, Herr Hitler invited the Austrian Chancellor to visit him in Germany, and pressured him into giving the Austrian Nazi Party a free hand in Austria. At the same time he made the Austrian Chancellor agree not to use his Army to resist German Forces, and although the Austrian Chancellor refused to appoint the Nazi Party leader as Chancellor to replace him, it didn't stop Herr Hitler's troops crossing the border in what amounted to an invasion of our country. The German's were welcomed by the Austrian Nazis, and others of our population, and the lack of resistance, allowed Hitler to annex Austria outright. I am afraid that Austria is now in all but name a part of Germany, ruled by the German Chancellor Herr Hitler, who is now using the title of Fuhrer. This does not alter the fact you are Austrian, and will remain so, but now our country is ruled by Germany."

The boys gasped at the news. They were Austrians, not Germans, and wished to remain so. Tears came to Joseph's eyes.

"What will become of us and our families?"

"Nothing will change for the moment, " said Kronfeld. "We are not at war, but there is no doubt that since Herr Hitler took power, he has militarized Germany, and may well do the same in Austria. What might change for you, is that you are at school in England, and you might have to stand some aggravation from certain sections of your fellow pupils."

"Well we have already suffered some, and that was before this bad news."

"What is clear your parents wish you to remain here, away from the troubles now heaped upon poor Austria. As you appreciate, not all Austrians welcome the situation, and I happen to be one of them. I would suggest you tell your friends what has happened as soon as you can, because the news will come out soon enough. Tell them how you feel. It might help if I walk you around the school, and talk to some of your fellow pupils and friends. I wanted to come again anyway, because I have arranged with, your headmaster here, and with the London Gliding Club, to take another party to Dunstable for tuition, and I would like you to suggest who might be interested. Perhaps this will help your cause at school. I don't know, but it cannot hurt. Come, boys. Let us walk around the school. Show me your classroom, and introduce me to your teachers and friends. While we walk around I will explain of what I know is happening in Austria. Just remember, what has happened is not your fault, you and your families are true Austrians. What has happened is beyond your control. Perhaps you could arrange for all the Air Cadets to meet later, and I can make an offer of tuition sessions to them. I can then make the arrangements."

The two boys then conducted Robert Kronfeld on a tour of the school, taking in their class where they introduced him to their teachers, asking Cavendish, on the way, if he could arrange a meeting of the Air Cadets at the end of the school day, so that

Kronfeld could make his offer to those who had not yet flown with him.

On the way round the school Kronfeld took the time to brief teachers and pupils on the ongoing situation in Austria. Most sympathized with Joseph and Walter. The only negative reactions came, of course, from Pilkinton-Ward and his cronies.

Later that day, the air cadets with their cadet commanding officer Squadron Leader Jacob Picozzi, and second in command Flight Lieutenant Cliff Wyatt, met in the six form common room. Among the crowd were Joseph's room mates, Cavendish, Menzies, Munroe and McKenzie, plus Pilkinton – Ward and several of his friends.

Kronfeld addressed the crowd and told them of the latest situation in Austria. He stressed he was Austrian by birth, and had left his country because of an atmosphere of persecution. He stressed that Austrians were not Germans, and most were not Nazis, although he admitted some of his countrymen had aligned themselves with the Nazi Party. He then offered to host a second glider tuition session, asking for volunteers to fly with him. All present put up their hands. Quickly eliminated were those who had already attended a session, and it was left to the two boys, in collusion with the commanders of the Air Cadets, to select the second group. Menzies and Munroe were selected as was Pilkinton-Ward and one of his cronies. Both smirked with a triumphant glare in Joseph's direction, as their names were announced.

"Good," said Kronfeld. "I will be in touch with the arrangements shortly."

Having said his farewells to the Air Cadets, he was escorted from the room by the two boys. "Remember what I told you. Keep your heads up. What has happened is not your fault. It is better you remain here in England until the dust settles and we see what the future holds for our country. I hope I have helped. I will see you again soon." He then left.

The two boys returned to their dormitory Cavendish and the three Em's, were present.

"What has happened in your homeland changes nothing as far as we are concerned. We all feel sorry for you and your families. Having to be here whilst Austria is in some turmoil must be very difficult. We know you are not Nazis. The headmaster has asked us to keep an eye on you, and that we will do. Now let's go to supper."

The group walked into the dining room, and there was no reaction from those present, with the exception of Pilkinton-Ward's group. As the boys passed their table, Pilkinton-Ward glared.

"Bloody Nazis," He muttered, loud enough for those close enough to hear. "Get back to Germany where you belong."

Cavendish grabbed Joseph and Walter by the arms and walked them past, then returned to Pilkinton-Ward, where he leaned into his face and was seen to whisper to him. At which Pilkinton-Ward looked furious but cowed. It was an uncomfortable moment for the two Austrians.

"If you get any further trouble from them," said Cavendish, "Let me know."

Two days later, Dr. Mozart and Herr Baumgarten came to the school to see their sons.

The boys were taken into the headmaster's office, where they stood in apprehension.

"I understand that you have been told of the Anschluss Joseph, " said his father.

Joseph nodded and said "Yes Papa."

"Well I want to update you on the situation in our country." He paused gathering his thoughts.

"The German Wehrmacht marched into Austria on 12 March. There were big parades, across the border and right through the heart of Vienna. Whilst you have been away the Austrian Nazi Party has further aligned itself with Herr Hitler, who now calls himself the Fuhrer. It would appear the welcome mat was laid out for his forces, and the border opened to them. Many of our Austrian Citizens welcomed them and now the Nazis seem to hold the power in our country. The rest of Europe has done nothing to stop this coup, despite it being contrary to the Treaty of Versailles, so we are effectively under martial law, and rapidly becoming part of Germany. This has many implications for us as citizens of Austria. For a start, and this will affect you and Walter. The Hitler Youth have now been introduced into Austria. All other youth organizations, including your beloved scouts, have been banned. The Nazi's did this in Germany some time ago, and now the ban has been extended to Austria. There are rumours unless you join the Hitler Youth you will not be allowed to go to further education, that means university."

"Can he do that Papa," said an incredulous Joseph.

"He has already decreed it, so it is fact. On the good side, it appears everything the scouts did, will be done in the Hitler Youth, including gliding. However, don't be fooled into believing this is their only purpose. I believe it is one of Hitler's tools to indoctrinate the youth of our country into the ways of the Nazi party. Many of the Nazi traits include persecution of our Jewish population. This has already started to manifest itself on our streets. I fear for the future of our country. As you know, I have already served in the medical branch of the army in WW1, and it looks like history is beginning to repeat itself. I hope I am wrong, but I fear it's going to happen all over again."

"I should come home father, " said Joseph. "If there's going to be trouble I should be there."

"That's the last thing that you should do at present," pleaded his father. "I and Herr Baumgarten wish you both to stay here in England, away from the trouble until we assess what is the best course of action. At least you will be safe here, and it will give us time to decide what to do. You both have your education to worry about. You shouldn't be worrying about politics. We came because we didn't want you to hear second hand, what has taken place. At least the Anschluss was relatively peaceful, we will have time to assess the situation as it develops. Meantime stay here and study. If you are to become an architect, which I believe is your ultimate ambition, then your studies are very important. So please stay until I advise otherwise."

"Yes, Papa," said Joseph.

Herr Baumgarten said, "The same applies to you Walter. Promise me you will stay and study. If the situation changes we will let you both know."

"Now," said Dr Mozart, "The headmaster has agreed that we can take you both out to dinner tonight, so we will return this evening to pick you both up. Meantime the headmaster has arranged for us to visit Westminster Abbey this afternoon. We are booked into an Hotel and we will be returning home first thing tomorrow. We will see you later."

Walter and Joseph returned to their class. Their minds racing with the news from their homeland. They were so absorbed in their thoughts that they showed no reaction to the glares, and silently mouthed threats coming from Pilkinton-Ward and his friends.

That evening the two boys waited at the main entrance to Westminster School. A taxi pulled up and Joseph's father, who was on board, indicated that the two boys should get in. They were taken to The Ritz. They travelled through grey drizzled streets, smoky motor vehicles belching out dirty fumes. The contrast when the taxi pulled up at the entrance to the hotel couldn't be more marked. The whole front was a blaze of lime- light. The top hatted doorman saluted as he opened the door to their vehicle. They walked through the glare of the entrance, blinking in the harsh light, into the lobby, and a world of opulence, glamour and gaiety, a far cry from the miserable and damp streets outside.

Waiting for them was Robert Kronfeld, a surprise for the two would be pilots. The men shook hands with him, and were directed to the dining room, where they were placed by the attentive staff, in a private room off the main dining room. The table was set for five, and began an evening of conviviality and conversation. From the boys came the inevitable questions on flight which Kronfeld patiently answered, and from the parents, the conversations centered around the political situation in their beloved Austria. It became clear Kronfeld, under the current regime in Austria, had no intention of returning to the country of his birth. As a Jew, he had closely monitored the situation under the Nazi's in Germany, and now as a result of the Anschluss, he foresaw the Nazi ideology being welcomed by certain sections of the Austrian population.

The two father's openly expressed the view that the Nazi's intended to apply their political ideology all across Austria, making it at one with Germany. The discussion, which the two boys listened to with avid attention, convinced them Austria would become aligned totally with Germany, and would be governed by Hitler and his Nazi government.

The subject which peaked the boy's interest the most was, with the rise of the Nazi's, came an intention to re-arm and reform the Luftwaffe. This was totally against the terms of the Treaty of Versailles, but Hitler had already run roughshod over the treaty without meaningful censure from the Allies. By including Austrians in his recruitment plan, he was openly pushing against the terms of the treaty.

Kronfeld had been monitoring the situation closely in his homeland and Germany, and he expressed the view the German's involvement in the Spanish Civil War was a prelude to all out war. By designing and producing new aircraft secretly in Germany, German forces were able to test war tactics and war machinery in a real conflict.

Doctor Mozart and Herr Baumgarten were concerned for their sons, as both had expressed a desire to go on to university. Joseph's ambition was to become an Architect, and Walter wanted to study medicine. In order to attend university and achieve their goal they would have to join the Hitler Youth on returning home despite their reluctance to do so..

The most worrying aspect of the discussions around the dinner table, was Hitler's ambitions would not stop at Austria. It was a strongly felt he wanted to extend his ambitions across Europe. The Sudetenland was to them an obvious target for Hitler's ambitions, and perhaps more. They would later realize how prophetic these words were.

A general discussion on glider training came with the pudding course. The boy's ears pricked. This was their territory. This was their interest. They both had ambitions to fly, and would avail themselves of every opportunity to do so. Kronfeld saw Hitler's policy of encouraging glider training as an obvious ploy to fast tract recruits to his newly formed Luftwaffe. Conversion from gliders to powered flight, was an obvious step and would shorten the necessary training time for pilots to qualify, and quickly swell the ranks of his air arm. However, the one drawback as far as the boys were concerned was that they were 15, nearly 16, and they could not join until 18 years of age although the air cadet arm of the Hitler Youth would be open to them. In their youthful exuberance they did not consider the consequences of joining the armed forces, or even consider that they might be required to go to war as a result, although all the indications were that Hitler's belligerence was moving his country swiftly toward aggressive confrontation with neighbouring countries.

The party moved, at the end of a fine meal, to the lounge, where Doctor Mozart and Herr Baumgarten talked to the boys about their immediate future. Both parents realized Hitler would gradually imposed his will over Austrian citizens, regardless of their political views. His policies would be advanced by Nazi sympathizers who had been agitating in Austria for years. They re-emphasized that the boys continue their education in England until the situation became clearer.

"We will speak to the headmaster in the morning, "said Doctor Mozart, "and apprise him of the situation as we know it. We will ask you both stay here in England until the position becomes clearer. Do you agree?"

Both boys agreed.

Robert Kronfeld said, "Now on less serious matters. I am due to take another party of trainees up at the London Glider Club next week. I will ask the headmaster if the trainees who have already flown with me, to accompany the next party to act as ground crew. This will all add to the experience. Would you think this a good idea?"

Both boys readily agreed. It was at least another day out.

That evening, in the dormitory Cavendish and their room-mates, quizzed the boys on their day out. They had obviously heard of the Anschluss, and wanted to know more detail. The boys brought them up to date with the situation as they knew it, which attracted a wave of sympathy for their invidious position.

Their room mates were cheered when they heard Robert Kronfeld wanted the first trainees to assist as ground crew for the second wave. They were sure the headmaster would agree to it.

The following day, Doctor Mozart and Herr Baumgarten came again to the school, where they had a lengthy session with the headmaster, It was agreed that the two boys would stay at the school at present, but the situation in Austria would be closely monitored. If there was any changes which would make their stay in England untenable, then their situation would have to be rethought.

The following Wednesday, the charabanc collected the next party of trainees from the school. Included in this party was Pilkinton-Ward and one of his cronies. They were their usual surly and menacing selves. The others sat at the back of the vehicle, away from the new party.

On arrival at the London Gliding Club they were met by Robert Kronfeld. He carried out a briefing in the clubhouse, before allowing the new trainees to don their flying overalls, and taking them to the gliders. He carried out his usual safety checks, taking the trainees through the checks one by one. Pilkinton-Ward, showing his usual arrogance and aloofness, was most dismissive of the need for the checks, and his distain was noted by Kronfeld who gave him a meaningful glare as he repeated the checks, to emphasize their importance.

The two gliders were ready.

"Are you ready to fly?" asked Kronfeld.

"Of course, that's why we're here isn't it? Sneered Pilkinton-Ward. His cronies smirked at his misplaced wit.

Kronfeld pointed at Pilkinton-Ward, "Please get into the co-pilots seat, then we will be off."

As Kronfeld got into the machine, he looked at Joseph and winked, smiling an evil smile. Joseph smiled and nodded in return, an unspoken pact passed between them, and the victim of this pact was always going to be Pilkinton-Ward.

The ground crew assisted in strapping the pilot into place, and hitching the machines to the bungee. Kronfeld passed a paper sick bag to Pilkinton-Ward.

"Should you feel airsick, please use the bag."

Pilkinton-Ward sneered with his usual distain, pushing the bag beneath him as he did so. Kronfeld shrugged his shoulders and looked meaningfully at Joseph again, his dislike of

Pilkinton-Ward obvious by his expression which could only have meant problems for his pupil.

The glider took to the air, bounding across the grass as the bungee released its energy. The ground dropped away over Dunstable downs, and the glider dipped ferociously as it tipped over the edge. This bought a scream of terror from PIlkinton-Ward, as the glider dived into space, before soaring into the heavens, heading for an obvious thermal where birds were circling.

The next few minutes saw the glider rise to 2000 feet, and Kronfeld allowed Pilkinton-Ward, once he had recovered from his initial terror, to take the controls. At first he was too savage in his handling but with patient and calm tuition, reluctantly taken, Pilkinton-Ward took control and improved his handling, growing more confident as he did so.

"Now, " said Kronfeld with a Machiavellian smile. "Let's have some fun. I have control, shall we try some fun stuff?"

With that Kronfeld suddenly put the glider into a steep dive, increasing the speed, then pulled up, so that Pilkinton-Ward lost sight of the horizon. His expression changing from one of sneering confidence to terror. Kronfeld, all sympathy gone, banked left as the machine reached the pinnacle of its climb, and he made the machine spiral down, corkscrewing first left and then right, before pulling up again into a thermal, which lifted them to 3000 feet as fast as an expresss lift in a department store. By this time, Pilkinton-Ward was started to go green, and he reached frantically for the bag he had scorned before the flight. Mercilessly, Kronfeld continued the aerobatics, moving the craft violently from one axis to another, until he saw Pilkinton-Wards head crushed into the bag with the smell of vomit permeating the craft, Kronfeld, maliciously, kept up the violent manouvres for a time, then relented, and landed the machine with a flourish. He energetically hopped out of the machine, leaving a pale and sweaty Pilkinton-Ward in a sorry and dishevelled state to climb from the machine on wobbly and rubbery legs. Pilkinton-Ward rushed to the clubhouse, his hand over his mouth, stained overalls showing his distress, leaving Kronfeld smiling in satisfaction. That will teach the arrogant little bastard, thought Kronfeld.

The rest of the training session went smoothly, everyone else enjoying the session. Pilkinton-Ward's friends having seen what had happened to him in flight, were particularly careful to be overly polite and subservient to their instructor's wishes.

The journey back to school was boisterous in the main, but Pilkinton-Ward and his chronie were very quiet. He was still pale and sweaty. His usual attitude of superiority and distain had gone, at least temporarily, much to the delight of the others of the party outside his immediate circle, who could not help but enjoy his discomfiture.

Once they reached the school, Pilkinton-Ward and his friends, thoroughly subdued, with their resentment obvious, quickly disappeared toward their dormitory, not to be seen again that evening.

For a few weeks, life at the school was peaceful. Pilkinton-Ward and his friends were keeping a low profile, but were often seen grouped together, talking sotto voce, and often glaring at Joseph, Walter and their group of friends. This was not so obvious when they were in the company of Cavendish, but It was obvious they were plotting and scheming some sort of retribution.

Meantime, taking care to mainly be in company with others, Joseph and Walter threw themselves into the activities of the school. They attended choir practice at the Abbey, they became embroiled in a game totally unknown to them, but which they grew to love, called rugby, and they avidly attended boxing training. They became fitter and more confident as a result, particularly as their language skills improved.

The weeks passed, and summer came. The boys were now introduced to the school's summer game Cricket. They had no idea what the game was about. They had never seen it, and never had they been involved in a game which went on for hours. Cavendish, their hero, was particularly enamoured of the game. He was described as an "all rounder". What that meant the boys had no idea, and they were utterly confused by the rules, and the way Cavendish attempted to explain the way a batsman was in until he was out, and they were totally bemused the way the fielding positions were described. Silly point and gully meant nothing to them, even after it was carefully explained to them. So confused were they that they decided to become spectators only, and to concentrate on their boxing training, at which they were much improved.

Over the summer weeks, they often received news from their homeland. It was not good. From what they were told and from what they were able to read from letters, and the English newspapers, Hitler, having taken control of Austria now had intentions to retake the Sudetenland which, although peopled by a German speaking population, since World War 1 had been part of Czechoslovakia. As the summer departed, so Hitler intensified his moves to absorb the Sudetenland, which resulted in leaders of Britain, France, Italy and Germany meeting in Munich agreeing to the annexation, in an effort to avoid another war.

Life for Joseph and Walter started to become difficult after this additional annexation by Germany. Pilkinton-Ward started spreading rumours about the boys being closet Nazi's, and some of the other pupils were beginning to take notice. Cavendish advised the two boys to always move around in company with friends.

As the summer faded into November, it was reported in all the British Newspapers, and announced on the radio, that in the early hours of 10th November violence against Jews in Germany and Austria, had resulted in mobs, led mostly by brown shirted S.A Stormtroopers, unleashing a whirlwind of destruction against Jewish owned businesses, and personal violence against the Jewish population in the streets. The newspapers labelled this "Kristallnacht", a night which would go down in global infamy.

Joseph and Walter, when they heard the news were thoroughly ashamed of their fellow countrymen, particularly as some of their friends, including Robert Kronfeld, were Jewish. Very few of the other pupils at the school however, understood their feelings in the matter and how ashamed they were, in that moment, of their fellow countrymen. It was noticeable some of the other pupils at the school, with the exception of their close classmates, and those sharing their dormitory, were beginning to whisper in groups when the two Austrians entered the room, obviously talking about them and associating them with the situation created by the Nazi's in their homeland. It made the two boys begin to feel uncomfortable, particularly when the most vocal group led by Pilkinton-Ward were deliberately loud and aggressive in their comments and condemnation. They were often overheard talking in loud whispers about Bloody Nazis, with accompanying malicious stares.

As November slipped into December, the situation reported from Germany and Austria, and now some of Czechoslovakia, grew much worse. Jews were being hounded and harangued without mercy, so it was reported, and the British Press kept the story as headlines for most of the time.

The headmaster called for the two boys and as they entered his study they saw, much to their surprise, their parents were there.

"Ah, Joseph, Walter. There you are," said the headmaster with a concerned expression on his face.

"Your Father's have come because things are happening in Austria faster than we all anticipated. I am aware there is now an undercurrent of bad feeling against Germans, and although we all know you are Austrian, I have detected an undercurrent at this school, which makes me believe the best course of action would be for you both to return to your homeland forthwith."

The boys looked at their parents, and then at each other, aghast at the news, but knowing in their hearts that what the headmaster had said was true. Anti- feelings were spreading from Pilkinton-Ward's group of friends, who were now taking every opportunity to stir up fellow pupils against them. It was not helped that the newspapers were constantly reporting the spread of Nazisim in Germany, Austria and now Czechoslovakia. Which country would be next?"

Doctor Mozart said, "Headmaster, you know we are not Nazi's and as far as I and Herr Baumgarten are concerned, we never will be. Thanks to you we now know our boys are being subjected to a barrage of hate from certain quarters, and it would be less than our duty to our families, if we allowed this to grow and fester. We have to be pragmatic, and understand the feelings which exist here in Britain. As far as we can see, it will only get worse. I cannot see Her Hitler being satisfied with just Germany, Austria and the Sudetenland. He is already growing his armed forces, and I have no doubt the Austrian Army will be absorbed into the

German Forces. There is persecution in Germany, now extended to Austria and Czechoslovakia, particularly against the Jewish population. Kristallnacht was an example of what is happening in our country, much to our shame, but what we cannot do, is leave our boys here to be subjected to harassment and perhaps violence. We need to get them home, where hopefully they will be able to continue their education. I know the Academy in Vienna is making similar arrangements for the English exchange pupils. They will be returning home shortly."

"Yes, I agree. I have been touch with Doctor Schmidt at the Akademisches Gymnasium and he is arranging for the English exchange pupils to leave as soon as possible, and under the circumstances, I believe taking your boys home is the best course of action," sighed the headmaster. "Your boys have been a credit to you whilst they have been here, but the time has come."

Doctor Mozart said, "We are staying nearby at an hotel. We will return by 9a.m. to collect the boys. I have arranged a ferry crossing for tomorrow to Holland."

He turned to the boys. "We want you both to return to your dormitory and pack. Say your farewells to your friends. We will return in the morning and take you home." He paused, took a breath and said to the headmaster, "Thank you Doctor Schmidt for all your help. I'm sorry it had to end in this way, but circumstances are beyond our control, and we must prioritize the welfare of our sons."

"I understand completely. These are difficult times. Let us hope that we can meet again some time in the future in an atmosphere of peace and understanding. I wish you all well, " said the headmaster as he shook hands with the two Father's.

"Now boys, go to your dormitory and do as your father's have asked. I will bring Cavendish up to date and make sure he is your guardian angel until you leave us. You leave with our friendship."

Joseph, in a tearful and choking voice said, "Thank you headmaster. I just wish you to know we are Austrians, not Germans or Nazis. I don't like what I have been reading about what the Nazis are doing, and although I might have to live with it, I will never like it, or become one."

They all shook hands in solemn farewell. The boys to their dormitory and their father's to their hotel.

Joseph and Walter, on returning to their dormitory, were surrounded by the three Em's.

"What's going on," they demanded. "Why did you have to see the head again."

The boys, suppressing tears, explained, and as they did so Cavendish walked into the room. He then briefed their room mates and they all helped the two boys to gather their belongings and get ready for bed.

Both boys walked along the corridor to the bathroom intending to wash. As Joseph reached for the light switch, and flicked it on, he felt a blow to the side of his head. He staggered, putting his arm up to protect his face, and saw that he and Walter were surrounded by Pilkinton-Ward and four of his cronies.

"Bloody Nazis," growled Pilkinton-Ward. "We will teach you."

With that, Pilkinton-Ward swung his fist at Joseph's face. He failed to understand that all year Joseph and Walter had been regularly attending rugby and boxing training. They were far fitter than they had been, more confident, had grown in stature, and immediately went into defensive mode.

As Pilkinton-Ward swung his fist to land a second blow, Joseph neatly blocked it, and hammered a straight right into his opponent's left eye, which closed and swelled. He swung again, and again Joseph retaliated with a short left jab to the end of Pilkinton-Ward's nose, which burst in a welter of blood and he sat on the wet and tiled floor with a thump, crying out in pain. Walter was meting out similar punishment to the other boys in the party, and although both were taking blows, none landed in vital places and they rode the pain as they had been taught. Their training found them able to retaliate with cool precision , leaving three of their attackers bloody and bruised.

The door flew open, and Cavendish and the three Em's rushed in having heard the noise. Very soon the whole of Pilkinton-Ward's group were either on the floor or leaning, bloody, against the wall, holding hands over their injuries. They would be a in a sorry state in the morning.

Cavendish stood, hands on hips, glaring at the injured. "Get out," he shouted, "And don't come back. The headmaster will hear of this. This is the second time you've picked on them."

"They're bloody Nazis, " sobbed Pilkinton-Ward. " I will tell my father, you wait and see," through bloodied and clenched teeth.

Pilkinton-Ward's ambush party limped out of the bathroom, in sorry state.

"Are you alright," said Cavendish to Joseph and Walter.

"Yes, fine, " said Joseph. Apart from a bump on the head. He forgot, we have been having boxing lessons. I think we surprised them."

"Serves him right," said Cavendish. I will tell the headmaster what happened. Don't worry. The truth will out. He will be mightily sorry. Well done, he deserved it."

Chapter Five

Liverpool Street Station was crowded. Apart from the normal passenger crowd, Joseph noticed large numbers of soldiers in uniform, some carrying kitbags, some standing in parade order, on the platform at the front of the train. As they walked to their carriage at the rear of the train, the order was given by the Sergeant Major and an orderly boarding commenced in military sequence.

"What's going on Papa?" said Joseph.

"It looks like the military are on the move. I don't really know, but I would guess, knowing the military as I do, then they are taking precautionary measures preparing for what is going on in Germany and our country. I would not be surprised if they were anticipating problems. But that is only my guess. I know the train passes through Colchester where there is a large barrack complex. Maybe it's just a normal troop movement," he said with a concerned note in his voice, and a troubled expression.

The boat train left London Liverpool Street, in a cloud of steam and black smoke, billowing up to the high roof of the station, creating a thick, smelly fog, through which the train punched a hole as it emerged into the open air. The journey home had begun, by leaving London and heading for the port of Harwich.

Joseph and Walter were staring out of the window for most of the journey in desultory mood. It was a grey, miserable day, which matched their feelings. They were reflecting on the friendships they had made as well as the enemies. As they had left the school at Westminster, they had seen Pilkinton-Ward and his group, nursing obvious injuries, standing outside the headmaster's office, all looking very sorry for themselves. Their last memories of them were the stares of hate directed at them as they departed.

They had shaken hands with Cavendish and the three Em's, promising to keep in touch, thanking them for their timely rescue the night before, and for their cheerful companionship during their stay. They were sorry to leave under the circumstances, but relalized their departure was inevitable under the circumstances. They were returning home more confident, fitter, taller, more grown up and fluent in English. They would miss the English way of life. The English sense of fair play, with some exceptions, and whilst they enjoyed sports which were new to them like rugby and boxing, and the strange and incomprehensible English obsession with cricket, which despite Cavendish's efforts to enlighten and enthuse them, they never fully understood.

The flat lands of Essex passed them by, without raising much interest as they passed through small towns and villages, until finally the train hissed to a stop in the country's oldest town. The Roman town of Colchester. The train remained in the station as it disgorged its load of soldiers, who were brought to parade status by their Sergeants on the platform. Once the troops had unloaded from the train, it recommenced its onward journey, billowing smoke and steam over the lines of soldiers as they stood in platoon order on the platform.

"I expect they are heading for their barracks in Colchester," observed Doctor Mozart, as he noticed the two boys clinging to the open window, fascinated by the military activity.

Half an hour later, the boys saw cranes in the distance, and the train slowed to emerge onto low lying land criss-crossed with tidal creeks. They rumbled over points onto an area of land festooned with railway sidings, platformed goods trucks, empty railway carriages, and stationary rolling stock. Some trains were carrying out shunting operations, and as they pulled into Parkeston Quay railway station, their destination, they saw two large ships tied to the quayside. They also saw large numbers of uniformed railway staff, some pushing luggage barrows, and other adults in civilian clothes, on the platform, ushering some 100 or so subdued and frightened children, all dressed in winter clothes, carry small suitcases, and all had cardboard numbers on a string around their neck. They were standing on the "up" platform waiting for the train to London, some were still descending the stairs from the railway bridge over the tracks to join the crowd, and there was a cacophony of noise and shouting, to establish some sort of order.

"What's going on Papa?" said Joseph.

"If it's what I think it is, "said his father, "it is an exodus of children of Jewish families, from Germany, Czechoslovakia, or Austria. There has been a lot of persecution of the Jews in those countries by the Nazis. There are rumours that some have been taken to labour camps, and you will remember what is known now as Kristallnacht, where the Nazis smashed up business premises owned by Jewish people. Well this exodus of children is as a result of that. It is not right. It is cruel and barbaric, but this is Germany today under Nazi rule, and this is why we are going home. I believe it will not be safe for you here, at this time, because of what Hitler and his Nazi regime are doing. I must emphasize to you both, that no matter what you see, no matter how you feel, you must remain silent. Particularly when we get home. It will not be safe for you or our families, if you are seen or heard to criticize any authority especially the Nazis. Much has changed in Austria since you have both been away, none of it good in my view, but I have to remain silent for the good of my family. Please understand and learn."

"But, Papa, we are Austrian. Not Nazis. We don't treat people like this."

"I know. We can remain true Austrians, but for now we are governed by the Nazi party, and you have to learn discretion. Keep this to yourselves. There is a feeling we will be going to war soon. Hitler has rearmed. War production has increased. We are making armaments, tanks, aircraft, and guns at an alarming rate. The armed forces are recruiting and training thousands and there can only be one conclusion to draw from all this. We will be at war soon. It is important that whilst you know what is going on, you never speak of it openly, or criticize. Walls have ears. You are approaching 17 and soon should be going to university, If you want to get there, you may have to join the Hitler Youth, because that is now the only route to university. You do not have to like it, but all other youth organizations have been banned. Scouts, the lot. You will have to grin and bear it, no matter how you feel about it. So be prepared, but keep your thoughts to yourself, no matter what."

They walked from the train, into the Great Eastern Hotel, where they went to the dining room for lunch. They had several hours to kill, before boarding their ferry to the Hoek van Holland. Through the window, they saw the forlorn and desultory group of children with the cardboard labels around their neck ushered onto a train, which would take them to London.

The bedlam on the station, subsided with the train's departure. Joseph felt an emptiness inside. An anger which he suppressed until it became a dull and powerful sadness. Like the arrival of sudden storm clouds which darkened the sky, so it darkened his mood. What was he returning to?

What did the future hold? He sighed. Resigned to a fate he had no control of.

Later that evening the party boarded the SS Amsterdam, and were allocated cabins for the night. The boys went on deck to watch the sailing, as tugs pulled the ship from the quayside. Once mid-channel, the ship slowly steamed away from Parkeston Quay, into the tidal waters of the river Stour. As They saw the lights of Harwich appear to their right, the lights on the quayside of Harwich illuminating the silhouettes of darkened ships moored within the confines of the Navyard Wharf. The boys could not tell if the ships were warships or commercial vessels in the darkness. Lights on the other bank of the estuary showed the port of Felixstowe, where the Stour and the river Orwell combined on their path to the North Sea. It was chilly on deck, and once the harbour lights had faded into the distance, the boys joined their parents in the first class dining room for an evening meal. It had been a traumatic day for them, to be suddenly pulled away from their exchange school, and return home to a very uncertain future made them feel sad. Seeing the refugee children on the station at Parkeston Quay affected their thoughts.

What were they returning to? It all seemed very depressing.

With these thoughts, after a meal, eaten in contemplative silence, the boys went to bed. They both laid awake for some time, until the rhythmic pounding of the ship against the waves, and the thud of the engines pushing them forward, lulled them to a fitful sleep.

Joseph and Walter were awake for a quickly taken breakfast, and then went again on deck to watch the berthing of the ship in the Hoek van Holland. They watched the now familiar process of the ship docking, pushed against the quayside by powerful tugs.

On embarkation, they walked onto the adjacent railway platform for their onward train, and there again on the opposite platform stood another group of about 100 children, again with numbered labels around their necks. They were being ushered into line by several adults, who shouted instructions above the hubbub. These children looked frightened, lost and just as miserable as those they had seen in England.

"Are they the same as we saw in England, Papa? " said Joseph.

"I'm afraid they are Joseph. It's going on all the time lately, I'm ashamed to say. They will be safe once they get to England. They are not safe in Austria or Germany anymore."

The Mozart's and the Baumgarten's were urged to board their train by the station staff and the last they saw of the group of children, as their train departed, was them moving in an ordered line, to the embarkation hall.

Joseph and Walter sat on the train in deep contemplation. What they had witnessed was the start of a pattern of behavior by the Nazis. What puzzled them both was that it was only an exodus of children. No corresponding numbers of adults. What it meant the boys could not fathom. It was most worrying and puzzling.

The train drove steadily on, passing through Holland, Germany into Austria. Late in the evening they arrived at a cold and drafty Westbahnhof Station in Vienna. A light dusting of snow lay on the ground. As the party alighted, they saw the first change. Some of the uniformed railway staff were wearing Swastika armbands.

At the ticket barriers, there were some military looking men in brown uniforms with swastika armbands.

"Who are they Papa?" Asked Joseph.

"The Sturmabellung or S.A. for short. They appear everywhere these days. They are Hitler's enforcers. You will have to get used to them, they are everywhere and full of their own importance. Don't give them cause to notice you. They are thugs in uniform, and they do Hitler's bidding. Keep away from them wherever possible."

There were other military looking men in smart black uniforms, with a skull and crossbones badge prominent on their caps. They also wore the swastika on their arm. They had the air of superior authority.

"Who are they," said Joseph.

"Joseph, please keep your voice down, and don't look directly at them. I will tell you all about them when we get home. They are the Schulzstaffel, known as the SS. They are chosen for their Aryan looks and loyalty to the Fuhrer. They carry out the orders of the Nazi party and are now very powerful. They are the more elite organization, and again you should avoid contact with them whenever possible."

The party hailed a taxi, which dropped the Mozart's at their house, leaving the Baumgarten's to go on to theirs,

Joseph's mother Emma waited at the door. When she saw Joseph, she burst into tears of joy, and hugged him.

"Joseph. Oh Joseph. You're back. Welcome home my darling. I've missed you so much."

She pushed him back, and looked him up and down.

"You've grown so much. You look stronger and fitter. They must have been feeding you well in England." She hugged him again tightly, broad smile on her tearful face.

"It's so good to have you back. Your old room is ready for you."

"It's good to be home Mama. But a lot has changed since I've been away. Everyone looks so serious and miserable. What's been going on?"

His father interrupted, "We have a lot to tell you my boy. A lot of what we tell you can never been repeated outside these walls. Austria is now in the grip of Hitler's Nazis. We have to refer to him as the Fuhrer. You saw all those people at the railway station in uniform. Well it appears that the whole nation is being militarized. The youth organizations you knew before you left have been banned, and replaced with one youth organization. The Hitler Youth. They do what you used to do in the scouts and air cadets, but in a more militaristic way. You are approaching 17 now, and will no doubt want to go to university. The only path to get there is by joining the Hitler Youth. All other paths are blocked. You will have to join if you want to further your education and achieve your goal of becoming an architect. Also if you want to continue to fly, you will have to do that through the Hitler Youth. It will take time to tell you of all the changes, but you saw some of it on our way here. You saw for yourself the exodus of the Jewish children. That I am told is due to continue. One thing you should know as that Ernst Bruen is now a local leader in the Hitler Youth, and he is throwing his weight around these days. Making himself as objectionable as ever, if not worse, and his father Heinz, who was our local Baker, is now working for the Sturmabellung, the SA, and he is worse than his son. I should avoid them both at all costs. They are nasty people and they love making people aware of their new found status."

"Ernst was always a bully," observed Joseph. "Give him some authority and he was bound to abuse it."

"Enough of this for now. I have prepared a meal for you both, and then I suggest you go to bed and get some rest. You have both had a long journey," said his Mother.

Later, in his room, Joseph pondered the changes he had been told of and those he had observed for himself. He was not happy with what appeared to be happening to his beloved country, and he slept fitfully.

The weekend allowed Joseph and Walter to re-familiarize themselves with their homes, their city, and the new oppressive atmosphere in the city. There were no smiles any more. Everyone walked around in gloomy silence, the exception being those that they saw swaggering around in uniform, showing off their new found authority.

On Monday, both boys returned to their school. The Akademisches Gymnasium in Beethovenplatz had changed little. What had changed was the atmosphere of the school. What had been a place of laughter, enjoyment and academic aspiration, had been replaced by an air of fanaticism. Some factions, having accepted the new regime and new way of thinking, welcomed the invasion of their country. Others found the situation they were now in depressing. Joseph now felt a stranger in his own country

The headmaster, Doctor Freiderick von Schmidt, called for the two boys during their first morning back.

Firstly he welcomed their return then said, "You have both been recalled prematurely because circumstances in this country have changed so much over the last few months. You have obviously been told of the Anschluss, and how the Nazis under the Fuhrer have taken over the government of this country. I have no doubt that your parents, knowing them as I do, have brought you up to speed on the political situation. I presume they have told you everything about Kristallnacht and its repercussions for the Jewish community."

Joseph said, "We saw groups of children in England and the Hoek van Holland being evacuated. But we saw none of their parents."

"The adults in their families have mostly been sent to labour camps. It has happened to some of our Jewish pupils, and their parents are no longer around," sighed the headmaster.

"It is very unfortunate. You will find the whole country has been militarized. Troops are billeted in every town, and many Austrians are now in uniform, having joined the Wehrmacht, S.A or SS or the Hitler Youth. All branches of the forces are recruiting at this time. We have had to replace our army and air cadet organizations with our own branch of the Hitler Youth. The hierarchy of these organizations is not in the hands of the school. The appointments are undertaken by the local Nazi party, which means if you are a member, you are now likely to have authority thrust upon you. Ernst Bruen is one example. He has been appointed a troop leader of the Hitler Youth. His Father is now a member of the SA. They appear to love their new found authority. I will say no more of that. However, what I will say is, if both of you wish to further your education, to achieve your goals in life, then the only route left open to you is to join the Hitler Youth yourselves. In this way, when the time comes, and in your cases that should be in a few months, you will be able to apply for university and will be able to carry on flying gliders. I would therefore advise you to urgently consider joining up, so please think very seriously about it. Talk to your parents, but take advantage of the opportunity. It's the only way forward as far as I see it. Now go to your class and consider very carefully what I have said, but please do not discuss what I have said here with anyone but your families. Please promise me that."

Both boys nodded their assent. As the boys left the headmaster's office, they saw Ernst Bruen in the corridor talking to a group of his cronies. They passed him by as he glared at them, with a malicious smile on his face. Portent of what the future might hold for them overcame them both like a thunderous wave crashing the shore. It was the dawn of a new era, and one they might be forced to embrace, like it or not.

Back home, after school, and when his father had returned from work at the hospital, the family discussed the future over their evening meal. Joseph told his parents of his interview with the headmaster.

"I believe Doctor von Schmidt is right," said his father. "The only way for you to further your education is via the Hitler Youth. Much as you might find this unappetizing, it is the only way. If you are to become an Architect, then you will need to find a place at a university which specializes in that subject. We have a fine university here in Vienna, but if you want a new experience I would suggest Innsbruck University. It has a fine faculty of Architecture, and there is a gliding club and the flying over the Tyrol is a first class experience, so I am told."

"I will research both. Innsbruck sounds wonderful."

"But first, you will have to join the Hitler Youth. If you go to Innsbruck, you can always transfer branches. I have taken the liberty of obtaining the application forms for the Hitler Youth. Please study them and if you wish. Fill them in and I will lodge them with the local branch. The sooner, the better. It will prevent you from being seen as an outsider. I am sure Walter is getting the same advice." Doctor Mozart then handed his son a sheaf of papers which extolled the virtues of the Hitler Youth, its activities and its creed. On paper it looked to be a wonderful idea and a great organization, but the Mozart's knew full well it was a way of training and streaming the youth of Germany and Austria into an Aryan culture and a disciplined and ordered way of life, a way of propagating the Nazi ideals. But what choice did they have if they wanted their son to achieve his ambitions in life.

Joseph read the application forms given to him by his father. He also read the accompanying pamphlets which extolled the virtues of the Hitlerjugend (Hitler Youth). He read, which surprised him, the organization had been introduced into Austria from Germany as early as the 1920's. Obviously starting in a small way, alongside Hitler coming to power in Germany. He read that all other youth organizations were now banned, but many of the activities he had been able to undertake in the Scouts, he could now carry out in the Youth movement, including gliding. His favourite hobby. Seeing this, Joseph filled out the forms and handed them to his father.

"I will look these over," said his father, "and I will talk to Walter's father, to make sure you can join together. You will feel more comfortable, knowing he can join with you."

A few days later Joseph and Walter presented themselves at the Hitler Youth headquarters in Vienna, where they were marched into an office before their Stammfuhrer (the equivalent of Major and the designated Unit leader). Stammfuhrer Jurgen Engel. He was sitting at a huge desk, which was fitting because he was a huge man in all respects. His white shirted belly hung over black trousers tucked into shiny leather boots. His belt buckle bore a metal swastika, and a long dagger was fixed to his left side. His dark hair was cut short and bristled, as did a pencil thin moustache, cut to emulate the Fuhrer he worshipped. Behind his desk was a banner which they knew to be the so called Blood Banner. Prominent on his left arm was a red banded swastika emblem.

He had them waiting standing to attention before him as he studied their applications.

He then rose, emanating self importance and said in a rasping voice, "So what makes you think you are good enough to join us in the Hitler Youth? What makes you both think you are ready to join our ranks."

Joseph looked at Walter, and said, "We were in the scouts. We have been training on gliders, and have done several flights, even being allowed to take over the controls. We both enjoyed the scouts, and of course we both want to go on to higher education. I want to be an architect and Walter wants to be a Doctor."

Engels said, "Ernst Bruen is one of our troop leaders, and he doesn't think very highly of you. He also told me you have both just returned from England where you were on an exchange. Bearing in mind that our Fuhrer's relationship with the British is at a pretty low ebb at the moment. Where does that leave you two. British sympathizers?"

"We were selected by our school to do a year in England to learn the language, exchanged for two pupils from the Westminster school. It wasn't our choice. It was our parents and our school. It was an experience, but we cut it short after the Anschluss. Some of the English pupils tried to make it uncomfortable for us. So we came home. We are Austrian."

"Well Austria is now part of greater Germany," Engels bristled, "The National Socialists are in power and I am proud to tell you that I am an active member of the party. We all support our Fuhrer, and we all support what he is doing for our country. Can you support him too?"

Joseph and Walter looked uncomfortable at the fervor which Engels displayed, and the fierceness with which he uttered the words. He was an obvious fanatic to the cause.

Tactfully Joseph said, "We all support our country, and abide by the law. We were born Austrians, and if Austria is now part of a greater Germany, then this is our homeland, whether it be greater Germany or Austria. We are loyal to our country."

"Hmm!" said Engels. "We will see. Are you prepared to take the oath of allegiance to the Fuhrer?"

Joseph and Walter, having been coached, said, "Yes, " in unison. Although both felt uncomfortable in saying so.

"Well, take these booklets, they tell you of the activities and purpose of the Hitler Youth. Get your parents to purchase a uniform for you. Details of where you can get them are in the documents, and report here next Friday evening at 7p.m.preferrably with your parents, where you will have your induction, and you will be required to take the oath. Once you join you can list your preferences of activities you want to undertake. I take it that you would like to resume your glider training. Umm?"

Both boys nodded enthusiastically.

"Well I can tell you. There is only one purpose to glider training in the Hitler Youth and that is to provide recruits to the Luftwaffe. If you are not prepared to follow that road, there is no point in you continuing to train on gliders. Understand?"

The boy said, "Yes."

"Yes, what?" Stormed Engels

"Yes, sir." Said the boys.

"That's better. Remember it. I am Stammfurhrer Engels. You will pay deference to my rank and always call me sir. Understand?"

"**Yes, SIR**" they shouted in unison.

"Dismissed. Next Friday 7 o'clock. Here, in uniform."

The boys turned and left quickly, feeling Engels eyes and wrath boring into them as they almost bolted out of the door.

"Phew," said Joseph, "He's something isn't he?"

Walter said, "Shush. Walls have ears, "and chuckled as they walked quickly away.

At 7p.m. the following Friday, both boys appeared in the main hall of the Hitler Youth headquarters. Both were dressed in the appropriate uniform.

White shirt, long white socks, black shoes, shined to perfection, neckerchief, and black Lederhosen. There were 20 other boys present, some from their school, whom they knew, and others they had never seen before. A motely bunch. Their parents stood, some displaying how proud they were, and others more subdued, at the back of the hall and there was a general babble of noise, as the anticipation for the coming swearing in ceremony grew. The potential recruits were called to order and placed in squad rows, cajoled by the squad leaders. They stood in silence, awaiting proceedings.

At 7.10p.m. the recruits were called to attention. The door to the commander's office flew open with a dramatic crash, as the opening bars of the Horst – Wessel-Lied blared from a speaker near the ceiling, with the opening line, "**Raise the flag.**"

Engels, in full Stummfuhrer uniform marched in, in time to the music, his feet stamping the floor, at the head of a small cadre of Hitler Youth officials. They marched in in close formation, one carrying the troop staff and banner. Halting in front of the assembled recruits, at his command, they turned in unison to face the throng. Halting with their backs to the Blood Banner of the movement, which was on a stand near the back wall. He stood, proud and bristling with pompous authority, at attention for a few moments, taking in the effect the entry he and his officers had created on the assembled gathering. Moustache twitching with the emotion of the moment, remaining statuesque until the last refrains of the anthem. The theatrical display was designed to shock and awe, and it had just that effect on everyone in the room, who stood rigid until the music ended.

"The Jugend will come to attention." Shouted Engels. Authority emanating from him like a magnetic force.

"You will now take the oath of allegiance to our Fuhrer. This is a blood oath taken before our blood banner, and will be taken each year on the anniversary of the Fuhrer's birth."

He then indicated to one of his staff, who uncovered a notice board at the back of the room, fixed to the wall adjacent to the Blood Banner. On it were the words of the oath.

"You will all repeat with me, the oath of allegiance. I want to hear it loud and clear. The oath will bind you to our movement and to the greater Germany. Now repeat with me."

So the ensemble, directed by Engels, chanted.

"In the presence of this blood banner, which represents our Fuhrer. I swear to devote all my energies and my strength to the savior of our country, Adolf Hitler. I am willing and ready to give up my life for him, so help me God."

Joseph and Walter, following the crowd, mouthed the words, soto voce, although they found them distasteful and contrary to their religious upbringing. But much as they disliked the terms of the oath they had both been coached by their parents to accept it as part of joining the Hitler Youth, in order to achieve their educational goals, and to be able to continue their flying ambitions.

Engels, the emotion of the occasion showing in his voice said in a parade ground voice, "You are all now members of the Hitler Youth. Welcome to our organization. Each of you will be given a copy of Mein Kampft. Study it, and heed our Fuhrer's words. You will also be given a copy of the Hitler Youth handbook, which lists the various activities you may take part in, some you can select for yourselves, such as air, army and naval cadets. Others are compulsory such as mountaineering, physical training, first aid, drill and camping. When we next meet I wish to know your chosen preferences, and we will try to accommodate you alongside the compulsory activities. Now, there are refreshments for all here, set out in the adjacent room. Please go through and help yourselves. I, and my officers will come among you and get to know you and your ambitions. Please, enjoy yourselves."

Walter looked at Joseph, then at their parents, and shrugged their shoulders with enforced acceptance of their future.

Chapter Six

The glider jerked to the pull of the bungee, gathered speed down the grass runway, and soared into the sky. Free of the earth, it climbed gradually into the cold but clear blue sky. The pilot pulled the lever to free the craft from the pull of the bungee, and it leapt further into the air as a bird escaping its cage. It was free of the earth's drag, and as it soared Joseph's heart sang to the tune of the rush of the wind.

Joseph and Walter had been lucky. Since joining the Hitler Youth they had been able to apply for university, Joseph's choice of Innsbruck University, where he wanted to study architecture and structural engineering looked promising, and Walter who wanted to study medicine had opted for Vienna with a similar result. Both had been absorbed into the youth movement, although their political views did not necessarily accord with the official Nazi doctrine, and been accepted for the Air Cadet branch. They were now at a camp where members of other Hitler Youth Units from all over Austria had sent their cadets for a whole week of glider tuition. A disparate group of youths with varying acceptance of the party political mantra preached to them at the opening part of each Hitler Youth meeting.

Again Joseph was lucky. His instructor was Fabien Von Weiser, whom he had previously met in Vienna, who was the son of Baron Von Weiser, and a qualified glider pilot, and with whom he had previously flown. He had been a particular friend of Robert Kronfeld and Joseph had been able to update Weiser on Kronfeld's situation in England, and the reason why he had to leave his school exchange in London early. Von Weiser gave the impression, but only to certain selected people, that he was not and never would be a committed Nazi, but he was wise enough to appear, at least in public, to toe the party line, as he knew the consequences of not showing the required amount of political enthusiasm in these troubled times. That Joseph accorded with Von Weiser's feelings, was unsaid but understood between them. They both were, however, forever patriotic Austrians.

"I will soar to 3000 metres, " said Von Weiser, then you can take over. By the end of the week I want you to be able to go solo. This will be my last session as an instructor. In two weeks time I am joining the Luftwaffe, to begin my pilot training."

This peaked Joseph's interest. "That's what I would like to do. I've always wanted to fly."

"Well if you are able to solo at the end of this week, you should be able to apply for your gliding permit. This will help you on the way to a pilot's license, but you won't need that if it is your intention to join up, for the Luftwaffe will train you."

Joseph pondered, "But I want to finish university before I apply. I have found that Innsbruck University has an air cadet branch of its own, so if I can get a place there, I would join their unit."

"Good choice," said Weiser. "Now concentrate. You have control."

The sailplane soared over the Tyrol, towards the majestic Alpine foothills. Joseph could feel the thermals and updrafts, and he used them to gain even more height. The views he saw were magnificent. White peaked mountains, shrouded in mist and low cloud, deep valleys, with rivers and waterfalls cascading down bare rock cliffs, all appeared in his view. He was entranced, and lost himself in the wonder of it all. He guided the glider down in a dive toward rolling hills, then soared above their peaks, to spiral round and repeat the exercise. He lost himself in the world where only he and the birds lived. The euphoria of the moment overtook his senses, until suddenly he realized that Von Weiser was talking to him. He blinked and zeroed his thoughts back to reality.

"Von Weiser said, "You were gone. Into another world. Am I right?"

Joseph sheepishly admitted he had lost reality for a time, under the spell of the mountains, the air, and the gorgeous vistas.

Von Weiser chuckled, "That's the magic of the mountains. That's the magic of soaring. If you felt at one with your aircraft, and were able to lose yourself in soaring with the birds, then you have the attributes of being a natural pilot. Well done. Now let's get back down and you can land."

Joseph turned the sailplane, dipping its wings and spiraling down. At 500 metres, he lined up the runway, and brought the craft down in a gentle glide, until the undercarriage kissed the ground, and they rumbled to a halt. The smile on his face told the story. It had been the best trip he had undertaken, the best views on earth. In the most majestic of lands and he knew he wanted more.

Joseph sat there, still in the spell of the flight.

"You can get out now and help the others, reminded Von Weiser."

Joseph shook his head to clear the euphoria.

" I will say my farewells at the end of the afternoon. Well done. If you do join up to fly, look me up. I feel you have the makings," smiled Von Weiser.

For the rest of the afternoon Joseph helped with launches and landings of the gliders as other pupils took their turn for instruction.

When the final flight finished, Von Weiser gathered the pupils around him.

"Gentlemen, you have all done well, some admittedly better than others, but your enthusiasm should lead you all to the enjoyment of flight. As I have told some of you. In two weeks time, I am off to join the Luftwaffe to train as a fighter pilot. What the future will hold, I would not like to predict, but I feel that the future will be out of our hands. I believe that the Fuhrer has ambitions which will mean that he will need an air force of some magnitude. We have already seen the involvement that Germany had in Spain, supporting General Franco's cause. If I am right, then you will all be needed in the future. So good luck gentlemen, and good hunting."

With a wave and a cheery smile he climbed onto his motor cycle, and roared off to his uncertain future.

Back at school, and now approaching 17 years of age, Joseph threw himself into his studies. He was determined to achieve his ambition of a degree in architecture and structural engineering. He had a busy life. He had to attend Hitler Youth activities at weekends, and was also involved with the local boxing club, having found he enjoyed the sport and the physical fitness it gave him. He had also to fit in glider training at his local club in Vienna, and within a few weeks of the tuition at Innsbruck, he obtained his gliding pilots license. A proud moment, he shared with Walter, and some others of his Hitler Youth group.

To celebrate their achievement, Stammfuhrer Engels, who vicariously took pleasure in the kudos associated with his unit's success, arranged for a presentation evening at the Hitler Youth Hall, where the entire unit was mustered to witness. Proud parents of the successful were also invited.

The euphoria of the evening resulted in various promotions, alongside the piloting awards.

Engels announced his promotion to Oberstammfuhrer(Lieutenant Colonel) and he proudly displayed the newly prepared shoulder epaulettes. He promoted the universally disliked Ernst Bruen to Obergefolgschaftsfuhrer (Lieutenant) who beamed at the honour and glared menacingly at Joseph but his menace was short lived when , much to Walter and Joseph's amazement, both were selected to be promoted to Leutenant (Second Lieutenant). The parade ended with a patriotic and sycophantic speech by Engels, followed by the singing of the Horst-Wessel-Lied, again in front of the blood banner. Engels then announced an officers call for the next day, where he would assign the newly promoted to their roles.

The following evening Engels assigned the newly promoted to their squads. Joseph found that because he was a glider pilot, his squad consisted of those who had a similar interest. They assumed the epithet "Eagle" squad. Walter found the same and he opted for "Hawk" squad. This meant that both squads would be able to attend flying training together. It made sense for squad members to have similar interests as they would be able stick together as a unit when training and mutually encourage one another.

There were four squads of 8 overall with a Lieutenant in charge of each squad. Two Obergefolgschaftsfuhrer's were placed in charge of two squads each, and fortunately the newly promoted Ernst Bruen was in command of two squads which did not include Walter and Joseph much to their relief. Oberststammfuhrer Engels was in overall command, and preening in his new glory, he became an even more ardent and committed Nazi.

Engels proposed a timetable. Nazi propaganda and indoctrination opened most meetings, followed by marching and drill and then some form of physical activity. He wanted intersquad competitions in shooting, boxing, and orienteering, and he also told them there would be, mostly during school holidays, camping expeditions and rallies with other Hitler Youth groups, which would be attended and led by members of the military. It was obvious to Joseph that the ultimate aim of the Hitler Youth was prepare and provide recruits for the armed forces, which accorded with the obvious expansionist aims of the Nazi party. When Joseph discussed these events with his parents, his father had to agree with his son's thoughts. The activities of the Hitler Youth were designed as a feeder to

Germany's military machine, and brainwash the members to total commitment and loyalty to the Fuhrer.

As the weeks went by Joseph learned more and more about the activities of Herr Hitler and his Nazi party. The more he heard the more disquiet he suffered and the more concerned he grew. He overheard his father talking about the Munich Agreement which took place in September 1938 whilst Joseph was still in London, apparently an agreement between Hitler and other European countries such as France, Britain, and Italy, where Germany was conceded the Sudetenland, and subsequent pressure by Hitler conceded more Czechoslovak territory. What really worried Joseph more, was when he overheard his own and Walter's Father talking about war. Joseph didn't fully understand the implications, but the tone of the conversation led Joseph to the belief that war was inevitable if Hitler kept up his policy of expansionism. Europe was being thrown into turmoil.

Alongside Hitler's expansionist ambitions, internal conflict was growing apace. The persecution of the Jews in Austria, Germany and other conceded lands was a policy being pursued with vigour.

Joseph had witnessed for himself the Kinder Transport situation, and there were rumours of Jews being transported to labour camps, and of ghettos being formed in major cities administered by the Nazis. It also became obvious to Joseph that the armed forces were recruiting on a scale unforeseen previously. His friend Fabien Von Weiser being an example Joseph knew about, who by now should have become a fully trained fighter pilot.

Joseph however, was intent upon his education. His application to the University of Innsbruck had been accepted, and in the new year of 1939, he was due to start his studies toward becoming an architect and structural engineer. This would mean leaving his Hitler Youth Group in Vienna, and transferring to the universities own group, where he could continue his hobbies of gliding and boxing. It would be a good move for him, because his time at the Vienna Hitler Youth was becoming uncomfortable mostly due to his increasing dislike of Ernst Bruen, who had made his ambitions clear he intended to join the SS or SA. With that authority Bruen would become unbearable.

Christmas 1938 came and went. The newspapers carried many stories about the negotiations between Hitler and other European countries. Meantime it became obvious Germany was recruiting and rearming its military, and exercising its power in Czechoslovakia, whilst putting pressure on Poland, which resulted in diplomatic missions by the British Prime Minister, Neville Chamberlain, and his French equivalent. This was a time of turmoil and unrest for all citizens under the Nazi regime, with rumours of dissent being quickly dealt with and quashed. It was a dangerous time for any resident to show resentment or to voice any disapproval of the regime and its policies. It was a wonder to the Mozart family that so many of their acquaintances believed in Hitler, his policies and the actions of the Nazi party. Normal people were being, in their view, brainwashed into believing this was the right way forward for the greater Germany. Of course, alongside the totalitarianism, the people saw a re-emergence of the German economy. Roads were being built. Manufacturing was up, especially arms and ammunition. Unemployment was down, and there was a new vigour to the economy. With the press under control, glowing reports on political rallies, where Herr Hitler with his ability to dominate an audience with his passionate rhetoric, was hailed as the saviour of the nation, the emerging economic growth only added to his charisma, some worshipping him and his policies as Germany raced out of recession. Germany, he ranted, was destined to become a dominant force in Europe and a world power to be reckoned with.

The defeat of the First World War, was to become a footnote in history, never to be repeated. The Third Reich would last for a thousand years.

Chapter Seven

Joseph, having said goodbye to his family and friends, especially Walter, stepped off the train at Innsbruck Marktplatz Station, and struggled through the six inches of snow, to the market place where he hailed a taxi to take him to the Universitat Innsbruck. He had just turned 18 and was almost at the end of his journey to university.

He struggled with two heavy suitcases, and was sweating inside his heavy clothing worn against the cold, until he obtained the services of a cabby who helped him load them onto his vehicle. The inside of the cab was warm, and he was grateful for the heat. The train had been cold, and there had been frost on the inside of the windows which had restricted his view of the snowbound countryside on his nearly 600 kilometer journey, which had taken an interminable 8 hours, although he was fortunate in one way that he had not been required to change trains en route.

The short taxi journey placed him at the main entrance to a five story imposing building, with an even more imposing colonaded entry built out from the front part of the building. Steps led up to three large oval topped doorways. The centre door was glass fronted, and inside was glowing with warmth and light, as if to welcome the freshers, of which Joseph was now one. He struggled with his cases to the top of the steps, puffing with the strain, and arrived, now red faced and sweating even more, in front of the main door, to see a notice. **"New students welcome. Report to reception desk inside main entrance."**

With some trepidation, Joseph, pulling his cases behind him, pushed his way into the main entrance to be greeted by a uniformed porter.

"Your name sir?" he said.

"Mozart," said Joseph "Architecture and Structural engineering."

The man consulted a list. "Ah, yes Herr Mozart. Table number 5. They will help you," as he pointed further into the entrance hall where a line of tables was set up, each separately numbered, with two or three staff behind each desk."

"By the way," said the man, "My name is Finck. I am head porter here sir, if you require my services, I can always be found in the porters lodge" he then pointed to an office with a hatchway located at the side of the main entrance.

Joseph nodded his thanks, and made his way to table 5, where he introduced himself. "Mozart," he repeated. Architecture and Structural Engineering."

"Joseph Mozart?" said one of the men behind the desk, raising his eyebrows in query.

"Yes," said Joseph.

"Welcome to Universitat Innsbruck Joseph. We will show you to your rooms. But first, here is a list of university rules, and there are forms for you to fill out. Full name, next of kin, home address, things like that. There is another form which lists your interests outside of your studies, such as skiing. If you would like to join the university clubs to join people of similar interests, you will be welcome, and on the list are probably some interests you may like to take up whilst you are here. If you fancy anything else on the list feel free to tick what you would be interested in. Please sit," and he indicated a chair in front of the desk, and fill out the first form before we take you up to your rooms."

Joseph sat, and began filling out the form, as the hall gradually filled with arriving freshers. The babble of voices echoed in the hall, sound bouncing off the high ceilings, white marbled walls and brown coloured marble columns.

He handed back the completed form, and one of the men behind the desk stood and said, " Let me introduce myself. My name is Johann Fischer. I am a 3rd year Structural Engineering student. I am also a Hauptgefolgschaftfuhrer of the college Hitler Youth, everyone is a member, and I am also an air cadet. I have trained on gliders."

"I have my glider pilots certificate, " said Joseph, "and I will be transferring from the Vienna Hitler Youth to the one here. I was a Gelfolgschaftsfuhrer in my old unit."

"We have a policy whereby you should retain your rank whilst here. Welcome comrade and follow me." He then picked up one of Joseph's cases, and walked toward the stairs.

"I'm afraid the first year students are housed at the top. It's a long climb. I hope you are fit."

"I do a bit of boxing and have trained twice a week lately. Hopefully I will be fit enough."

"Good," said Fischer,"You can join our boxing team too."

At the end of the climb, no matter how fit Joseph thought he was he was puffing and sweating. Lugging a heavy case up numerous flights of stairs was indeed hard work. He was relieved to find that Fischer was also out of breath.

They stopped outside a door bearing the number 11. There was a key in the door, which Fischer opened. Joseph saw that his room, held a bed, a wardrobe, a locker, a desk and had a large window which overlooked a quadrangle at the back of the building. It was light and airy.

"When you have settled in and unpacked, come down again to the desk. We will then take you to our faculty common room, where you will meet your fellow freshers, plus some of the 2nd and 3rd year students. Fill out that hobbies form and bring it with you to the common room and we can give you the timetables for the various clubs and events. In 2 hours time, there is a meal laid on and you will be taken there after you have finished in the faculty room. Welcome, I hope you enjoy your stay. Oh, before I forget, the bathroom facilities are out of your door, turn right and three doors down."

He then shook hands and left Joseph to his own devices to assimilate his surroundings and settle in.

He experienced the now familiar onset of homesickness. Shook his shoulders, and told himself to "get a grip", then concentrated on his unpacking.

Later, in the common room he was introduced to fellow fresher and second and third year students. He handed in his hobbies form to Johann Fischer who seemed to have taken responsibility for looking after him.

Fischer said, "I will guide you through your transfer to the college Hitler Youth, and as you have gliding as one of your main sports and we share that as a common interest, I will introduce you into our air cadet group, if that is what you want."

"I want to continue gliding. I have always loved it, and I would love to continue gliding here. I have flown once in the Innsbruck area. It's a beautiful part of the world and the thermals and updrafts are fantastic," enthused Joseph.

"I believe we have the best gliding in the world here. The Tyrol and the foothills of the Alps make sure of that. I see you have your gliding pilots certificate so you have obviously soloed. I expect however, you will have to convince our instructor before being let loose on your own, but I expect that should be a formality. I will also introduce you to our Oberstammfuhrer. His name is Rudolf Leitner. He is also our glider instructor. His brother is in the Luftwaffe. He's a good teacher and a good Austrian. Come, meet him, he is here."

They walked over to a group of youths surrounding a very tall, thin man, with dark wavy hair, dressed in the Hitler Youth Uniform, showing the insignia of an Oberstammfuhrer. He was holding court to a group and the conversation Joseph overheard as he approached was all about flying. They stood waiting their turn and Fischer excused his interruption.

"Sir, let me introduce our latest recruit. Joseph Mozart."

"Ah yes," said Leitner, "welcome to Innsbruck University. I have received your transfer notification from Vienna. You will retain your rank in the Hitler Youth whilst you are here, and I hear that you are a qualified glider pilot already and are a keen boxer?"

Joseph nodded his assent.

"Good. We can make use of your talents. Fischer here is a boxer too, and you would be a useful addition to our team, and as for the gliding. Fischer will bring you to our next meet where I will assess your skill. We will need pilots, I am sure in the future, and your glider training will prove very useful in putting you on a fast track to flying aircraft with engines. What are your intentions."

"Well sir, I want eventually to become an architect, so I am here to study that and structural engineering, and if I have to go into the forces I would want to join the Luftwaffe to become a pilot," said Joseph without much enthusiasm.

Ignoring Joseph's reluctance Leitner said, "We are Austrian, and since the Anschluss, we are part of the greater Germany, like it or not. We would be fools to think otherwise." He continued with a meaningful and warning expression. "Any dissent from that view would not now be acceptable. There is no doubt the greater Germany is rearming apace. The build up of our military forces means there is only one conclusion in my view. We are heading for war, I don't know when or whom we will be fighting but our Fuhrer's expansionist program is already under way with the taking over of the Sudetenland and now the rest of Czechoslovakia and I feel there will come a time fairly soon when the rest of Europe will object to the Fuhrer's plans, so we will need all our young men. Qualified pilots will be at a premium, so we will do our best to provide you with the right training. Meanwhile, of course, you are here to study, but I feel that we will have to prepare our air cadet force for what I believe will be inevitable. I will get Fischer here, to look after you and mentor you. He is a good chap and knows the ropes. He will look after you.   Right Fischer? " he said purposefully, looking directly at Fischer.

This gave Joseph much to think about. He had effectively been told, like it or not, he was destined to join Hitler's war machine at some time in the future and because of his training, he would be an obvious candidate for the Luftwaffe. Meanwhile he had to accept that if he wished to study, he had to be a member of the Hitler youth, and to continue his glider training.

Fischer interrupted his thoughts. "Come, I will show you round. I will show you the lecture rooms, the common rooms, the library and our Hitler Youth HQ." He added, when he saw Joseph's crestfallen expression. "I am Austrian too you know. I came here to study fine art and history. Now we, as a nation seem to be making history, I hope we have time to finish our studies, but something tells me we are on a roller coaster which we have no control over, and we cannot get off, no matter how much we would like to. A word of advice. Just be careful in expressing your views and to whom you express them. There are certain people here who are committed totally to the Nazi regime, and its tenets."

With that subtle warning on his mind, Joseph was conducted on a hour long tour of the university, and was grateful to observe during his tour Fischer was very much Austrian first, and not a committed Nazi. He was however, just like Joseph, a patriotic Austrian and would be compelled to commit to his duty for his country.

The next few days for Joseph were settling in days, where he got to know the geography of the university and got to know his fellow students and members of his Hitler Youth Unit, the boxing club and air cadet wing of the Hitler Youth.

Apart from Fischer, whom he shared empathetic views, he found a particular friend in Tomas Jager whose home was in Saltzburg. He was also on the same course, lived two rooms away from Joseph and was also involved in glider training. They found that they shared the same views on life and hit it off almost straight away. As time went on they became firm friends. Tomas's father was an architect in Saltzburg and he had two slightly younger sisters. His political views accorded largely with Joseph's. Neither were persuaded to the Nazi cause, but both had the realization that in the present political climate, they had to be seen to toe the line, especially if they wanted to achieve their ambitions.

The University Hitler Youth Unit, stood to attention, in the Innsbruck Town Square. The Blood Flag in evidence held by appointed flag bearers. The officer cadre of the unit, stood in a line at the front of their unit, and on a flag pole in the centre of the square fluttered the Nazi flag.

The University groups was only one of several units, all paraded in the square, with banners proudly fluttering in the evening breeze. Several hundred Hitler Youth, stood in total silence, all flags displayed. On a rostrum stood an imposing figure, resplendent in the uniform of a Bannfuhrer . He was the district commander of the Hitler Youth. Around the podium were grouped three Oberstammfuhrer and three Stammfuhrers. All were stiffly to attention, awaiting the words of their leader. Set in front of him was a bank of two microphones.

"I am Bannfuhrer Ernst Mayer," he boomed, his small moustache bristling, his chest puffed out.

"We are here today for the first district parade of our Hitler Youth." He paused, looking over the assembled squads, beaming with pride and passion. His voice rising.

"You are here this evening to show your allegiance to the Hitler Youth, your unit, and to our Fuhrer, Adolf Hitler. You will retake the Blood Oath tonight, and we will march proudly through our town, to show you are all part of our future and the grand plan of our Fuhrer. To show we are One People, One Reich, with One Fuhrer." He then raised his right arm to the Nazi salute, shouting with fervour, **"Seig Heil. Seig Heil. Seig Heil!"**

With that, the officers around the podium took up the chant, whilst raising their arms into the Nazi salute, and the chant was taken up by all the Hitler Youth on the parade. The shouts of Seig Heil echoed around the square, the voices of the parade added to by the watching population, until the pigeons rose into the evening sky, frightened by the noise.

It reached a crescendo, echoing on and on, until the Bannfuhrer nodded to the Hitler Youth band, waiting at the side of the square, and they struck up **Das Lied der Deutschen,** which, led by their Bannfuhrer, bellowing the words over his microphone, was joined with much enthusiasm by the assembled parading youths and some of the watching crowd. All stood with raised right arms, the passion and fervour of the moment swelling the breast with nationalistic pride, starting some of the more fervent with tears of joy.

Joseph, caught up in the moment joined in. He found himself in strange circumstances. There was no doubt that he was not an absolute Nazi, but the passion of the moment gripped him, and left him bemused at his own behaviour. He did not understand the effect the scenario was having on him. He was caught up in the moment despite his logic telling him he was being manipulated, and carried along on a wave of crowd passion and near hysteria.

The anthem came to a close. Mayer bellowed once again. "We will now take the oath of allegiance."

He repeated, and the crowd followed the words of the Hitler Youth oath to their Fuhrer. Again raising their arms in salute to the flag. With that Mayer left the podium, and the band struck up the Hitler Youth marching tune, **Forward, Forward, Blare the**

Bright Fanfare. Followed by his officer cadre, he stepped out in time to the music, and marched round the square, followed by each squad in turn, who followed him finally off the square, and through the public lined streets to the University, where the parade was halted in unit order outside the main entrance.

Mayer addressed the parade with passion again, bellowing his loudest, "Remember, **One People, One Fuhrer, One Reich. You are the future of a greater Germany! Parade dismissed.**"

Inside the university food hall, a light meal had been laid on for the participants. At the informal gathering many talked about the parade and its effect on them. Joseph singled out his friends, Tomas Jager, and Johann Fischer.

"What did you think of the parade, " said Fischer a sardonic smile on his face whilst raising one questioning eyebrow.

"Well, " said Joseph. "Interesting. I found myself caught up in the moment. The fervor and passion stirred something inside which I could not explain. It was exciting and frightening at the same time. I don't really know how to explain my feelings. I can understand why people get caught up in the rhetoric of the moment, the stirring music and patriotism shown. It takes on a force of its own and carries you along with it. It's like riding the waves. A strong and unstoppable force.

"I agree, " said Fischer. "If you think that about this parade, you should go to one of the National Rallies. I have and our Fuhrer is the most dynamic speaker I have ever heard. It is hard not to be caught up in his vision of Germany, of how it should be according to Nazi principles. A kind of mass hysteria. However, viewed dispassionately, as all thinking men should, if we carry on believing we are the master race, persecuting people, and taking over territory, there will be much trouble ahead for us. I believe we are just a few steps away from war, and if that happens, Germany will need all its young men."

He gave both Joseph and Tomas a meaningful stare, cocking his head in query and raising expressive and questioning eyebrows, leaving them in silent contemplation as he walked away.

The boys looked at one another. "He's right you know," said Joseph. "Where will it all end?"

Chapter Eight

Joseph quickly settled in to his new surroundings and his studies. In his free time he attended Hitler Youth meetings and pursued his hobbies of boxing and gliding. As time went on the intensity and fervour of the meetings increased as the successes of the Germany Army increased. More of the membership were sucked in by the constant Nazi militaristic propaganda. National pride at the loudly heralded government achievements swelled the ranks of the believers, until an almost religious feavour gripped the more malleable minds of the young recruits. Joseph tried to remain detached and clear thinking as he had always been taught, but it was hard to maintain a detachment with such fervour gripping the majority of Hitler Youth members when coupled with the constant bombardment of propaganda. Joseph's father would probably describe the situation as brain washing. His belief that once you have bent the minds of the young to a certain way of thinking, you probably had them for life, was prophetic. He had always desired his son remain a free thinker, whilst being a patriotic Austrian.

To maintain a certain detachment and to retain a semblance of individuality Joseph ensured he was always busy and honed his fitness to a peak. He took part in several boxing tournaments at middleweight, representing both the university and his Hitler Youth Unit. He improved over time, winning more than he lost. He also honed his skills as a glider pilot, and now flew solo over what was becoming familiar, but still breathtaking territory. The Tyrol was one of the most picturesque places on earth, in all seasons, and it was these activities, in serene surroundings, which cleared his thinking, returned him to logical thinking, and gave him the confidence to maintain a certain detachment from the mass hysteria being perpetrated on the ground. He was not a fool however, and kept his independent views to himself. It would be extremely foolish to broadcast his private thoughts in such a charged atmosphere.

During his first term Joseph also took skiing lessons, and by the end of his first year became a proficient skier. The constant activity made him as fit as he had ever been in his life. He was promoted within the ranks of the Hitler Youth to Obergefolgschaftsfuhrer (Lieutenant), a promotion which he did not necessarily want or seek as it cemented him more fully into the Hitler Youth, an organization that he did not whole heartedly approve of, as it was becoming more and more martial, as Germany rearmed. However, he was in a dilemma, as he loved the physical side of the Youth movement, and he enjoyed the companionship of some of his fellow members. He avoided the more committed and fanatical members of his group as he considered their blind acceptance of the Nazi mantra as dangerous.

During his first year it was apparent that Germany was expanding, mainly in the first instance, to the detriment of Czechoslovakia, but as the political machinations of the Nazi party increased its power and hold over the German people, dissent was dealt with, usually violently, by the thuggish behavior of the S.A Storm Troopers, who having been established in 1922, had become more powerful as the Nazi party's domination increased. Scapegoat minorities were persecuted with vigour.

As 1938 gave way to 1939, the newspapers reported on negotiations between France, Britain, and Italy, and as the year went on, various agreements were made with Hitler to prevent him increasing any further expansionist ambitions. In particular the allies wished to curtail his obvious and blatant ambitions toward Poland and the Baltic states. The British and French governments were represented by their Prime Ministers, who held frequent and more desperate meetings with Hitler, seen particularly in the British press as a one sided appeasement to a dictator to whose tune they danced. These meetings, whilst frustrating for the French and British Governments, seemed to have the effect of increasing Hitler's popularity at home, cementing and consolidating his power over the German peoples, both in Germany, Austria and in its captured territories.

On 1st September 1939, a momentous day in world history, Hitler's army invaded Poland, despite his promise not to. With its well practised Blitzkreig, or lightening war, honed and perfected during the Spanish Civil War, Hitler's army quickly overran Poland and it's armed forces, despite the valiant efforts of the Polish Airforce and it's brave pilots to hold him off, leading to its final capitulation within 35 days. As a consequence Britain and France declared war on Germany. Joseph was shocked at the news, especially as he remembered fondly his time in England and the friends he had made there. His university was abuzz with rumour and counter rumour. Joseph's group of Hitler Youth were generally delighted at the news, and parades in the town square became more frequent. Marching to rousing martial music, swaggering with pride at the successes of the German Forces, singing patriotic songs whilst marching around the town spurred a recruitment drive, swelling the units numbers considerably, all born on a wave of apparent patriotic invincibility. Many of the older boys in the movement began volunteering for the German armed forces, their studies and home life put on hold.

Despite his training in gliders, and being of age to join up, Joseph was reluctant to give up his studies. He was in a minority however, as most of his compatriots showed a keenness to join the various branches of the armed forces. The majority of his compatriots in the Air Cadets, of course, wished to join the Luftwaffe, and to fly the latest aircraft. They were looked upon as the new heroes of the Reich.

Posters were displayed in all public places and within the university, urging those over 18 to join up. This was, after all, the underlying purpose of the Hitler Youth, to provide fit and committed young men for Hitler's forces . Obedience, fitness and fighting spirit. Joseph lacked none of these attributes, but he was determined to finish his studies before making any final decision.

In October 1939, at term break, Joseph returned to Vienna to his parent's house. He was welcomed with open arms by his family, and he was reunited with his friend Walter Buamgarten who was also on a break from his studies. They had missed one another, and over the next few days reignited their life- long friendship. Both were now over eighteen and of the age when they could join the armed forces, both being trained glider pilots, but they both had the desire to finish their studies.

The Vienna they both knew was changing. The number of people in uniform seemed to outnumber those in civilian clothes. Militaristic parades became a regular occurrence. Martial music filled the coffee houses, cafes and squares. Grim faced, black uniformed SS patrols roamed the streets, as did the brown shirted S.A. There was an undercurrent of apprehension and fear whenever they appeared on the streets, usually in squad formation, marching with purposeful stride, their intent to ensure the civilian population toed the Nazi party line in all respects. Any dissent was crushed immediately and forcefully . Prominent among their number was Ernst Bruen, a natural bully and ex-pupil of their school in Vienna. He was now parading the district as a member of the S.A., and seemed to thrive on being able to throw his weight around in the name of the state. He had always envied Joseph and Walter, and whilst at school had always tried to make their lives uncomfortable. He and his like were to be avoided whenever possible.

The cafes and restaurants were doing a roaring trade, but many of the shops, particularly those whose previous owners had been Jewish, were boarded up with anti-Jewish slogans still prominent on the shop face. Much of it the work of local S.A. who seemed to revel in the terror they caused in the name of the Reich. The aftermath of Kristallnacht, the Kindertransport operations, reports of Czechoslovakian Ghettos filled with Jewish people and their subsequent transport to what was euphemistically called "labour Camps" was reported sparingly in the newspapers, alongside the headlines of triumphs of the German Blitzkreig operations. Posters urging recruitment were everywhere.

Doctor Maximillian Mozart, Joseph's father, was a trauma surgeon at the main hospital in Vienna. He had been a field surgeon just after qualifying from medical school, during the First World War, only returning home at the end of hostilities. The war had affected him deeply. As a newly qualified physician he had been thrown into the deep end of trauma surgery, and some of the horrors he witnessed stayed in his conscious mind for the rest of his life, but his experiences made him an excellent and eminent surgeon when he applied the skills he had learned during the First World War, to his civilian role at Vienna's main hospital.

He sat, as if in a trance, alone in his living room. He had received an official letter. Will we never learn, he thought. History repeating itself. It was postmarked in Frankfurt, and came from the office of the Adjutant General. He had read and re-read the content. It summonsed him to the Army Recruiting office in the Rathaus der Wein (Town Hall of Vienna) off Rathaus Platz at 10am the following day. He was being recalled to the German Army Medical Service. He would find out more at the Rathaus.

He sat, alone in the dark. His wife, Emma entered the room. She switched the light on.

"What's the matter my darling. Why so glum?"

He handed her the letter, without saying anything.

She read it, gasped, putting her hand to her mouth. Tears starting to flow.

"They can't do that. You've done your bit in the first war." She whispered, her voice choking.

"They can, and they have it appears," said Doctor Mozart with a heavy sigh.

"I have to report tomorrow at the Rathaus, as you see."

"It's not fair. You are wanted here. The Hospital needs you." She sobbed.

"If I don't go, they will come after me. I will go and find out what they want of me."

They sat holding each other for a long moment, taking comfort from each other at the dread news. As they sat, Joseph opened the front door and switched the lights on. He saw immediately his mother had been weeping, and his father looked grim.

"What's a matter?" he asked.

His mother handed the letter to Joseph, who read it quickly.

"Can they do this?" said Joseph. "Just like that. Take you back into the Army?"

"It would appear so," said his father. "They are obviously expanding the war. I expect Herr Hitler is set to invade other countries now that France and Britain have declared war on Germany. He will obviously want more troops, and of course if the war expands, so will the dead and wounded increase. This summons makes me believe he is intent on expanding the Third Reich. It will mean much bloodshed I fear." He gave a heavy sigh, and a final hug to his wife, before standing, resigned to his fate.

As he stood, he looked at Joseph and said, "I want you to finish your course at university if you can. You are now a trained glider pilot, and the next obvious step is for you to join the Luftwaffe. Please try and put this off until you have your degree. The war will not last forever, and architects will be in high demand rebuilding what is destroyed. I fear we as a nation are making too many enemies and we have a long hard road to travel. Please go back to your studies. Will you do that for me?"

"Yes Papa," said Joseph. "But what about Mother. How will she get on without you?"

Frau Mozart said, "Joseph, don't worry about me. I will still be needed at the hospital. I have responsibilities as Matron, and I feel I will be as busy as ever now. Your Father is right. Go back to your studies. Write to me, and come and see me in the next holidays."

Joseph looked crestfallen, but nodded his assent. "I will Mother."

The following day Doctor Mozart attended the Rathaus, and was directed to an office on the first floor. Sitting behind an antique desk, on which were a bank of three telephones, sat an Oberleutenant, who was speaking into one of the telephones. He ignored Doctor Mozart whilst he finished his conversation. Once he finished speaking he continued to ignore the man standing in front of him, whilst he made notes and shuffled papers. After a long moment, he looked up, and in an officious voice curtly demanded, "Yes?"

Patiently Doctor Mozart passed over the letter he had received the day before. With a sigh the Oberleutenant snatched the letter officiously, read it, saying curtly "Wait here!"

He then got up, straightened his uniform tunic, and went to a door behind his desk. Rapped smartly, and at the "Come!" Went inside. He was gone for a short time, and when he came out, said, in a more courteous and chastened manner, "Please go in Sir."

In the inner office sat an Oberst dressed in the uniform of the German Army Medical Service. He stood as Doctor Mozart entered the room, and held out his hand in greeting. Mozart took the hand and shook it, surprised that he recognized Doctor Boris Schaffer, an eminent surgeon from a hospital in Berlin, with whom he had served in World War One, when both held the rank of Hauptmann.

"Max," said Schaffer. "We meet again after all this time. I followed your progress over the years. It's been a long time since we served together on the western front, and a lot of water has passed under the bridge since then."

They chatted of times past and caught up with their respective family circumstances. Then Doctor Schaffer became more serious.

"It is unfortunate we meet under these circumstances. But as you see I have been called back into service, just as you have. There is nothing I can do about it, and the same applies to you. The Army needs our services, and the Third Reich, in other words, our Fuhrer, places demands on our profession, to bolster the numbers of army surgeons. In my view this can only mean he has expansionist ambitions, which will mean we will both be in a war again. You and I are needed, and I have written orders for you. You are to report in two weeks time to the Adjutant General's office in Frankfurt. You will be given the rank of Oberslieutenant. Where you will be posted and what training they have lined up for you I have no idea. But with your skills, I would imagine that you will be a chief surgeon somewhere. All I can say, is I am sorry to be the harbinger of bad news, but as you see, I am back in the army, and it looks like you are too." He shrugged in helpless resignation.

Doctor Mozart said, "Well. It's good to see you again. I don't like the circumstances of our renewing our acquaintanceship Boris. But I see your hands are tied as much as mine."

"I will come out with you. Between you and me, my adjutant is a dyed in the wool party member. He's nasty, creepy, and as far as I am concerned not to be trusted. I suspect him of spying for the SS. But they have foisted him on me, I suspect to keep an eye on me. So watch what you say in front of him. If he shakes your hand then count your fingers." He said with a throaty chuckle.

"Come, I will get him to give you your travel warrant."

They entered the outer office and the Lieutenant sprang to his feet and clicked his heels, displaying his subservience to the authority of his Colonel.

"Muller. Please give the Obersleutenant his travel warrant."

At the mention of his newly acquired rank, Muller became obsequious. His attitude changing from officious and rude to overly polite and subservient.

"Of course, Oberst. I have it ready."

He then handed Doctor Mozart his travel warrant. Mozart shook hands with Doctor Schaffer. "It's was good to see you again Boris," he said, "I wish the circumstances were better."

"Good Luck Max." said, Schaffer, shaking Mozart's hand. "I hope we meet again."

Muller rushed to the door, opening it for the departing Mozart, clicking his heels and raising his right hand in salute shouting "Heil Hitler."

As Doctor Mozart looked back he saw that Schaffer had raised his eyebrows in silent disapproval of Muller's absurdity. He stifled a sympathetic chuckle and swept from the room before he gave way to uncontrolled mirth at the behavior of such an obvious party member and would be martinet.

A few days later Joseph said goodbye to his Mother, Father and his friend Walter, and returned to Innsbruck to resume his studies. As he travelled, he saw newspaper headlies. The British Expeditionary Force (BEF) had travelled to France to reinforce the French Army. They bolstered the numbers manning the Maginot Line, on the border of Germany and France, and had landed forces in Cherbourg, Nantes and St Nazaire, supplementing the French forces with an estimated 300,000 men.

Once back at university, there was much discussion on the news of the British and French combined armies, and the effect their numbers might have on the ambitions of the Wehrmacht, but after the initial headlines, there followed a quiet period where a stalemate appeared to be in place.

It was well known the French thought the Maginot line was formidable and impregnable. However, after some months of inaction, headlines announced the Wehrmacht had bypassed the Maginot line by a lightening push by mechanized brigades through the Forest of the Ardennes, and were now located both in the front and rear of the line. British and French troops were steadily falling back towards the coast of Northern France and Belgium.

The news became the talk of the university and of the Hitler Youth. Many more were encouraged to leave the youth movement and join the forces. Several of the older members left to join the Luftwaffe, and pressure was growing on those left behind to join up in their turn. Joseph determinedly stuck to the wishes of his family, and remained at his studies. The German air force and army were doing well without him.

The news and newspapers reported in late May 1940 that the British Expeditionary Forces and their French allies, were surrounded in Belgium. The victorious German Army had become an unstoppable force, and was laying siege to the British troops on the beaches of Dunkirk. It was reported the Luftwaffe were carrying out regular bombing and strafing operations in the area and on the beaches, against an armada of ships and small boats attempting to carry the British and French troops off the beaches, and the heroic pilots of the Luftwaffe were engaged in aerial warfare with the Royal Air Force, and showing great success. The Dunkirk operations lasted for about two weeks, until finally the Wehrmacht overran the defenses and captured over 40,000 British and French defending soldiers. That over 300,000 British and French troops had been evacuated back to England, was largely ignored in the German press, but a clear and decisive victory was heralded and celebrated by the Fuhrer and his Generals. Victory Parades were held in major cities, and again the Innsbruck University Hitler Youth played their part in the celebrations, by parading around the town, with bands playing, being cheered by the local population as they marched.

The rest of France capitulated and pictures of the Fuhrer in Paris were shown on the newsreels. It was a heady time. Greater Germany now held the territories of Czechoslovakia, Poland, Luxemburg, the Netherlands, Belgium and France, and the German army gradually consolidated their territorial gains, occupying and setting up coastal defenses whilst only Britain remained defiant.

Another period of calm, where the German Invasion Forces consolidated their manpower preceded what Hitler heralded in large headlines as "Luftschlacht un England" (Air Battle for England) and which the British later called the Battle of Britain. It trumpeted his ambition for a seaborne and airborne invasion of Britain, known as "Operation Sea Lion".

From 10th July 1940, regular news update reported the bombing of British airfields, and the victories achieved against the defending and beleaguered Royal Air Force. Air Aces of the Luftwaffe were honoured as "Heroes of the Reich" by Hitler awarding them various grades of Iron Cross Decorations, and their battle achievements were heralded in the German Press. It was a heady time for the German nation, with victory following victory, and following the successes, recruitment to the services proceeded apace.

Joseph visited his parents a few weeks later. They had requested he go home to say farewell to his father, who was now in the Army Medical Corps, and on his way to his first posting. He was now an Obersleutenant. His re-introduction to the military had been swift and re-training rudimentary, as he had held the rank of Hauptmann the first war, and remained familiar with military ethics. Joseph admired his father, whom he saw as an imposing figure in his new uniform, carrying his new rank with inborn authority. He had been, after all, a senior surgeon at the main hospital in Vienna and was used to dispensing medicine with the inbred authority of a senior medical practitioner. He was to be posted to run a surgical unit at Hopital Litie-Salpetriere, in Paris, located on the banks of the river Seine, and which, since the invasion and occupation of France had been taken under German control. Its main function now, was the treatment of wounded military personnel, and Doctor Mozart was tasked to re-organize the hospital to accommodate the wounded.

Joseph had little time to be re-acquainted with his father, as that very afternoon, Doctor Mozart had to catch a train to Paris. The family stood on the station platform in Vienna to say their farewells. The train was emitting steam as it prepared to leave, consequently the farewells were brief.

"Joseph. Try to stay at your studies," said his father, "And look after your mother."

"Yes, Papa," said Joseph tearfully, as he hugged his father. "I will do my best."

"Goobye my love, " said Doctor Mozart to his wife Emma. "I know you will be busy at the hospital. We live in strange times. Please take care of yourself." He briefly kissed his wife, shook hands solemnly with Joseph, and then stepped aboard the train.

He stood at the open window, as the train moved away from the platform, and stayed watching and waving until the bend in the tracks took him from view.

The following day Joseph met his friend Walter, who was also home from University and they met for coffee at their favourite café, the Café Central near the Vienna Rathaus, where they enjoyed a convivial morning swopping stories of their university life and catching up in general. As they left to go home, a squad of brown shirted S.A. Troopers, surrounded them. Their leader was their old nemesis, the bully Ernst Bruen, wearing the insignia of an S.A. Sturmfuhrer.

"Mozart. Baumgarten!" shouted Bruen. "We have been looking for you. You are to come with me right now. You are to be taken immediately to the Luftwaffe Recruiting office in the Rathaus . Your country needs you." He said with a vicious smile on his face.

Joseph's reaction was to pull back his fist and punch Bruen's face. He was half way through the blow, which brought a look of fear onto Bruen's face, when he felt a vicious blow to the back of his head, and he felt arms grab him and force him, reeling, to his knees. Bruen then stood over him and struck him full in the face with a swagger stick, causing blood to start from his nose, and a cut under the eye. Walter's arms were similarly pinned by two burly S.A. troopers.

"Don't give me any more trouble, either of you. I have here your conscription papers. As I said, your country needs you. You are both trained glider pilots, and the Luftwaffe wants you. Give me any more trouble," he said with a sneer, waving the papers in their faces,"and you will go in the cells."

By now a crowd had gathered, watching the bully boys of the S.A. secure the two youths, giving way as they cut through the crowd frog-marching Joseph and Walter across the Rathaus Park, and up the main steps of the imposing Rathaus buiding.

Once inside the building, they were frog-marched to the first floor, and into an office marked as Luftwaffe Recruiting Centre. The squad with its unwilling recruits came to a halt in front of a desk, behind which sat a Luftwaffe officer showing Hauptmann (Captain) insignia.

"What's going on here?" demanded the Hauptmann.

Bruen interjected with a leer, "I have served these two with their call up papers. They are under orders to report here to join up."

The Hauptmann looked at the two boys, still being held by the troopers. He noticed Joseph's injured face, and said to Bruen, "Well they are here now. Release them."

When their guards still held on to them the Hauptmann roared in a parade ground voice, **"I said release them."**

Their escorts jumped as if electrocuted. Stepping quickly away from their charges.

The Hauptmann stared with disgust at Bruen, shouting, "You can go." When they didn't move quickly enough to his command he again roared, **"Go. Get out. Now!"**

Bruen jumped, flung the call up papers at the two boys, and leapt for the door his squad tore after him, looking fearful, and in their haste jammed themselves in the doorway anxious to escape the wrath of the Hauptman, who smiled to himself when he saw their comical efforts to exit.

The Hauptmann looked at Joseph, smiled, and said, "Are you alright."

"Yes, " said Joseph, "I've had worse in the boxing ring. Bruen took us by surprise that's all. We went to the same school as Bruen, he was always a bully and now he's a bully in a brown shirt. We were having a quiet cup of coffee having come home from university, when he turned up. We were hoping to finish our university courses, before we needed to join up, but it looks like we will have to put our education on hold for a time."

The Hauptmann smiled sympathetically, as said, "Sit down and tell me your stories. Let me have a look at the call up papers."

He studied the papers for a while, looked at Joseph and said, " My name is Hans Reiter. I am a Hauptmann in the Luftwaffe, on temporary assignment as recruiting officer for this district. I normally fly ME109's. Your conscription documents are issued from the Ministry and your service is mandatory I am afraid. I see from the document you have a glider pilot's permit, and you are a member of the Hitler Youth in the rank of Obersgfolgschaftfuhrer, and you study at Innsbruck University."

"Yes," said Joseph. I am in my second year studying architecture and structural engineering."

"And you want to fly?"

"Yes," said Joseph. "I have always wanted to fly, but my father wants me to complete my degree course at university. I was going to complete my course and then if the war was still on, I was going to volunteer. I saw my father off yesterday. He is a surgeon and has been recalled to the Army Medical Service, being posted to Paris."

"I am afraid it will not be possible at present to complete your university course, but the Fuhrer has decreed that all students who have not completed their courses, may do so at the end of the war. I have to instruct you to attend Schleissheim Luftwaffe Air Base in Bavaria near Munich, in one week from today, for assessment to undertake flying training."

He looked at Walter and said, "The same applies to you Herr Baumgarten. I will issue you both with travel warrants. You are now, both of you under military orders to report for training. I would suggest that you both return home, make you farewells to your family. Inform your respective Universities and your Hitler Youth Units. These orders supersede all and every other instruction you have or may be given."

He then handed each a folder of instructions. "Please read what these documents contain very carefully. Good luck Gentlemen. If you have any further questions, I am here to provide the answers. Welcome to the Luftwaffe."

He shook hands with each of them and showed them to the door.

Chapter Nine

Joseph and Walter arrived on the platform of the Schleissheim Railway Station, carrying their cases, looking apprehensive. They were in a crowd of similarly aged young men, all chattering excitedly. They walked through the exit arch, to see a large covered truck waiting near the entry point. As they got near a man jumped down from the vehicle. He was in the uniform of a Luftwaffe Obergefreiter.

"All those for Schleissheim Air Base, line up beside the lorry." He shouted.

Most of the young men from the train shuffled into a semblance of a line.

"Straighten up. Straighten up," he shouted. "Put those cases down, and let me look at you."

He then walked the line, staring into the eyes of each one, and stepping back to view the overall image.

"Well, I don't know what this country is coming too," he screamed, turning a shade of purple. "If this is the best we've got, then God and the Fuhrer help us. Now, get into the back of the lorry. Sharply mind!"

They shuffled quickly toward the back of the lorry, and helped one another into the back. It was crowded, a tight fit. Joseph and Walter felt every bump as the lorry roared its way toward their destination, leaving a trail of black exhaust fumes in its wake.

The lorry slowed and came to a halt after a 20 minute journey, and Joseph saw that they were approaching the main gate of the air base. He could see aircraft in the distance, and just inside the gate, was a single storied wooden building, painted black. It had a wooden veranda, on which stood an officer.

"Out, " shouted the Obergefreiter. "Out and line up for inspection. The officer wants to see what he's got coming. Lively now."

They jumped down from the lorry and lined up in a semblance of parade order. When the Oberefreiter had settled them to his satisfaction, the officer walked purposefully along the line, inspecting his new recruits.

Once the inspection was completed, without any words being spoken, the Obergefreiter consulted a list on a clip board. He walked the line, standing in front of each person, and demanding their name.

When he received a reply, he shouted. "Obergefreiter! Get it." He got to the next person in line shouting.

"You will say your name and then address me as Obergefreiter. Right?"

The next person in line got it right with the addition of "Obergefreiter."

Thus the intake of some 20 souls were introduced to the rituals of life in the Luftwaffe.

Once the Corporal had finished his head count, he reported that the intake numbers were correct and the officer deigned to speak.

"You men have been conscripted into the Luftwaffe, and you are here to assess whether you are good enough to fly. A lot of you will fail. If you fail, you will be shipped out to other duties. We only take the cream of the crop. I understand you have all qualified as glider pilots but that does not necessarily mean that you will be good enough to fly one of our Fuhrer's aircraft. They are expensive machines, and only the best will qualify to fly them. Over the course of the next few months, if you last that long here, you will be taught to fly. If you succeed in flying, you will then be taught tactics, basically how to fight in the air, and how to win.

Winning is important, and must be your ultimate goal from now on. You will be taken from here, to the trainees mess, where a meal is prepared for you. When you have eaten, you will be assigned barracks, and given time to settle in. In the morning you will all undergo a medical examination, and be issued with a uniform. Once that is completed you will undergo a written examination to assess your capabilities, and the results could influence whether you become Non-Commisioned Officers or Commissioned Officers. If you fail your flying aptitude, then you may be reverted to other ranks. It is largely up to you, your ability, and the effort you put into your training. Obergefreiter. Take them to the trainees mess."

At the officer's command he shouted, "Pick up you cases, form two lines and follow me. Left, right, left right!"

They marched to a huge wooden building, and leaving their cases in the entrance lobby, entered the mess set with long dining tables. Food was steaming in big trays and pans, on a long table at the end of the room, manned by a dozen cooks, armed with ladles. There were others present in civilian clothes and some newly uniformed young men already sitting at tables, eating.

The babble of noise quietened as everyone present stared at the newcomers.

Self-consciously the new recruits made their way to the table laden with food, and were served a hot meal of potatoes, sauerkraut, sausage and gravy. They were then directed to a vacant table, embarrassment showing visibly on each of their faces. It was strange times, and strange surroundings. As they ate, they got to know those around them. Some had come in a group and others alone. Joseph and Walter sat together gathering comfort from each other's presence. The room went quiet again, as another group of trainees entered. The new arrivals suffered the same attention from the room as Joseph and Walter had experienced, until they too settled to their meal.

Once the meal was over, the same Obergefreiter collected his charges and directed them to a line of black painted wooden barrack rooms, about 100 metres from the mess hall. It was marked in large while letters on the door J20.

"This is your barrack room. Your home for the next 9 months if you make it that far. To save squabbles, I will allocate the beds. Unpack your cases, and put your things in the bedside locker. Hang you coats in the wardrobes and stay in here until morning. We rise at 0600, and by 0630 I want you all standing in a line outside. I will then take you to breakfast, then for medical examination. You will then be taken for your aptitude tests, and uniform issue. I will look after you just like your mothers. The toilets and ablutions are in the end room. I would remind you. You will be washed, shaved and dressed and outside by 0630."

Joseph looked at Walter. They were lucky as their beds were opposite one another and they could talk without walking the length of the room. Joseph looked around. He saw that the only heating in the room was a large pot- bellied stove beside which was a large bucket full of coal. Another bucket on the other side contained chopped sticks of wood. The unlined walls were painted black like the outside walls, adding to a depressive atmosphere. Joseph felt strange and despite Walter's presence, a weird kind of loneliness. He shrugged his shoulders and told himself to get a grip of his feelings. He was where he wanted to be.

Joseph spent the evening, as did the other trainees, putting away his clothes, and getting to know his companions. At lights out he laid in the dark, listening to the heavy breathing, snoring, bed creaks, and guttural noises of those who managed to get to sleep before him. He tossed and turned for what seemed to be ages, before finally he managed to sleep. It only seemed a very short while, until the lights in the room where switched on. A stentorious voice bellowed.

"Wake Up. Wake Up you lazy lot. It's time. Rise and shine." It was their ever loving Obergefreiter shouting with a malicious grin on his face at their discomfort.

"You have 30 minutes to be washed, dressed and outside. You lucky people!"

The rush for the bathroom became a stampede. Cold water was splashed. Razors flashed across cold faces, some creating bloody nicks. There was no hot water, but it did not matter, there were too many people to share too few sinks, showers, and baths. Somehow, Joseph completed his ablutions, and dressed in time to join the assembled trainee squad outside. Where they stood, yawning and scratching under the scrutiny of a very wide away Obergefreiterl, who surveyed them with contempt. They were disorientated, disheveled and indisciplined. Yesterday they were students, leading the indolent life of the campus and civilian life, today they were subject to the rigours and rigid routine of the military. A vast change for most of them, even those who had been members of the Hitler Youth. Joseph vowed to get up earlier the next day and make a habit beating the crowd. He hoped that none of his companions would adopt the same policy so he at least would have a free run at his ablutions.

The Obergefreiter marched them to the parade ground, shouting at them to keep in step, where others were assembling in squad order. They were pushed and cajoled into rough formation, and told to stand to attention. Some squads were in uniform, and some newly arrived were not.

As they stood in the cold dawn, silent and wondering what would come next, a Stabsfeldwebel, resplendent in uniform and carrying a cane beneath his left arm, marched onto the parade ground. He marched to the centre of the square, came to attention with a crash of heels, and stood, looking along the lines of uniformed and civilian clothed trainees, his moustache bristling. He obviously disliked what he saw before him as his complexion purpled with restrained fury.

"The parade will come to attention." He screamed. Not liking the first efforts, he shouted "At ease!

Now wake up and let's try again. PARADE. ATTENTION!"

This time, although it was still a shambles, he let it go as a group of officers, resplendent in full uniforms of the Luftwaffe, led by Oberst Heinz Weber, walked from what was obviously the headquarters building to the centre of the square.

In the silence that followed, the officer group, led by the Oberst, walked along the ranks of those squads which were in uniform. He walked slowly, carefully inspecting them, pausing occasionally for comment to the Stabsfeldwebel who attentively followed.

When he had finished with these squads he had the Stabsfgeldwebel dismiss these men to the mess hall. Those not in uniform, were the newly arrived, and remained.

"I would like to welcome you all to the Luftwaffe. Here it is intended to train you all to be pilots. But first your are to be trained to our military ways. For those who succeed, the course will last 9 months. For those who do not succeed, you will be assigned to other duties within the Luftwaffe. Today you will be taking an aptitude test, and depending on the results, you will be assigned to your training group.

You will all be required to pass a medical, and uniforms will be issued according to the results of your test. Some will become officer cadets, others will not, depending upon ability. For now, welcome to the finest and most successful air force in the world. Only your best will do, as we set the highest of standards. Obey all orders of your superiors. I wish you luck."

He turned to the Stabsfeldwebel. "Dismiss the men, and send them to breakfast. I'll leave it to you Stabs."

The Stabefeldwebel stamped to attention, "Sir! Heil Hitler!" he shouted, his arm extending into the Nazi salute.

The officer party walked off the parade ground, returning to the headquarters building, and once they were out of sight, the Stabsfeldwebel shouted for the to dismiss their charges in squad order and take them to the mess hall for breakfast. Thus started Joseph's first day. A day to remember.

After a quick breakfast they were all marched to a large hall, set out as an examination room, with individual desks and a chair at each desk. The next three hours were consumed by silence, as the trainees undertook a written examination. This would be part of their overall assessment. Once the examination was over they were marched to another wooden building, where they lined up and were subjected to questioning by a panel of aviators and psychologists, assessed their flying experience and their mental stability.

They were marched to the mess hall again, for a midday meal and from there they were marched in squad order to a large wooden building where they were lined up and issued with a uniform.

Carrying armfuls of uniform, they were marched back to their dormitory hut, where the Obergefreiter went through instructions on how to wear and look after their new clothes. He included instructions on laundering their clothes, and showed them the ironing facilities within their hut.

"You now have two hours to prepare your uniform, and put it on. In two hours time I will return and you will parade outside this hut for inspection. You have a lot to do. So get on with it. I will return."

As he left the hut, it became a bustle of frantic activity, as the trainees tried on their clothes. They queued for the ironing equipment, polished boots, creased trousers, and tied ties.

The Obergefreiter returned, shouting, "Outside you lot. Form up. Smartly now."

They stood in a line, displaying their new uniforms in various states of disorder. The Obergefreiter walked the line slowly examining each trainee. Pulling here, straightening there. Criticizing and cajoling, until he had each trainee looking like the Flight Cadets they now were. By the time he was semi-satisfied with their turnout, he marched them again to the mess for their evening meal, after which he marched them back to their billet, where he proceeded to lecture them on the care and presentation of their newly acquired uniform. He also showed them how he wanted the spare uniform folded and stored, a system alien to most of the trainees.

At lights out, they were exhausted. Joseph and Walter looked at one another and with a sigh of relief, collapsed into their beds, where they quickly fell asleep, only for the whole mad scramble to be restarted the following morning.

The following days and weeks blurred into a whirl of activity. They were paraded each morning, taught to march, drill, handle weapons and fire them. They were double marched, made to run across country wearing packs on their backs. They swam, took part in unarmed combat, and one afternoon each week they participated in sport. This time of the year is was mostly skiing on the nearby slopes. For a month they were not allowed near an aircraft.

The newspapers were reluctantly reporting German setback in the war against Britain. Operation Sealion had not gone well. The Fuhrer made the decision to abandon his plans for the invasion of England. The whole of Joseph's intake of trainees were marched on to the parade ground. They stood in silence as a cadre of officers marched, grim faced, from the Headquarters building to the raised saluting platform in the centre of the parade square. The Commandant, Oberst Heinz Weber mounted the platform. He stood momentarily in silence surveying the sea of faces looking with anticipation at him.

"This is a sad day for the Reich and our nation," he shouted. "Our Fuhrer has abandoned his plans to invade England. Operation Sealion, reported widely in our newspapers and on the radio, will not now take place."

A hum of noise rose from the assembled trainees as they absorbed the bad news. The Stabsfeldwebel standing below the platform shouted, "Quiet in the ranks. SILENCE!" The noise abated.

Oberst Weber continued, "This is the only setback in our Fuhrer's plans. But it is only a setback. We still control Czechoslovakia, Poland, Belgium, Holland and France. We have been victorious in all these theatres, and the British RAF is licking its wounds as we speak. As I said, this is only a set back, which will be put right by your efforts in the near future. It reinforces our need to train pilots. You are the future of the Luftwaffe. As a consequence, I have received orders to speed up your training. We are therefore bringing forward plans to shorten and intensify the training program. You will all have to work harder to achieve your goals in a shorter time. Your instructors will tell you more in the following days. Your Fuhrer, your Reich, your Luftwaffe need you more than ever," he shouted, his voice rising in crescendo.

He stood smartly to attention, raised his arm in the Nazi salute and shouted, "Heil Hitler. Heil Hitler!"

The parade took up the call, the noise was thunderous. "Heil Hitler," echoed and re-echoed around the parade. It was a heady moment, turning a set back into a hope of future triumph. It roused the trainees to a fervour of patriotism, and stimulated their collective determination to achieve an ultimate victory.

The noise subsided and the Oberst and his cohort of more junior officers, left the platform, returning to headquarters. The Stabsfeldwebel bellowed. "SILENCE." He paused and then shouted again, "DISMISSED!"

As the trainees left the parade ground a cacophony of noise rose from the departing crowd. The announcement had made a huge impact on them in many different ways. To some, dedicated to the Nazi cause, it increased their fervour and blind obedience to their Fuhrer. For others, who were less committed, it showed in their more logical minds that the Reich was not as infallible as was heralded by the newspapers and radio announcements. However, this was not a time to show any sort of disloyalty, even though it showed a definite chink in the Nazi war machine and planning.

After four weeks, the training program suddenly went into overdrive. They were marched to the airfield, where they saw an array of aircraft lined up in front of a large hanger.

Standing waiting for them they saw an Oberstleutnant, and a cadre of other officers. They were brought to attention in front of them.

"I am Oberstleutnant Boris Konig. I am your chief instructor, and these officers are your instructors. You are now all to begin your flying training on an accelerated program, to meet the needs of the Reich and of the Luftwaffe. During this training you will be constantly assessed on your flying ability. You will start on two seater trainer aircraft, and if you are suitable you will progress to other more advanced trainers, until finally selected for fighters, bombers or transport aircraft. Your progress will depend upon your ability. Some will fail, and will leave this training program to be sent to other non-flying units. The training is designed to find those suited to flying. We will not condemn you for failing the course, as some people are just not natural pilots. However, be assured your country needs pilots at this time, and we will do our best to help you achieve your wings. Now inside the hanger, you will be issued with your flying suits, and when you have been kitted out your instructor will call out your name and your will join his group of trainees."

The group were marched into the hanger where there was a long table, stacked with neat piles of flying overalls, helmets and goggles. The clothing store staff quickly assessed the sizes of the trainees and they spent the next two hours drawing and wearing their kit. Joseph felt self conscious in his new unfamiliar gear, and there was a general atmosphere of levity as the students paraded around showing off their new clothes.

A mobile canteen vehicle arrived to provide the students with refreshments, which paused the levity, after which the cadre of instructors reappeared and started calling names.

Joseph was called to a group of four students by a Major, and he saw Walter called to another instructor. The Major addressed his group.

"I am Major Horst Leitner, and I will be your flying instructor for the first part of your training. I see from your profiles that you all have gliding experience, and have all soloed on gliders. That is a good start. Now this afternoon I will be taking you up in one of our trainers. Follow me."

He then took his squad to the side of the hanger, where stood a two seater biplane.

Leitner indicated the aircraft saying. "This is the Focke Wulf 44 primary trainer. This is one of the machines which you will initially fly. Once you are proficient, you will move on to the Arado 66 advanced trainer, and depending on your ability, you will then be directed to an advanced flying school, where your suitability for Fighters, Bombers or Transport Command, or not, will be assessed. So, now prepare yourself. I will take you up initially in alphabetical order." Joseph found he was to be the third in line.

With his instructor, Major Leitner watching, Joseph walked around the aircraft checking the wheels, flaps, tail, and engine cowling for leaks. Joseph climbed aboard the machine, settling himself on his parachute pack, in the front seat of the FW Trainer. He plugged in his intercom lead, as he had been instructed, and strapped himself in.

The voice of his Instructor said, "Make sure that your seat is as comfortable as you can make it, sitting on your chute pack, and make sure that your harness is done up and tight." Sage advice if he was to sit in the aircraft for hours, and carry out aerial manoeuvres.

Joseph pulled at the straps to ensure he had carried out the instruction.

"Now, let me run through the controls. Your will be familiar with most as you hold your gliding license, but as you know this aircraft has an engine, and you will also have to be aware of the difference that makes when in the air. Obviously thermals mean little when you have an engine as your power source, however you may still feel their effect, when your aircraft takes a sudden dip or rise. It is something you have to be aware of and be ready to counteract when it happens. Okay, let's get started."

Leitner signaled to the ground staff, who went through the startup routine, and the engine burst into life. The chocks were removed, and Leitner opened the throttle, whilst talking Joseph through the procedure step by step.

"Take note of what I am telling you, because you will have to master the startup procedure and very soon, you will be piloting the aircraft yourself."

Leitner taxied the aircraft to the main runway, and Joseph heard him ask the control tower for permission to take off. With permission given, the engine note rose as Leitner held the machine against the brakes, until it had reached the optimum revolutions for take off. He then released the brakes, and the aircraft started to accelerate. In a surprising short time Joseph felt the bumping of the undercarriage cease as the aircraft left the ground, and they were airborne. They climbed slowly to 1000 metres, then banked left toward the foothills in the distance. The noise of the wind increased in the open cockpit, and Joseph was grateful for his flying helmet and goggles. It got considerably colder as they rose, but the views were magnificent, and Joseph found himself again lost in the wonder of the panorama, until Leitner's voice brought him back to reality.

"I am handing control over to you now."

Joseph felt a lurch, as he gripped the joystick, in a panic at the sudden responsibility handed to him.

"Easy now, "came the calm voice of the instructor. "Handle the machine like you did when gliding. Easy stick movements, and push the revs up a bit when you turn. Now make a wide left turn. Don't forget the revs."

Joseph made his turn, overdoing the revs, but correcting when instructed. Over the next hour he was encouraged to bank, dive, climb, fly level, and turn the aircraft, whilst remaining aware of the compass heading of the machine at all times.

It seemed but minutes until the instructor broke his concentration again. "Right let's head home. Head on 135 degrees, that will take us back to the field."

Joseph did as instructed and a few minutes later the airfield came into view. Leitner resumed control and brought the aircraft down in a wide sweep, expertly kissing the ground with the wheels, and taxiing to a halt on the concourse of the hanger from where they had started.

Joseph blew out his cheeks, as he sat in the cockpit, bathed in sweat, as Leitner ran through the details of their flight, encouraging and criticizing where appropriate, on Joseph's first efforts at mechanized flight.

"Well, did you enjoy that?" said Leitner.

"Yes, " said Joseph. "But there is a lot to think about all at once."

"My brother, Rudolf, has told me about you. He said you were a good glider pilot. Now I have to make you into a good pilot on mechanized aircraft."

Joseph gasped, "Leitner". Of course he thought. Rudolf Leitner had been his Hitler Youth leader at Innsbruck University. He now recognized the family resemblance.

"How is your brother?" asked Joseph.

"He's joined up. He is now a Hauptmann in a Panzer Unit. Most of your youth group at your age are joining up." He paused, becoming professionally serious.

"Now let's talk about your first flight. For your first time you did okay, " came the comment.

"However, if you want to become a fighter pilot, all we did up there has to become second nature, and on top of that you will have to learn to fight your machine against an enemy who wants to bring you down. When in combat you should never fly straight and level for more than a few seconds. It's the quick or dead."

Joseph climbed from the machine and raised his hand in thanks to his instructor. He pulled off his helmet from his dank and sweat soaked head, and felt the welcome cold air drying his skin. What an experience! What a thrill! He wanted more.

He stood with his group chatting to those who had flown before him, comparing experiences, and detailing successes and failures in equal measure, as the aircraft taxied away with the final member of his group on board. The wait for the return of the aircraft allowed Joseph to calm down, and for his adrenaline levels to return to normal.

Once the aircraft returned with the last pupil, the group were taken into the hanger by Leitner, who ran through each of the flights.

"I feel that it is important to bring out the highs a lows of each of your flights, in front of all of you. That way you can all learn from each other's mistakes."

They spent the next hour discussing each flight and all absorbed the lessons not only from the instructor but from each other's experiences.

"Right," said Leitner. "Let's get something to eat. It's been a long day."

They marched to the mess hall, where all the students assembled. Joseph caught up with his friend Walter and they compared notes on their experiences. Both were full of excitement at the prospect of more flying time.

Chapter Ten

Weeks passed, and the days of the student pilots blurred into a whirl of lectures, sessions with mechanics in the hangers where they were shown and instructed on the workings of the engines and airframes of various aircraft. They were subjected to parachute training, ditching in water procedures, navigation, and radio procedures, Information came at them thick and fast, followed by written tests at every stage of their development.

Some students disappeared, having failed to make the grade, and the numbers of their intake shrank. The groups were shuffled and re-shuffled as the numbers diminished. Those left moved on to the Arado 66 more advanced trainer. It was still a twin wing open cockpit machine, but with a more powerful engine and was a faster machine.

Joseph thrived on the challenge, but he ended each day exhausted from the mental and physical activities. He was not alone. All the students were effected in the same way, and each night they climbed into their beds and slept deeply, groaning each morning at the call of reveille, and going through their ablution routine on automatic pilot.

As the weeks went by the dormitories were reshuffled, as their intake diminished further. Joseph and Walter remained, tired but still determined to succeed.

The remainder of the intake one day were in class, when the Commandant, Oberst Heinz Wagner, and his cadre of instructors entered the room. The students sprang to attention.

"At ease," he barked. "Sit." As they resettled at their desks, he continued. "You have all done well in the initial course and I have come to tell you that you will all be moving on to the next stage of more advanced training. Some of you have been selected for fighter school, some will go on to learn to fly bombers and others will be directed to transport command. Lists will be placed on the main notice board this evening, directing you to your next assignment. Tomorrow you will all be granted leave for a week before moving on. Travel warrants will be issued to all of you, for your homeward journey and for you to get to your next assignment. But tonight there will be a farewell dinner and evening in the bar of the mess."

This raised a cheer from the students.

The party in the mess that evening became a riot. After many weeks of intensive training, the remaining trainees really let their hair down. The training staff were VIP guests of the students, and they too enjoyed the party atmosphere.

Joseph had seen the bulletin board before the start of the evening festivities. He was posted to a fighter training station near Paris. He was overjoyed as it meant that he might be able to see his father, who remained as Chief Surgeon in the main hospital, sequestered by the Wehrmacht when France had fallen, and which was now used to treat the wounded of the Reich, and a limited amount of Vichy French allies.

The one sadness Joseph had, was that his friend Walter had been selected for training on Bombers, and after his leave, which he could share with Joseph, they would go their separate ways. He was heading back to Bavaria, to the Landsberg Air Base in Upper Bavaria, to be trained to fly the Heinkel HE 111.

The following morning, with suitable headaches all round, the trainees were transported to the local railway station, where they boarded trains for their various destinations. Sad goodbyes where made to the new friends they had made during their initial training. Of the sixty recruits who had presented themselves initially for training, only 32 remained. 14 where scheduled for various fighter schools throughout the Reich and its captured territories, a further 14 were to be trained as bomber pilots, and 4 were heading for transport commend.

Joseph and Walter shared a compartment with two others heading for Vienna, and on arrival at Vienna Main Station, they parted from each other, heading home. Joseph arranged to meet his friend Walter the next day as they intended to spend as much time together over their precious week of leave, before their parting of the ways.

Joseph let himself in to his house. He called out to empty rooms. It all looked the same and he felt a wave of nostalgia and home sickness as he looked around at the familiar surroundings. The housekeeper they had before the war had gone, she had joined up, volunteering for the Wehrmachtelferin, the Womans Wehrmacht Auxilliary army, she was employed as a driver attached to an artillery regiment. His mother, a matron at the main hospital in Vienna, he guessed was at work, no doubt keeping herself busy in the absence of her husband in France, and her son in flight training. She would have a pleasant surprise upon returning home.

Joseph unpacked in his old room. His familiar belongings still around him. His civilian clothes still in drawers and his wardrobe. He longed for the luxury of a warm bath. He poured the steaming water, testing the temperature of the water. He stripped and gently lowered himself in, gasping at the heat, but wanting its comfort. His flesh turned a healthy pink, as he withstood the sting until his flesh became used to the hot water. He felt his pores open to the luxury and he laid back contentedly as the water lapped his flesh in a hot embrace. He lay back, eyes closed, luxuriating and dozed until the water started to chill, when he added more hot. After thirty minutes of contentment he heard the front door open and slam shut. He stayed, listening, as he heard footsteps on the stairs. He called out, "Mother, is that you?"

He heard a gasp. "Joseph. You're home. Where are you?"

"I'm in the bath. Hang on, I will get out." He heard the door handle click.

"Don't come in Mother. I've no clothes on."

"I've seen it all before. I'm a nurse, don't you know." She said, laughing with joy.

"Mother, stay where you are. I'll come out." An embarrassed Joseph quickly left his bath, dried himself and put on his dressing gown. He opened the bathroom door, to be engulfed in the frantic embrace of his mother, who burst into tears of joy.

After a time, she pushed him away.

"Let me look at you. You've lost weight. You're skin and bone. Don't they feed you in the Luftwaffe."

The motherly concern and rapid questions forestalled any answers he might have given, and she carried on with a torrent of motherly concern, until Joseph said, "Mother. Let me get dressed. I will come down and have coffee with you and tell you all."

He managed to get to his bedroom, where for the first time in months, he dressed in his civilian clothes. He came down to the kitchen to find his mother waiting in anticipation to hear his news, with freshly brewed coffee filling the kitchen with its enticing aroma. He was home and now he felt at home.

"How's father, have you heard from him?" asked Joseph

"He is well. Extremely busy. It appears that the hospital he is working in, is the main hospital in France for the wounded, and he is called upon to operate daily. He works long hours, and then of course, he is responsible for the whole surgical team, which means organization and paperwork on top of his surgery. He is extremely busy."

Joseph said, "Well, I have some good news. I have passed the initial training, and I am now posted to Paris-Orly Airfield for advanced fighter training. So I will be able to go and see Papa, as it's just outside Paris."

"Fighters?" worried his mother. "That's dangerous work."

"I'm not there yet. I've a long way to go. But I love to fly and fighters would be my first choice. So I would be doing what I want. If I must fight, then the best way I can fight for my country is in the air. The Reich demands that of everyone these days. I came home with Walter, " said Joseph quickly changing the subject, "He has been posted to bomber training in Bavaria, but first we have a whole week off."

"I am scheduled to work every day," she said with concern. "I will try to take some time off to be with you." She pondered, "Yes, I will arrange time off. They owe it to me."

"Mother, to celebrate my homecoming I would like to take you out to dinner. Shall we do that?" asked Joseph.

His mother beamed. "That would be very nice. I will bathe and change. Please wear your uniform."

Later they ate a typical Austrian meal in one of their favourite restaurants, the Zwolf Apostkeller, where the family Mozart were well known as customers in more peaceful times. The atmosphere of the cellar with its subdued lighting, welcoming ambiance, and soft music of the resident string quartet created a warm and pleasant atmosphere. Enhanced when the owner met them at the entrance seeing Joseph in his uniform for the first time. He made sure his staff became effusively attentive to their needs, and even had the quartet play the Eine Kliene Nachtmusik and other selections by Wolfgang Amadeus Mozart in deference to their family name and occasion of Joseph's return. They had a very pleasant evening of reunion, with one missing element. The presence of Joseph's father.

The following day, in the late morning Joseph, now in civilian clothes, met his friend Walter for coffee at their favourite café. They talked of their respective homecomings, and of their future in the Luftwaffe. Walter was disappointed he was not to join Joseph at fight training, but he seemed content to be posted to bomber training, particularly as the training base was located in Bavaria, a beautiful part of the country and so far untouched by war.

They spent a very companionable few hours together, but as they left they saw a group of brown shirted S.A. members on the far side of the street. Standing with them was a brown shirted S.A Officer, who looked somewhat familiar. They were in the process of beating a man, who lay on the ground in the fetal position, being kicked. The poor unfortunate wore a Star of David arm band. Joseph and Walter went across the road at speed to intervene, only for the SA Officer to shove them to one side, shouting "Mind your own business!" As he turned, both recognized Ernst Bruen, now a Leutenant in the feared SA.

He snarled, "You two. I might have known. If you know what's good for you, you will piss off."!

The SA personnel meting out the violence stopped what they were doing and surrounded the two, threatening with their menacing presence and backing up Bruen, as he glared at the two who had attempted to interrupt.

"What are you two doing here?" demanded Bruen. "You're supposed to be in the Luftwaffe."

"We are, " said Joseph. "We're on leave between transfers. Why are you beating that poor man?" Indicating the man bloody and sobbing on the floor.

"It's none of your business. It's state business. He's under arrest. He's a Jew."

"Why are you beating him. What's he done," persisted Joseph.

"It's nothing to do with you and unless you want to go with him, Piss off!"

The SA then pulled the man to his feet and marched off with him.

"This is SA business. I said Piss Off!" shouted Bruen.

He then walked away following the prisoner being dragged by the SA escort down the street.

Joseph looked at Walter, his anger palpable.

"Calm down Joseph," said Walter. "Bruen's now in the SA. You don't want to mess with them. They're big trouble. He's ideally suited to them. He's a dyed in the wool Nazi and will always be a bully. Be careful around him, now he's in the SA he wields a lot more power."

"It makes my blood boil," said Joseph. "That they can get away with such violence on the streets and no one stops it. They're thugs. Out and out thugs."

"I wouldn't voice that opinion in public if I were you. Now calm down. Let's go."

He then pulled Joseph away down the street in the opposite direction from Bruen, with Joseph still seething with indignation at what he had witnessed.

It was now June 1941, and Vienna basked in summer heat. Joseph was enjoying his weeks rest, and re-familiarizing himself with his home town. Not many of his friends were left as most were now serving in some branch of the armed forces. He was at home when he heard the shock news, German Forces had invaded Russia. The news bulletins covered a speech by the Fuhrer where it heralded "Operation Barbarossa".

The rest of Joseph's week went all too quickly. He and Walter met nearly every day, and discussed at length the implications of the latest territorial invasion. They reached the conclusion that the invasion of Russia meant their services would be needed more than ever and sooner rather than later.

After fond farewells with their families, the two met at Vienna's main station. They had a final drink together and then Walter, as his journey was shorter, saw Joseph on to his train, westward bound.

Joseph's train journey would be overnight, a distance of over 1000 kilometres. Because of the war, there was no direct train to Paris. He would have to change trains at Stuttgart and again at Strasbourg. He could not book a sleeper compartment and had to share with other servicemen retuning from leave, most destined for occupied territory in Holland, Belgium, Luxemburg, and France. There were delays at the train changes, the first of two hours and the second of an hour. At 0600hrs the following day, a very tired and disheveled Joseph found himself standing on the platform of the Gare du Nord with his luggage around him. He found a porter who directed him to another platform, to catch a local train on the 45 minute journey to Orly station. By the time he arrived at Orly he was exhausted. As he exited the station he saw a Luftwaffe Obergefreiter standing next to a canvass backed lorry bearing Luftwaffe marking, the back being almost filled with Luftwaffe personnel.

He approached the Obergefreiter, who clicked his heels and saluted.

"Are you providing transport to Orly?" said Joseph.

"Yes, sir," said the Obergefreiter. "My instructions are to wait for two trains. Yours is the second. May I see your papers?"

Joseph showed his papers, and satisfied, the Obergefreiter took Joseph's bags from him and placed them in the back of the truck.

"You can travel in the cab sir, " he said. "There is one other officer there, but there is room for two. Let's go."

Joseph climbed into the cab, saying "Hello" to the Hauptmann already ensconced there.

"Hauptmann Hermann Rickter," he said, "Just joining us."

"Joseph Mozart. Yes. I am posted here to start more advanced training from Schleissheim."

"I am one of your instructors, just returning from leave. No doubt we will meet over the next few days. I hope you settle in and do well. We need all the pilots especially now since Operation Barbarossa got underway and is causing us to fight on two fronts. I believe there will be even more pressure on us to turn out pilots in as short a time as possible. It's a big commitment."

The lorry pulled in through the gates of Orly Air Base, and stopped at the gatehouse, where they disembarked. The Feldwebel in charge of the guard, saluted Hauptmann Rickter and let him through immediately, the rest he checked against a list before letting them through. He inspected Joseph's papers and pointed toward a building some 200 metres away.

"Please report to the Adjutant in the Headquarters building over there," he said pointing towards a large double fronted building, with steps leading up to its main entrance."

Joseph gathered his belongings and walked to the building. He went up the front steps and through the main entrance which led into a large entrance hall. It had a polished oak floor, large chandeliers, and a sweeping staircase leading to the upper floors. Sitting at a desk near the stairs was a Luftwaffe Sergeant, who directed Joseph to a doorway marked Adjutant. He knocked and entered.

Sitting behind a large mahogany paneled desk was a Hauptmann, who was studying papers on his desk. Joseph stood silently in front of the desk at attention, until the Hauptmann looked up.

"Leutnant Joseph Mozart reporting for duty sir, " said Joseph.

"Ah, yes," said the Hauptmann. "We have been expecting you. You have come from Schleissheim I believe, and passed your initial training. You have been sent here to undergo more advanced training. Correct?"

"Yes," said Joseph.

"My name is Hauptmann Erik Schaffer. I am the adjutant. You are one of an intake of 20 for advanced training. We have about 60 students here at the moment. There are two courses ahead of you, 20 on each course, and you are the newest intake. I will get an orderly to take you to your billet, but before he does, let me tell you a bit about the base. Orly is a both an operational airfield, and a training base. There are combat fighter and bomber units operating on the East side of the airfield and our training facilities are set up using some older airship sheds at the opposite side of the airfield. They have separate facilities and we have to be careful not to interfere with their operations. The training facility uses old airship sheds to house and maintain our trainers. You will find out more in the next few days. Some of your intake have arrived before you and we are expecting the others to arrive soon. You will start training first thing in the morning. Once you have settled in, feel free to use the mess. The orderly will show you where to go, and tell you the times you may get your meals, but I suggest that you settle in first and introduce yourself to your course colleagues."

He then called the front desk Sergeant into his office, saying, "Get an orderly to show Leutenant Mozart to his quarters, and show him where the mess is."

Joseph was led to a row of wooden huts at the rear of the headquarters building. It contained a row of beds on each side, some taken and other unoccupied. There was a pot bellied stove at the far end, and most of the occupied beds were at that end, where they would get the maximum heat. As Joseph entered all conversation died much to Joseph's embarrassment, as the occupants looked questioningly at the new arrival. Joseph walked to a bed fourth from the end and said to the, tall well built, fair haired occupant of the next bed, "Is this one taken."

"No," came the answer, "It's yours if you want it."

"Joseph Mozart," he said, studying the good looking aryan but open and honest features of his neighbour.

"Petr Muller. Welcome to hut 24." He then shook hands with Joseph. "Where are you from?" He asked.

"Vienna. Innsbruck University studying architecture and Structural Engineering, via Schleissheim Luftwaffe base near Munich, where I did my initial training. You?"

Petr said, "A village near Hamburg you have never heard of. Tespe. It's on the banks of the Elbe. My family own a hotel there. The Gasthov Zein. I initially trained at Berlin-Gatow, and now I am here for advance training, hopefully to fly fighters. I was pulled off my university course as well. I was studying to be an engineer at Hamburg University. I hope to finish my degree when the war is over."

Joseph looked at the others in the room and went round introducing himself to them one by one. Each told him of their origins, and where they carried out their initial training. All had a similar tale to tell. Recruited through the Hitler Youth Air Cadet scheme, some pulled from university courses before completion. Whilst he was doing the rounds of introduction two more trainees arrived, and were welcomed to the hut.

A short time later a Luftwaffe Obergefreiter opened the door. "Gentlemen," he shouted. "Lunch is about to be served. I am instructed to take you to the officer's mess, where you will meet the station commander. Please follow me."

They were marched back to the headquarters building, and taken to the first floor, where the Obergefreiter threw open the door of a room crowded with officers of all ranks. The babble of noise ceased as the newest recruits were shown inside.

A stout and flush faced Generalmajor detached himself from a group at the bar, and drink in hand, came to the entrance to the room to greet the new arrivals.

"I am Generalmajor Otto Schwarbe, Commandant of this advanced flying school. Welcome gentlemen." He said with loud and effusive bonhomie. "Come, meet some of your instructors."

He then took them to the bar, where a round of introductions were made to the cadre of senior officers he had left to greet them.

"It is my tradition to buy you each your first drink in the mess," he said with a smile of largess.

He nodded to the barman who served the requested drinks. Once all the new recruits had a drink the Brigadier-General shouted, "Prost," then he downed the remains of his drink in one long draught. "To table," he commanded, and led the ensemble to the dining room, set out with a top table at which the Commandant stood, with other long tables at ninety degrees to the top.

Joseph and his newly arrived compatriots stood at the end of one of the tables, as indicated by a mess orderly, a long way from the top, waiting for the order to sit. The Commandant paused, looking imperialisticly around him, until complete silence was achieved, he then nodded to a Major next to him who shouted "You may sit."

A babble of conversation erupted, as the doors to the kitchen opened, and a stream of serving staff brought in steaming dishes, which they placed on the top table. Each table was then served in rotation, until at last Joseph and his new friends were served their meal. They were last at every serving, but spent the time usefully, getting to know their fellow students. Joseph took a particular liking to his new friend Petr Muller.

After a long lunch, Joseph was drooping with fatigue. He had had a long journey, as had the others. They were allowed to return to their billet to settle in and unpack properly, being told they were free until reveille at 0600hrs the following morning. Most went to bed and slept deeply.

Chapter Eleven

0600hrs came too soon, with the arrival of a Stabsfeldwebel, all red faced and shouting.

"Rise and Shine. Rise and Shine. Outside in 30 minutes. Full uniform."

Joseph, startled to fully awake jumped from his bed and ran to the washroom. He was first there, he had been caught before.

The Stabsfeldwebel walked the room shouting and screaming at those who made attempts to continue sleeping, until they too joined the mad scramble for the ablutions.

Thirty minutes later the group stood to attention, stifling yawns, in squad formation. Whilst the Stabsfeldwebel walked the line, inspecting his latest victims. He didn't like what he saw, and he told them so.

After 30 minutes of close order drill, they were fully awake, alert to his commands, and fully receptive to his orders. They were marched to the mess where they were given 30 minutes to break their fast. They were then assembled at high speed, in front of the headquarters building, where they stood to attention in the cold morning air, until the same cadre of instructors they had met in the mess the night before, walked smartly down the front steps of the building to stand in front of the squad.

A major stepped forward. "I am your chief instructor, Major Heinrich von Graf. These officers, indicating his companions, are the instruction staff. Groups of four will be allocated to one instructor, and you will begin your more advanced training today. There are four more trainees coming. They have been delayed because their train was attacked overnight, and derailed. They will be here later and will have to catch up. Time is now of the essence. Since the invasion of Russia, we are now fighting on two fronts. The British are fighting us still, sortieing across the English Channel, and now we have the Russia front to occupy our resources. Therefore your training time has been shortened again, and so you will have to work harder than ever to graduate. Each instructor in turn will call out four names, if he calls out your name, then upon dismissal, join him. Understood?"

The line of instructors then called out four names each, in turn. Joseph was gratified to find that Petr was in his group. It was to be the start of a firm friendship.

A Hauptman stepped towards the group. He called out four names including Joseph and Petr, checking he had the right people.

"Follow me," he said, stepping away from the main body of men. As he did so, other instructors stepped forward and gave similar instructions.

He took his group toward two enormous hangers, which he told them were constructed many years ago for airships, where standing in front of the hanger was an aircraft.

"My name is Hauptman Erik Jager, " he said. I will be your advanced instructor. The program of training we are just starting is to be accelerated. We need pilots urgently to feed into both the Eastern and Western battle areas. You are all familiar and competent flyers and have passed your initial training. You have all shown competence at navigation, and all the other aspects of your initial training. You all now need to be taught to fly the latest aircraft, and more importantly be taught how to fight in the air. The next few weeks will be concentrated on aerial combat, ground attack, night navigation, and getting you familiar with more powerful aircraft, hopefully leading you toward qualifying you to fly our latest fighter aircraft. If you pass the course, which has now been shortened to three months, you will be posted to a combat squadron." He paused for effect looking at each of his trainees in turn, until he saw them nodding in assent.

"Good, "he said, "Now this aircraft," pointing at the one immediately behind him, "is the Arado 96 B – 2 armed, two seater trainer. It will not be armed initially, but later in your training, when we teach gunnery, it will be. It is a single engined low wing monoplane with a Argus AS 410A V12 air cooled piston engine . As you see it is of all metal construction, produced by the Arado Flugzengwerke factory. It is 9.1metres in length, has a wingspan of 11 metres, a maximum speed of 330 km/h and a range of 991 km. It also has a variable pitch propeller, and automatic flaps. Now, come closer, and we will show you the controls, and the cockpit setup."

The party climbed onto the aircraft and Jager pointed out the seating, instrumentation, and the controls. Joseph saw the other parties going through similar routines on a line of identical aircraft, a little further away.

"Please familiarize yourself with the aircraft over the next hour." He then handed each of his trainees a handbook.

"As you look around the aircraft, "he expounded, "Check the details in the handbook against what you see. In our shortened training program it is important that you familiarize yourself with its detail. The Luftwaffe needs you in its squadrons as soon as possible. You need to hit the ground running."

The group spent the next hour climbing all over the aircraft, testing the movement of the rudder, flaps, and taking note of the instrumentation.

"Right, " said Jager," Let's now take a break for lunch, and then your first flights will be this afternoon. To shorten time we have arranged for you all to have a light meal inside the hanger, so follow me."

He then took them inside the hanger where a canteen wagon was parked, surrounded by benches and tables. Joseph took his light meal of sausage, bread and sauerkraut to a table with his trainee colleagues, and spent the short time getting to know his fellow squad members, whilst eating.

Once the meal was over Jager barked, "Right, let's get started. You have your flying gear. Muller, you're up first. You others study your manuals in the hanger whilst we are away. There will be questions later."

Petr put his parachute harness on and climbed into the front seat of the aircraft, Jager settling himself in the back. A ground crew mechanic stood by, whilst Jager went through his pre-flight checks, watched intently by the other students in the group. The engine was started and the remainder of the group stood back, whilst the instructor went through the pre-flight routine with his pupil. The aircraft then taxied away toward the main runway, gathered speed and took off, disappearing quickly towards the horizon.

An hour later, the aircraft returned and a sweaty but joyful Petr climbed down from the aircraft.

"That was great, once I got the hang of the controls," he said beaming.

Jager shouted, "Mozart. You're up next. Get your kit on and get in."

Joseph donned his parachute and climbed into the front seat. He connected his intercom cable and the instructor's voice came to him immediately.

"We will climb to 3000 metres, heading north, and once I have got her up I will hand the controls to you, and we will go through some basic manouvres. Understand?"

Joseph acknowledged.

The engine was restarted, and the aircraft taxied to the main runway. Joseph heard Jager ask permission to take off, which was granted. The craft then gathered speed down the runway, with Jager giving Joseph a running commentary as they reached take off speed. Suddenly the aircraft left the ground and soared into the air, banking right to avoid the take off area of the operational side of the airfield, with Jager continuing to comment on every nuance of the flight. They reached 3000 metres, heading out over the east of Paris which Joseph could see spread out beneath them, as he felt the familiar thrill and wonder of flight. He sudden jerked back to reality when Jager's voice came over the intercom.

"You have control. Head us north on 130 degrees."

Joseph, now no longer a complete novice, held the craft straight and level for a moment, then banked turning onto the required compass heading. He then followed each instruction he received from Jager, banking, climbing, diving and even, when Jager felt he was ready for it, looping. He was so busy following instructions that Joseph had no time to admire the view. He was put through a complex routine which required his whole attention.

Jager's voice interrupted Joseph's concentration. "Good. For a first time in an Arado, not bad. Now take us home. Let's see if you can land it."

"Are you sure?" asked Joseph. "This is my first time remember."

"I think you can do it. Have confidence. Now head us back home."

A sweating Joseph saw the airfield come into view. His nerves jangled, his confidence eroding as he approached the critical point.

"Steady," came Jager's voice. "You can do it. You have shown me you can fly. Now show me you can land. Adjust the pitch of the propeller. Put the undercarriage down. Remember the craft has automatic flaps. Bring the speed down to 180kmph."

Joseph made the adjustments.

"That's good, now down, gently, gently does it!"

Joseph drained off speed to the required amount, and with sweaty palms brought the aircraft onto the runway. He bounced once, and then the aircraft smoothed out its run along the runway, with Joseph braking to taxiing speed.

"Turn right off the runway and stop beside the hanger" Came the voice. "Now, cut the engine."

Joseph did as instructed, and let out a huge sigh of relief.

An amused Jager said with a chuckle in his voice, "That wasn't so bad, was it?"

Joseph gave a nervous laugh. "Unexpected, so soon. I thought I would be given much more time before landing the thing."

"There is no time, " came the voice. "Next time you will be taking off."

Joseph climbed from the machine controlling the wobble in his legs. He had the sudden realization that this training would be very intensive indeed. There was no time to waste.

Later, in the mess his group compared notes. Petr and Joseph had been allowed to land the aircraft, the other two were not. All had been told however, because of the urgent need for pilots, they would be thrown in the deep end, and by the end of the week would be both taking off and landing the aircraft, and within one month would be taught tactics and instrument flying. It was to be a crammed program. This gave them all food for thought.

The first week passed quickly, Joseph's head was crammed with new information. He had progressed to both taking off and landing his aircraft, and at the end of the second week he was flying the machine throughout the entire flight.

In the second week they progressed to instrument training, and longer cross-country flights which taxed his navigational skills. On top of the flying, the students were subjected to advanced navigation, parachute training, physical training, radio procedures and under the tuition of a Feldwebel Mechanic, the mysteries of the servicing and fault finding in the engine, landing and cockpit gear.

In week four, they were subjected to flying by instrument, and they had their first taste of night flying, a different type of flying indeed. Being totally reliant on instruments was a different science to daylight flying, with the sense of sight cut off, the isolation Joseph felt was palpable. It was a skill he would have to master if he was to succeed.

Once they were proved competent in all these skills, they were taught combat tactics, and gunnery. Both ground attack methodology and aerial combat. They had no time to themselves, and mostly at night they collapsed, exhausted into their beds too tired for anything other than sleep.

It was announced, after the students had completed week four, they could have four days rest. Joseph decided to seek out his father at the main Paris Hospital. He explained his intention to his friend Petr, and they both left the base to seek out the fleshpots of Paris. They begged a lift to Orly station and caught a train into the centre of Paris, where they booked into a hotel.

Joseph rang the main hospital to speak to his father. He discovered he was busy in the operating theatre, but he left a contact number and when his father rang him back Joseph, together with Petr arranged to meet at his father's favourite restaurant that evening, the famous Ritz Hotel in the Place Vendome.

At 7pm that evening, Joseph and Petr walked into the Ritz restaurant and were directed to a table where Joseph's father sat. He was in the resplendent uniform of a full Oberst of the German Army Medical Corps. He looked tired, he had had a busy day carrying out some tricky operations on wounded military personnel. However he was animated enough by the contact with his son, and they spent the first few minutes catching up on family matters. He told of his life as a military surgeon in Paris and Joseph told him of his efforts to become a fighter pilot. They were careful to include Petr in the conversations, and Doctor Mozart was interested to hear of Petr's village life and his route to becoming a Luftwaffe pilot.

The two boys were slightly overawed by their opulent surrounding. Despite the war and occupation, the Ritz had maintained a certain independence and its grandeur never suffered despite the hardships of the time. The restaurant seemed reserved for the German Officer class. They were surrounded by high ranking officers of all branches of the service, some with elegant women accompanying them, and others not. The subdued lighting added to the atmosphere, and it was obvious that some officers had found French companions despite the national feeling of oppression and anti-collaboration.

The meal, despite the hardships of war, and shortages was excellent, and the wine made Joseph and Petr effusive as they expanded on their experiences whilst training. Doctor Mozart listened with interest to his son's adventures, concerned that he would soon be seconded to a theatre of war. Joseph however was so enthusiastic about his flying, his father approving of his son's enthusiasm, which resulted in the evening becoming most convivial. When asked about his role in Paris, Joseph's father saddened slightly. He was seeing how much the war was effecting the German armed forces. His hospital was only one of a large number catering for the sick and wounded, and he and his team of surgeons were constantly required to complete twelve hour days to cope with the incoming patients. Some of the injuries were horrendous and the death rate appalling. Doctor Mozart was seeing the bloody consequences of Hitler's war.

Never-the-less Joseph was glad to have caught up with his father and their reunion was an overall success. Doctor Mozart was at pains to include Petr in his bonhomie, and altogether they had a very pleasant evening.

As they left the hotel, feeling mellow and well fed, a military staff car pulled up outside the main entrance. A woman soldier in uniform got out and opened the door for Doctor Mozart.

"Good evening Herr Oberst, " said the woman. "Back to the hospital?"

"We will drop my son and his friend off first at their hotel," said Doctor Mozart. "Where are you staying?"

"Le Chat Noir. Montmatre," said Joseph. "Not as grand as the Ritz, but one we can afford on our Leutenant's pay. We have a two more days before reporting back. "

The car pulled up in front of the Le Chat Noir, the two boys got out waving goodnight to Doctor Mozart.
"Goodnight boys," said his father, "Enjoy the rest of your leave." And he waved as the car drew away.

"A good evening," said Joseph in an alcoholic haze, "It was good to see my father again. He looks tired. He's not having an easy time."

"There are obviously too many wounded. It makes you think who's winning this war, " said a similarly hazy Petr as they entered their hotel.

The two trainee pilots returned to base Sunday evening, ready for their training to restart the next morning. They had enjoyed the entertainments in full , those they could afford, which the French Capitol put on offer. They had eaten well, socialized as young men do when in company of liberated young ladies, and drunk far too much. They were tired but happy and collapsed, in a satisfied stupor in their beds. They were not alone, the others in their dormitory were in similar states of alcohol and sexually related euphoria. Their dreams were happy recent memories.

Reveille the next morning grated on their ears, their dreams shattered, as the Stabsfeldwebel, in his usual ebullient style roused them from their beds. The usual physical torture he subjected them to, produced more than the usual groans, but it did have the desired effect of waking them up to a new day with new challenges.

The squad of trainee pilot stood to attention, in squad order, outside the largest airship hanger, which had been their assembly point from the moment their advanced training began. In echelon beside the hanger was a line of 20 MF Bf109 fighter aircraft.

The Chief Instructor, Oberstleutenant Boris Konig, stood in front of the squad, with the remainder of the instruction staff behind him.

"You will delighted to know that your training program has been advanced even further. You have had the last six weeks flying trainer aircraft. The Arado 96 B is a good trainer, but now you are moving swiftly on to the ME Bf109, the fighter of choice for the Luftwaffe. You will remain in sections of four, with your current instructor, who will instruct you on the workings of the aircraft, and who, when he feels you are ready, will lead you into the sky. Now the hard work starts. This session of your training will encompass air to air combat tactics, air to ground tactics, gunnery, and target acquisition. You will operate in fingers of four, unless in combat when you will become a pair, a leader and wingman. The aircraft you see beside the hanger are the aircraft you will use. Your own instructor will allocate a machine to each of you, and that will be your aircraft for this period of your training. Treat it well, do not bend it. It belongs to the Luftwaffe. Now break off, and assemble with your own instructor."

Joseph and Petr found Hauptmann Erik Jager. He led them to the line of aircraft. Standing beside one, he said, "Gentlemen, this is the BF, commonly known as the ME Bf109 E fighter aircraft. It has a fuel injected V12 engine, and is capable of 530km per hour. It has a range of 660 km. It is not the latest in production, but it is the one you will use in training. It has a retractable undercarriage, and when taxiing and during takeoff the angle of the nose prevents full forward vision until take off speed is achieved. Therefore weaving side to side during take off is essential to see ahead. During takeoff you will notice a tendency for the aircraft to swing to the right. This is due to the propeller wash across the airframe and you will have to learn to counteract that, or you will crash. I suggest therefore that you slowly build to take off speed at first until you get used to the little foibles of the aircraft. Now we will climb on board this aircraft and I will show you the instrumentation."

He then allowed his squad to view the controls and the instruments, and walked the around the aircraft to help familiarize them with the airframe.

Jager then said, "When we get going, I will allow each of you to taxi on the taxiways, so you get used to the feel of the aircraft. Keep your eyes on your instruments, and remember the swing. Weave slightly so you retain a near straight line. Do not try to take off at this point. I will take the lead when we do, and guide you through it. Right," he said pointing at Joseph. "You are first, get into your aircraft, and we will go through the startup procedure."

Joseph climbed aboard, and went through the startup as instructed by Jager with the help of a ground crew member. He built the power up to half, released the brakes and began to taxi along the taxiway. His vision was restricted by the nose angle of the aircraft so he weaved slightly as he had been told. He found the aircraft responsive, and wanting to take to the air, but he held it on the ground braking at the far end of the taxiway. He then turned the aircraft and repeated the process, halting and switching off in the place where his aircraft had been originally.

The trainees spent several hours repeating the taxiing process until they all felt competent in the manouvre.

After a break, they spent several more hours repeating the same process until Jager expressed his satisfaction at their efforts.

"Tomorrow, we take off and fly the machines. You will use the same aircraft through this period of your training unless you prang. My advice is listen to what I tell you. Do not exceed your instructions and you will be fine. Now dismissed!"

The following day Joseph and Petr stood beside the line of ME Bf109 aircraft. They were listening to Hauptmann Jager.

"Yesterday I got you to familiarize yourself with your aircraft by taxiing it and getting used to its idiosyncrasies. Remember them, it could save your life. We are again going to practice taxiing, and then we are going to fly the machines."

Jager then watched as each of his group of students practiced for an hour. Then he said, "We will now take to the air. Heed what I say. We will take a short flight and this afternoon we will practice take offs and landings, known as circuits and bumps. Gentlemen, to your machines."

They each moved to their machine and started to climb aboard.

Jager shouted, "What have you forgotten."

When the students looked puzzled, he shouted, "Walk round inspection. Tyres, flaps, rudder, filler cap. Check for fuel, oil leaks. The check list you have been taught should be routine by now."

Chastened, his students carried out their inspection routine, and then, with the assistance of their assigned ground crew, climbed into their machines and carried out instrument checks, whilst being strapped in. Having plugged in their radio leads they heard the voice of their instructor."

"You may start your engines. In line astern follow me."

The engines fired in unison, and with Jager leading, they taxied toward the runway. They heard Jager ask for permission to take off, and he lined up on the runway. His engine roared and he gathered speed, weaving slightly from side to side, until his tail came off the ground, and he then soared into the air.

The students, one by one, followed him, emulating his routine, until they were all successfully airborne.

"Form up on me, line abreast," came Jagers voice. "We will head north on 175 degrees, speed 200kph, and climb to 3000 metres."

The formation gradually rose into the sky. The outskirts of Paris appearing below them, the Seine glittering in the morning sun.

Jager's voice came over the radio again. "Your formation for combat will always be finger four. Should you become involved in combat, the four will become two twos. A leader and a wingman. It is the duty of the wingman to stick with his leader, and to protect him. In combat never fly straight and level for more than a few seconds, and the golden rule is always check for your enemy coming at you from out of the sun. You have to be able to see all around you. That is why most pilots wear silk neck scarves, as their heads are swiveling all the time, and silk will not rub your neck and make it sore. It should be your first purchase when we land."

They carried out formation flying to the instructions from their tutor, for an hour until he called time and they headed back to base. He then circled slowly as he watched his charges land in echelon, seeing faults as they bounced along the runway before returning to park beside their base hanger.

Joseph feathered his aircraft onto the ground, but still bounced twice before running fast and smooth. He found, when he landed he had to look sideways from his cockpit, because the nose of the aircraft was above his line of vision, to keep to the centre line of the runway. He was sweating profusely when he stopped. The aircraft had its own foibles. He would have to get used to its tricky handling and tendency to pull to the right.

Once they had all landed they held a debrief, and Jager offered advice and criticism to each of his students in turn, his intent was for each of the students in his care to learn they had all made mistakes, and by hearing the faults of others, they would learn more quickly. The students were embarrassed at first but finally saw the benefit of an open critique.

Jager took them to a classroom within the hanger, where he went through the finer details of their first flight in an ME Bf109, and where he offered individual advice. He ran over their program for the coming week. The students realized the accelerated program would require intensive concentration and effort, if they were to succeed.

Chapter Twelve

Six weeks from the start of their flying program, they were told they were in their final week, before being posted to a Gruppe. They had each completed 100 hours of flight, which had gradually intensified leading to simulated dog fights against each other and Hauptmann Jager. They had held live firing exercises, against static ground targets, and moving drones. They had completed countless circuit and bumps, practicing until they were competent and confident. They had taken part in instrument flying at night, and during the day. Had completed cross country navigation, formation and finger four exercises, and had taken turns in leadership and wingman flying until they could do these manoeuvres automatically. The whole training program had not been without incident. There had been two crashes. Fortunately not in Joseph's squad. One trainee pilot had died crashing on landing, and another had run off the runway on takeoff, slamming into a truck. The pilot was alive, but was in hospital with a broken arm and a broken nose. He would be back-coursed upon recovery. There had also been one instance of a student landing without lowering his landing gear. Fortunately he was not injured, but he was seriously embarrassed, and the dressing down he received as a result was heard by most of the staff within the headquarters building. He would never forget again. His aircraft was used for spares.

The day came for the award of pilots wings to the successful students. They were paraded in full uniform in front of the headquarters building and awarded their wings by the Commandant of the flying school, Generalmajor Otto Schwarbe, who gave a rousing speech extolling the virtues of the 1000 year Reich, and the Fuhrer. The students had been so busy they had forgotten what a politically motivated and nasty war they were to be involved in, and that they were fighting for a cause some of them were not fully committed to. Without question Joseph and now Petr were patriots to their country and would do their duty, but they were intelligent enough to question in their own minds the need for European domination, and the cruelty of oppressing minorities to achieve success. However, it would be dangerous for them to express any disquiet or disaffection. They had seen how the regime dealt with those who did.

The party in the mess that evening went into overdrive. The students mingled with the instruction staff, with drinking games loosening inhibitions. With the mess piano going full belt, singing of bawdy songs, with words altered to hearty Luftwaffe themes, filled the air. Everyone present seemed intent upon releasing the pressure of the past few weeks, by drunken and exuberant behavior. There may be regrets in the morning, but tonight was their night and the riotous behavior acted as a release for the pent up tension of the last few weeks.

The following morning, the students had a rude awakening. The sound of explosions shook the air, and forced the hungover students to instant wakefulness and terror. The explosions were accompanied by the sound of multiple aero engines, and the staccato sound of machine gunning. The airfield was under attack.

The students leapt from their beds in panic, they needed no reveille on this their last morning. British bombers were achieving what the Stabsfeldwebel could not. Instant wakefulness and accelerated exit from the dormitory. Joseph pulled on his trousers, hopping to the doorway as he did so, to see a darkening cloud of Wellington Bombers, accompanied by what he recognized as Mosquito fighters, with other smaller aircraft circling high above. Orly Base was being heavily attacked. Fortunately for the students, it was the operational part of the airfield on the far side from the training facility, being bombed and strafed.

Joseph, with his colleagues ran for the bomb shelters. As they did so, an echelon of Mosquito ground attack craft loosed a rocket attack on the balloon hangers and the adjacent parked aircraft used by the students. Smoke and debris clouded the air, explosions came nearer, accompanied by the anti- aircraft guns adding their crescendo to the already chaotic scene.

The attack was over in minutes, but it seemed like hours to those taking shelter from the mayhem. Joseph, together with the other students emerged from the shelters to see palls of smoke coming from the far side of the airfield, and from the area of the balloon hangers where they had parked their training aircraft. Fire and rescue vehicles were racing toward the destruction, and bodies lay inert on the ground. Joseph then saw the training headquarters had taken a hit, and was on fire. He and the other students rushed towards the building, and began pulling bodies from the rubble. Some were wounded but alive and others dead. Ambulances began to appear, and Joseph and his friends helped carry the wounded to them. Joseph thought his father would be very busy this day. There were dozens of wounded in the training facility, but many more where the operation squadrons operated on the far side of the airfield.

Joseph's last day before posting to a squadron was to be a busy one, and his posting would be delayed for a least a few days, as he and his fellow students were required to help put the base back to some sort of normality.

After three days of back breaking work, the students were assembled in the remaining balloon hanger, where the Commandant, who had survived the hit on the headquarters building, posted a list of their names, together with their new postings. It was an inauspicious start to their first posting to a combat squadron.

"Gentlemen. I would like to thank you all for your efforts over the last few days. Your help in clearing the debris and with the dead and wounded was appreciated. I am sorry it delayed your posting to your squadrons, however. Those posting have now been put on the notice board in your dormitory " The Commandant continued, "It would appear that there was a larger raid further west, which our fighters were scrambled to deal with, and 100 plus enemy bombers with fighter escorts spilt off from the main formation, targeting our airfield. It caught us by surprise, and was some time before we had proper cover back. However, our aircraft downed at least 8 enemy bombers and three fighters. Some of which crashed on our airfield and others further afield. As a result of this raid, it seems prudent to move the training school further back into Germany. Therefore you are the last course to finish here. The rest will transfer over the next few days to another training site. I therefore wish you all good luck for your futures."

The assembly was dismissed and Joseph with his flight colleagues hurried to their dormitory to read their posting. All four were posted to Alakurtti Air Base in Finland to take part in Operation Artic Fox, an operation designed to ultimately capture the Russian port of Murmansk, starting by capturing the town of Salla and blocking the main railway route to Murmansk.

There were gasps of amazement as they realized the year was coming towards autumn and winter, and how cold it might be. Russia was not a popular posting.

As they read the dread news they were joined by Hauptmann Erik Jager. "I see you have read your postings gentlemen. You don't seem happy about it."

Joseph said, "It will be pretty cold at this time of year and winter will soon be upon us. The snow will be pretty deep."

"I don't see this as a long term posting, " said Jager with a conspiratory smile. "The weather will end the campaign, I am sure. There will come a time soon, when the snow will prevent take offs and landings. But by then Murmansk will be iced in and probably unusable. Anyway, the good news is. You are not getting rid of me. I am coming with you, as your wing commander. I have been promoted Major." He waved his hands to quiet the congratulatory remarks. "If you look at the list again. I don't suppose you have noticed, but you because you have now successfully completed your training, you are all now promoted Oberleutenants," This caused a cheer and back slapping of congratulations all round.

"Now," said Jager. "Gather your gear. We are to catch our transport to Berlin, and from there fly to Alakurtti."

Jager led his party to the runway beside the now bombed out balloon hanger they were so familiar with. Parked there with its engines running was a Junkers JU52/3m Trimotor transport plane. Old design but reliable. They boarded as instructed and settled into its uncomfortable seating. Once loaded with its passengers, it took off heading for Berlin. Joseph looked out of the window, to see that there was another identical aircraft in formation with his, and slightly above and behind were two ME Bf109's acting as escorts. The flight was boring for the newly trained pilots, they mostly attempted to catch up on their sleep. The route they took meant that the flight would be longer than normal, but should be safe from enemy activity.

4 hours later they landed at Berlin-Gatow Air Base. The JU 52 rumbling to a halt over the grass landing field. They were told they were to stay overnight before going on to Finland and were taken by an orderly to a barrack block, where above the door was a bust of WW1 Luftwaffe Ace, Rudolf Berthold. Once settled in, they were taken to the officers mess for a meal, after which they focused on the bar to talk about their coming new adventure in the far north.

The following morning, the transport flew them on, via Oslo, where some passengers were dropped off. The plane then took off again to Alakurtti Air Base, landing on a snowy runway. Alakurtti Air Base was bleak, cold, dusted with light snow, with a freezing cross wind which penetrated their unsuitable clothing. The group were taken to a hanger used as the stores, where they were issued with sheepskin flying jackets, and padded winter overalls, donning them immediately as the appropriate dress for the conditions, and it wasn't even autumn yet.

The newly arrived pilots were shown to their accommodation, and then taken to the officer's mess for a hot meal. They were tired from their journey and soon went to their hut, gathering around the glowing stove for heat, until warm enough to contemplate sleep. Eventually they undressed and went to their beds, sleeping deeply, having learned the trick of sleeping at every opportunity, even in strange surroundings and strange beds.

When, the next morning, they awoke, there was a rime of frost on the inside of the windows, despite the heat from the stove. It was as cold as Joseph had ever been, even though it was only approaching autumn. Ablutions were rudimentary. There was no hot water. They all wore the cold weather clothing they had been issued with the day before, and felt the benefit on the walk to the mess for breakfast. The group were met at breakfast by the now Major Jager, who was also dressed in his cold weather issue.

"This morning will be used as orientation. I want to have us taken on a conducted tour of the base, and then this afternoon you will be shown the aircraft that you will be flying. The main difficulty here in the north will always be the weather. Storms can come out of nowhere, the weather changing unexpectedly even whilst you are in the air. It is important to take notice of the signs of change and to rely upon your instruments if you get caught out. Correct navigation is essential, because in the snow, more of which I understand is imminent, landmarks can be covered. Landings and takeoffs are particularly tricky. The principle goal of Operation Artic Fox is to capture the town of Salla, and eventually block the railway to Murmansk. Our troops are fighting with Finnish troops, who are better suited to the territory and these conditions, and it is up to us to support their advance. You will find the Soviets are pumping in reinforcements to the area so it will not be easy. If we get time this afternoon, we will complete a short sortie, to familiarize ourselves with the terrain. I will lead, and we may do some circuits and bumps to get used to the landing conditions. The cross winds here can be tricky at times, so we practice. Do not be under the illusion that the Soviets fly outdated aircraft. They don't. Their pilots are good. They have men and women pilots. If we come across them on sortie then treat them as expert pilots, flying lethal machines. Our ME Bf109's will outturn them, so remember in combat never fly straight and level for more than a few seconds, and wingmen, make sure you stick to your leader. Now let's explore the base."

They spent the next two hours on a conducted tour of the facilities, including the hangers, inside which was a line of ME Bf109's.

"These are your machines," said Jager. "We will allocate them later."

They continued the tour of the base until lunch time, after which they assembled in the briefing room. The stood when an Oberst entered the room.

"Please sit, " he said. "I am Oberst Karl von Kaufmann. I am the Base Commander. I would like to welcome you to Alakurtti. As you have realized, this is a Finnish Air base and you are here to reinforce our numbers for a push on Murmansk. Our role will be to support our ground troops as they push forward, firstly to Salla, and then on to Murmansk. Our other task will be to disrupt the railway route to Murmansk. Our time is short. Firstly the weather will shortly be closing in making flying conditions very difficult, and secondly we have intelligence which suggests that the Soviets are sending some of their more experienced troops as reinforcements, to prop up their defenses. The Soviets, as I am sure you have been told, have some good aircraft, and the British are sending convoys to the Russian northern ports including Murmansk, loaded with Hurricanes and Spitfires. Of course our navy and airforce are trying to stop the convoys getting through with their cargo. This should be a short campaign because by the end of October, Murmansk will be iced in. The sooner you all get acclimatized to the cold and snow, the better. You will be flying the ME Bf109, an aircraft I understand you are familiar with, so I will leave you to the tender mercies of your flight leaders to get you all up and running. Good luck!"

He then marched from the room as the pilots stood to attention.

An hour later the newcomers were assembled in a cold and draughty hanger. Each had been allocated an ME Bf109, and they were carrying out visual checks of their machines. It was very cold and windy outside and they were advised to mount their aircraft inside the hanger. Jager was towed outside first, followed by his group including Joseph and Petr. As soon as they got out into the cold air they were advised to start their engines, which they did. Once assembled they taxied to the runway, and upon being given authority to take off by the control tower, in pairs they gunned the engines, and followed Jager down the runway, counteracting the buffeting wind as they did so and the torque of the engine as it tended to pull right.

In the air they formed up behind Jager, and climbed to 3000 metres. The panorama opened in front of them. Snow clad mountains showed in the distance, and they headed north towards the Kola Pennisula, passing over numerous lakes and rivers.

"Keep a good lookout, we are in Russian territory. Remember to check the sun. What there is of it, " came Jager's calm voice.

As the formation approached Salla, Petr excitedly reported, "Bandits, One O'clock high."

Joseph looked ahead and up and saw a formation of four aircraft. They were too far away to identify, but they were approaching head on and above, the closing speed bringing them very quickly into range.

The Russian aircraft were identified by Jager as Yakoulev Yak 1's. These were fast and nimble aircraft. They had obviously seen the German formation, and now were diving towards them, gathering speed.

"Break, break," shouted Jager, as he took evasive action. Petr stationed himself on Joseph's wing as they dived, and turned away from danger.

They gathered speed, as two of the Yaks closed on their tails. Joseph jinked his aircraft first to port and then starboard, and when his speed was sufficient for the manouvre, looped to port. The pressure of pulling out of the dive made him grey out for a split second, but he recovered enough to bank violently as bullets sythed the airspace he had occupied just before. The two Soviet aircraft in their haste to make what they thought of as an easy kill, were pulling up from their dive, when Joseph and Petr completed their loop, to come behind the Yaks. As they closed, the Yaks split left and right. Joseph followed the one to the right,

Petr following the one to the left. Joseph's target was now weaving, and spiraling. Joseph briefly had a target and opened up a 2 second burst, but the Yak banked away from the bullet stream. As he was concentrating on his intended target a stream of bullets hit the end of his starboard wing. Joseph banked violently left and suddenly a Yak he hadn't seen burst into flame alongside him, tumbling from the sky shedding debris as it fell. Sweat beaded Joseph's face at his near miss, despite the cold his palms were soaked with sweat, and his googles misted. He had been lucky.

"One down, three to go," came Major Jager's calm voice. "Form up one me."

The Yak Joseph had been pursuing was now nowhere to be seen. The sky appeared clear. The whole action taking seconds, which seemed like hours. The other aircraft formed into a finger four formation, with Jager behind and above, and he ordered them to turn for base. Blue Two had damage to his engine and was leaving a trail of light coloured smoke. He was obviously loosing oil.

"Blue two, can you make base, it's not far," asked Jager.

"I believe I can, " said its pilot.

"We will stay with you. You land first. Straight in and switch off as soon as possible."

"Will do."

The formation nursed their wounded companion back to base, the light coloured smoke, now turning black on the injured aircraft. The formation circled as they saw the damaged Blue Two, land safely, and taxi to the side.

They then landed in rotation. Jager bringing up the rear.

Joseph sat in his aircraft, numb from his first experience of combat. It had all happened so fast. The sweat on him dried quickly in the cold, and after a while the adrenalin activated a tremour in his right leg, which took time to settled down. He slowly climbed from his machine. He had been lucky. He had not seen the Yak closing on his tail, his attention was on the Yak weaving in front of him. He had learned a hard lesson, and had luckily come through his first encounter thanks to the experience of his leader Major Jager. The bullet holes in his wing enforced how lucky he had been. Joseph felt weary beyond words. Totally drained.

At the debrief, Jager listened with interest as the individuals on his flight recounted the details of their first encounter with the enemy. He then went through the details of the battle, advising and criticizing so they all learned from their experience.

"Come on. I'll buy you all a drink in the mess," he said finally with a grin of condolence at their discomfiture. "The main thing is you survived your first combat, and the enemy are now one less. Let's celebrate your survival."

Later, in their hut, the four of Jager's flight, talked through their encounter, getting it out of their system, and calming them down enough to be able to sleep. Sleep they did. The sleep of the exhausted, only the rousing of the Stabsfeldwebel the next morning shaking them from their deep slumber, and spurring them on to a new day, awakening them to another day of possible danger.

Operation Artic Fox, they learned the next morning was a small part of a larger operation designated Operation Silver Fox, which planned to capture the port of Murmansk.

Murmansk, they learned, was vital to the Russian war effort in that it received supplies of military equipment, including aircraft, mainly from Great Britain. It was planned by the German High Command to take the port and prevent these shipments of supplies reaching the Soviet Army and Airforce.

In the pilot ready room, the progress of the Operation was discussed. It was a joint operation by Finnish Artic and German forces, to advance on the town of Salla in a pincer movement with other German Forces from the west, with air support from Alakurtti. A roster of continuous daylight patrols to support the advancing troops was ordered, and Joseph and Petr found that they were on the second patrol of the day.

By 0900 they were in their aircraft, the holes in Joseph's wing now patched, and the engine of Blue Two now repaired, with engines running awaiting the order to take off. Major Jager was in his usual lead position, and would act like a shepherd tending his flock. Whilst not part of the flight he would always station himself above and slightly behind his flock. They were still his boys and they were combat virgins. They needed to quickly learn the facts of life.

They took off in pairs again, and formed up at 3000 metres. It was colder than yesterday. There was snow on the higher ground, and the light dusting on the runway had been swept away. Autumn would soon give way to winter, when flying would be almost impossible as the snow would lay too deep for operations to take place.

They navigated towards the town of Salla, the front line was within 10 kilometres of the town, but beyond the town and further east were a line of Soviet fortifications, and it had been reported that the Soviet Army were rushing reinforcements by rail to the area to protect Murmansk. The sortie intended to carry out a raid on that railway. They were to rendezvous with a flight of JU 87 Stuka dive bombers who were to attack the Kandalaksha and Kirov railway line.

Petr, with his sharp eyes, was again the first to spot the other German aircraft. Jager made contact over the radio, and his flight positioned themselves 100 metres higher and behind the Stuka formation.

As they neared Salla, ground defenses opened up and the sky became pockmarked with explosions of flak. Joseph saw one Stuka hit and fall to earth in flames, but the others carried on to target. As they neared the railway, an Intensive barrage of anti aircraft fire rose into the sky. As the Stukas dived to attack, a flight 6 Soviet Yak fighters appeared from the east.

"Bandits, five o'clock, 500 metres below, " came the calm voice of Jager. "They are going for the Stukas. Let's get after them."

He led a dive towards the Yaks, which broke formation at the sight of the ME Bf109's descending on them from above.

Joseph, closely supported by Petr, got on the tail of a Yak, which made a violent turn right, spiraling down towards the earth. The Stukas forgotten for the moment. Joseph followed The Yak down, the pressure of the dive pressing the breath from his lungs, but he managed to give the enemy aircraft a 2 second burst from his wing mounted machine guns. He was gratified to see bullet holes stitch along the fuselage into the engine cowling, which then emitted a large plume of black oily smoke. The plane inverted in its dive, and a body hurtled from within the cockpit. Joseph saw, several hundred metres below the now flaming aircraft, a parachute open. This scene was short lived as Petr engaged another Yak, hammering bullets into its tail, which shredded causing the craft to spin towards earth.

The action then became a general melee of banking, weaving, and diving, with neither side scoring much more than superficial damage.

Suddenly the air was clear again. The Yaks had disappeared east low to the ground and at speed and all but two Stukas formed up having acquired their targets, leaving the railway damaged and unusable at least for the next 24 hours, until the repair teams moved in.

Jager's flight escorted the Stukas away from the area, and returned to base. Joseph had achieved his first kill.

The pattern of operations continued unabated for 8 weeks more. Joseph achieved one more victim, but in the main their operations were to support the ground offensive, where concentrations of troops and artillery were the main targets. Petr, however, did secure his first verified kill in aerial combat.

The weeks went by in a pattern of sleep and flying. The constant pressure and terror of air battle turned the novice pilots slowly into veterans. They had fought and survived the first real shooting war of their short lives. They had learned the first rule of war. Kill or be killed, despite an underlying feeling of compassion for his victims. They had learned how to fight in the air. Politics and government meant nothing to these young pilots. Power was not something they considered.

Captured territory had no meaning other than to those wielding the power of leadership. Patriotism was ever present for the zealots, but faded into the distant mists for those doing the actual fighting. As the intensity of war increased so, survival meant everything.

These thoughts ran through Joseph's head as he flew his missions. He had to keep his thoughts to himself, it was dangerous both to him and his family in the present climate to express his true thoughts. He concluded he was a reluctant protagonist.

Chapter Thirteen

The campaign to capture the port of Murmansk was only partially successful. The German and Finnish Forces finally managed to capture the town of Salla, supported daily by air from Alakurtti Air Base, but they could not penetrate the old line of Soviet fortifications to the east which were defended by increasingly reinforced and determined Soviet troops. The weather by this time had made flying sporadic. Winter was setting in. Snow lay thick on the ground, and the cold was so intense, maintaining the aircraft, let alone flying, was hazardous in such weather. Before each take off and landing the snow had to be cleared from both the runways and the aircraft, to give the pilots any chance of undertaking air operations. Sometimes the weather predictions just precluded or cut short operations, as storms could quickly close down the airfield whilst the aircraft were still airbourne.

The troops on the ground managed to advance within 30 kilometres of Murmansk, but got no further. A stalemate was reached, where the opposing forces could go no further without major reinforcement and improvement in the weather.

With the weather situation making air operations impossible, Jager and his flight received orders to leave Alakurtti. A transport aircraft arrived during a lull between snow storms, to take them to Olso, where they stayed overnight, flying on to Berlin, the following day. Landing at Berlin-Gatow air base. There they were accommodated until given the good news they had been granted a 7 day furlough. They were ordered to report back to the airfield for onward posting at the end of their leave.

Petr and Joseph travelled into the city centre of Berlin. The city was on air raid alert having suffered allied air raids from early 1940, but normal life seemed unaffected as the streets were crowded with civilians and military personnel in uniform. The night life continued unabated. Joseph and Petr were determined not to let the danger of an occasional air raid spoil their furlough. They were young, with the energy of the young, and they were members of an elitist group. They were pilots of the Luftwaffe and admired as such. They booked in the hotel Adlon Kempinski, on the Under den Linden, with its view of the Brandenburg Gate. It would deplete their accumulated pay but this could be their last hurrah for some time. They could be dead or wounded in the coming weeks, so what would they need to save money for. Their future was so uncertain. They needed to release the tensions of combat flying, and Berlin was still an open town with all the delights a large city had to offer.

They were welcomed by the owner of the hotel, Herr Louis Adlon as heroes of the Reich. He offered the two young airmen special rates for their shared room, recognizing that having two active pilots in his hotel would add to his kudos with the Nazi regime. High government officials and hierarchy of the Nazi party, Luftwaffe and other armed forces, who regularly inhabited his establishment would note and approve of his actions towards these young airmen. He would exploit their presence in the way a good businessman would when presented with a good public relations opportunity. He ensured his wider clientele knew of these two young heroes. He would publicly show his delight at their presence in his establishment, and make sure all the right people would know of his generosity. Joseph and Petr were the epitome of young and vigorous German Youth serving and defending their country, and their stay at his establishment was to be exploited by the canny businessman to its fullest extent. Not that it didn't benefit the two young men. As they became known, they were subjected to the favours of the rich and famous clientelle. They hardly had to pay for their own drinks in the hotel, finding it astounding they were feted as heroes of the Reich, but wallowing in the unsolicited attention.

On the second day of their furlough, sitting at dinner in the luxury of the sumptuous dining room, a waiter brought a bottle of champagne to their table. It was on a silver tray.

"We didn't order this, "said Joseph.

"No," said the waiter, "It is a present from the Baroness." He indicated two beautifully attired, elegantly dressed, and sophisticated woman, in their mid thirties, at a table near the window. He poured two glasses. Joseph looked over to the two elegant ladies, raised his glass in salute, and sipped the bubbling liquid. His salute was acknowledged by an imperious wave of the hand and a nod of recognition at the gesture.

"Wait here," Joseph said to Petr. "I will go and thank them."

Joseph walked over to the two ladies, who were both looking lasciviously at him and smiling.

"Ladies, " said Joseph, "I wish to thank you both for your kind consideration on behalf of me and my friend," indicating a watching Petr. "It was most thoughtful. We are here on leave from the Russian front, and your gesture has made our evening. May I introduce myself. I am Oberleutnant Joseph Mozart from Vienna, and my friend is Oberleutnant Petr Muller from Hamburg." He said, clicking his heels together. " May I have the honour of knowing your names?"

The dark haired, slimly built, aristocratic lady,wearing a shimmering light grey silk evening dress, drew on her cigarette in its long holder, blew smoke at Joseph and raised a quizzical eyebrow, looking at him as a hungry leopard would when anticipating a kill . She was beautiful, assured, and spoke with a husky voice which held the promise of the unknown.

"Baroness Ursula Von Ritter. My companion here," indicating the blonde haired buxom lady on the opposite side of the table, "Is Marta von Hase. " She looked at Joseph with a knowing smile playing on her lips. "You are heroes of the Luftwaffe. Herr Adlon speaks highly of you both. Would you and your friend care to join us?"

Joseph waved Petr over, who came clutching the bottle of champagne, with a broad smile of lustful anticipation on his face.

"Good evening ladies. Thank you for your generosity," said Petr his voice lowering as his arousal at the sight of the two elegantly dressed women raised his hormonal activity to the point of recklessness. He kissed the Baroness's hand in a slow meaningful gesture, gazing into her vivid blue eyes as he did so, with a smile playing on his lips. He then did the same with Frau Von Hase, clinging to her hand for a long moment whilst staring into her eyes.

"Would you care to join us," repeated the Baroness, in a sultry voice. "Please sit."

The bottle of champagne did not last long as the two young men were captivated by the enchanting women. Another bottle was ordered and mutual toasts of admiration were given and returned, as the sexual atmosphere worked into overdrive. The women were cool and sophisticated, but oozed sexuality, and both young pilots were drowning in its implied promise.

"What are you both doing whilst on your leave?" inquired the Baroness.

"We are just exploring the possibilities and wondering what night life in Berlin has to offer," offered Joseph with a questioning raise of his eyebrows.

"The possibilities are many and various in Berlin," purred the Baroness. "We are going on to a nightclub. Would you care to join us?"

It took both captivated young men milliseconds to agree with an eager nod of their heads. They were too overcome by the obviously loaded invitation to even think about refusing.

They finished the second bottle of champagne. Baroness Von Ritter called for her bill, and in a wave of unexpected generosity paid both bills. The ladies called for their wraps, and the party swept from the dining room, with an obsequious Herr Aldon bowing them out of the hotel with a knowing smile playing on his lips.

The doorman called a taxi. "Nollendorfplatz," said the Baroness to the driver.

The taxi dropped them off at the end of a darkened alley. The party walked arm in arm down the alley following a faint light. As they neared the light they heard the faint sound of music. They came to a large studded door, with a closed hatch set in the structure.

"Knock twice, then once," said the Baroness.

Joseph did as instructed. A face appeared at the hatch.

"Tell him, Aldon sent us," said the Baroness.

The door opened, a curtain was drawn aside and they entered into a smoke filled corridor, with stairs going down. Music and voices filled the air.

As they descended the stairs the music got louder, as did the voices.

"I though the Fuhrer had banned nightclubs," said Joseph.

"It's not always what you know. It's who you know," whispered the Baroness. "This is strictly illegal. But ignored. No doubt by paying substantial bribes."

They moved into the main room of the cellar which was wreathed in tobacco smoke, the dim lighting playing on the haze as it danced in the air. A slow jazz number was being played by the quartet on a small stage, and a singer in a slinky black dress crooned to the music. Couples swayed, locked together, on the tiny dance floor.

The party were shown to a table in a side booth. The brick of the cellar at their backs. A waiter appeared like a wraith in the gloom and they ordered a bottle of Schnapps. Couples at other tables were groping and fondling, the atmosphere highly charged with sexual promise.

Joseph looked around him. This was a first for him, he had never been to such a nightclub before. The openness of the couples in various stages of dress, couples, some wearing heavy makeup, others male, dressed as women, people of the same sex dancing together. It was all new to him. He looked at the Baroness, charged up by her obvious excitement at being in a place banned by the Nazi regime, but being enjoyed by the mostly Lesbian and Gay customers. How did they get away with it, he thought. He knew that the authority's had banned all such places and made such contact illegal, but here it was. In the Capital City, right under the noses of the officials at the Chancery.

They sipped their drinks.

"Would you like to dance?" said Joseph to the Baroness.

She slipped into his arms as if slipping into a sleek dress, and they gyrated to the music. The dance floor was so crowded with other couples, their closeness was unavoidable. Not that Joseph objected, as their gyrations had a very arousing effect on him.

He saw his friend Petr was now in a similar position to himself. He was dancing with Marta von Hase in similar close contact.

They drank and danced. Danced and drank for an hour, the sexual temperature reaching toward a crescendo, when suddenly the atmosphere was destroyed by the sound of whistles, and the crashing of hammer blows.

The music stopped abruptly. A waiter appeared suddenly at their startled side, from among the screaming and panicking crowd.

"Baroness," he shouted above the din. "This way, quickly, follow me."

He took them through a curtained doorway, which he bolted on the other side, and down a passage. Through more doors, and up a staircase, three floors to a roof. The screams of those left in the nightclub faded. He then led them to a fire escape.

"Down there," he said, you will be two streets away. This is the roof of the building next door. My boss said you were too important to be caught by the Police. Now go Baroness, quickly."

The Baroness pressed a wad of notes into the waiter's hand and they all descended the fire escape stairs. As they got to the street with Joseph and Petr helping the women, they saw muted flashing lights at the top of the narrow road. They turned in the opposite direction, walking swiftly away, until three streets away when they hailed a taxi.

The Baroness, now laughing at their close encounter, gave the taxi driver an address, and quickly Joseph and Petr found themselves deposited outside some evidently elegant apartment block, with a concierge in its entrance lobby.

"Good evening Baroness, " said the concierge.

"Good evening Schmidt," said the Baroness, totally unfazed by the encounter, even though Joseph and Petr were present. "We will go up."

They walked arm in arm across the foyer to a set of lifts, taking one up to the penthouse. The Baroness opened the door to an astoundingly beautiful and exceptionally sumptuous apartment. It was all the latest furniture in the modern mode. She drew the blackout curtains, and turned on soft lighting, threw her wrap on a luxurious settee, turned and said, "Now, where were we? Drink?"

She mixed drinks at a stylish modernistic drinks trolley and Joseph found a cognac of the finest quality pressed into his hands. Delivered with a long lingering kiss which hinted at much promise.

"Now, do make yourselves comfortable. Excuse us for a few minutes. We have to make ourselves presentable," she purred, as she and Marta disappeared into what was obviously a bedroom.

Joseph looked at Petr. Shrugged and sat down on the enormous settee, sinking into its comfort, as he loosened the collar and undid the buttons on his tunic. His example set, Petr did the same with a grin of conspiracy at their luck.

Here they were. Surrounded by luxury. In the company of two, obviously titled, sexually charged and married women. Sitting in anticipation, in elegant surroundings, sipping the best quality cognac, having had one of the best meals for some time, experienced some of the illicit nightlife of the Capital, and having escaped a Police raid, now waiting in highly charged states, awaiting the next chapter in their adventure to evolve.

The bedroom door opened and the two women glided into the room wearing frilly diaphanous night dresses with over gowns of similar material. The baroness sat close to Joseph, drink in hand, devouring him with her eyes, as she quizzically assessed him and slowly sipped her drink. Joseph glanced at his friend and he was similarly engaged.

"Would you care to stay. The streets are dangerous at this time of night. There are air raids and Police everywhere. Criminals and nasty people too. It would be much safer if you stayed," she cooed.

Joseph gulped at his drink. The realization hitting him that he was in the home of a married woman.

"What about your husband?" He queried.

"Oh, he's away. He's in the Luftwaffe somewhere in France. There will be no bother."

"What about the concierge? Said Joseph.

"What about him. He is totally loyal to me. Forget him."

Two drinks later the Baroness led Joseph to her bedroom. She turned and kissed him lingeringly and deeply until his head spun with arousal. He pulled at her clothing, such as it was, but she pushed him away.

"Slow down. There is no rush. We have all night," she whispered in a husky voice, as she moved toward the huge bed with silken sheets, where she sat looking at him as he frantically tore at the buttons of his tunic, her half smile indicating her approval as his lithe and muscular body was gradually revealed to her.

He move towards her and she seemed to glide into his arms, pressing her body into his. Joseph was lost in the moment. Soon they were lying on the bed, naked and caressing each other. She again slowed him down.

"We have time. Enjoy." She whispered in his ear, her teeth sinking into his lobe in a gentle bite, which made him almost frantic with desire.

She climbed on top of him, massaging him across his shoulders, his chest, his abdomen and lower. She slowly kissed him, tongue seeking and dancing with his. Joseph had never been so entrapped. She was the ringmaster, calling the tune. He was her puppet.

They gyrated together in rapture. Joseph had never experienced such physical and emotional wellbeing. He soared, she gasped. They climaxed together. He sank down, replete and at peace with the world. The war forgotten, his fears, his worries for the future, lost in the moment.

He lay there, dormant, his mind replaying the act.

"Stay there," she whispered. "The night is young, you have much to learn, and I will teach you."

His breath returned to normal and he was somnolent. A deep peace pervaded his being. His breathing regulated, he was in a place of soft light, and music.

She bit his ear again, but harder. He emerged from his trance-like state with a start.

"Stay with me, " she said. "There is more."

He felt her move against him, and this time it was slower, deeper and more meaningful.

At last they collapsed into sleep. She had touched his very soul. He was replete in every way. The war was far away.

Joseph awoke to find himself alone in bed. His clothes still scattered where he had left them the night before. He laid back comatose, enjoying the luxury of his surroundings and the feeling of contentment coursing through his body. He stretched, feeling the silken sheets whisper beneath his naked body.

The door opened, and the Baroness, now dressed in a fresh silk dressing gown entered bearing a large silver tray from which issued the delicious smell of freshly ground coffee, and freshly baked bread rolls. There were cheeses, ham, honey and jams. He sat up, unashamed at his nakedness, and they breakfasted.

"Will I see you again," asked Joseph.

"How long is your leave," she queried.

"Five more days before I have to report to my new posting."

"Then we have four more days, and nights?" she said questioningly.

"Marta and I have things to do today. We will dine together. I will arrange it and telephone you at your hotel later. Leave it to me."

After breakfast Joseph bathed, and dressed. Petr, in the same soporific state, was in the sitting room talking to Marta, who smiled a knowing smile as he entered.

"We will see you both later then," bantered Marta.

"We will look forward to it, " Joseph replied, smiling.

They walked through the lobby of the apartment block, nodding to a knowing concierge, who smiled to himself as they left the building. Another of the Baronesses young men, thought the concierge. Lucky boys, he thought with envy.

They returned by taxi to the hotel. They saw the owner Louis Aldon, who beamed when he saw his young heroes, with a knowing and envious smile. He knew about the Baroness and her peccadilloes. She was a regular and valued customer. He was all knowing and always discreet. His lips were always sealed. He was the perfect hotelier, the soul of discretion.

The two young pilots met the two ladies again that evening. They went to a very expensive but discreet restaurant, not far from the hotel, and enjoyed a convivial evening, ending again at the Baroness's apartment, where she continued

Joseph's sexual education, giving him the benefit of her maturity and experience. The learning curve of both young men was the most enjoyable tuition they had ever experienced in their lives. They learned to give as well as take, and that speed was not necessarily the panacea to sexual enlightenment.

Four days later, having learned so much about human nature from their willing tutors, sexually sated, having passed out in the university of life with flying colours, they reported back to Berlin-Gatow air base, tired but happy. They were given orders to proceed to Orly Air Base near Paris. This time they were assigned to the fighter Staffel which operated on the other side of the base from where they had completed their training. They were directed to an officer's waiting room, where half a dozen more young pilots were awaiting transportation. These were newly trained, fresh faced and very young looking pilots, and they looked up nervously as Joseph and Petr entered the room. It was obvious to the newly qualified that Joseph and Petr were more experienced pilots, their faded shoulder insignia showing them to be full Oberleutenants, which probably meant combat experience.

The wait was short before a Stabsfeldwebel entered the room.

"Gentlemen, your flight to Orly is waiting on the tarmac." He announced.

Led by Joseph and Petr, and carrying their bags, the group walked across the tarmac to a waiting Junkers JU52 Trimotor transport aircraft, affectionately known as "Tante Ju"(Aunt JU). Joseph and Petr grabbed the front seats, stowed their bags, leaned back and dozed, smiling as they recalled the dreamy days of their leave, when they had both been welcomed into proper manhood. The new pilots, in awe of the two more experienced Oberleutnant's, chattered excitedly amongst themselves in nervous anticipation of their first posting.

The flight of just over 1000 kilometers took just over two and a half hours, and at last the Junkers entered the glide path over Orly. The runways looked familiar to Joseph and Petr. It was, in a way, a home coming.

They were ushered Into a briefing room, where they settled for the usual greeting from a Senior Officer. A short time later, the door opened, and a Stabsfeldwebel shouted, "Attention." As a cadre of senior officers of the Luftwaffe marched in unison into the room, led by a General.

The new arrivals stood rigidly to attention. The General, in his mid forties, in the full panoply of his rank, with bristling moustaches, stepped forward on the platform at the front of the room..

"Pleas sit." The ensemble sat, and the General continued, "My name is General Eberhart Von Ritter, and I am here to welcome you," he barked with assured authority.

Joseph looked at Petr, with amazed horror written on his face. It couldn't be, could it? he thought. Petr looked at Joseph, raised his eyebrows in silent panic. Was the General the husband of Baroness Von Ritter. It must be, it fitted with what they had been told by the Baroness, and Joseph then remembered a family photograph he had seen at the apartment. It was him. He was certain. They were doomed.

Both sank into their seats, bowing their heads. Sweat beading their brows as the realization hit them full on. What had fate thrown at them now?

Chapter Fourteen

After his welcoming address, they stood to attention as General von Ritter left the room, with his ADC. Joseph and Petr studiously avoiding any eye contact with their would be nemesis. Others of the senior officer cadre remained.

A Major stepped forward. I am Major Reinhart Wagner. I am the commanding officer of Jagdgeschwader (JG) 54, which fly ME Bf109's. Two of you," he said consulting a list,"Muller and Mozart," he then paused and laughed, "It's the first time a Wagner played with a Mozart," he quipped, " are to join us. Both of you please stand and give your names and experience."

Petr and Joseph stood.

"Petr said, "I trained on 109's here at Orly, then was posted with my friend here, " indicating Joseph, "to Alakurtti Air Base in Finland, where we were involved in the Murmansk campaign. It was stalemate when we left, the Russians had stopped the advance about 30 kilometres from Murmansk. The weather stopped us flying after a six month deployment, the snow was 3 metres deep, so we were redeployed here."

"Good, " said the Major. "You are combat experienced. We can use you."

He looked at Joseph and said, "You?"

"Similar," said Joseph. "Trained here on 109's with Leutnant Muller, and we both served at Alakurtti in the Russian Campaign."

"We will get to know you soon enough. I will have a Corporal take you to your quarters. You will be sharing, and I will see you both in the mess at lunchtime where we can get to know one another and I can introduce you to the rest of the staffel."

He nodded to a Obergefreiter at the back of the room who guided them away to find their accommodation. As they did so, another Major stepped forward, to address the remaining new pilots, who were replacements for Jagdgeschwader 21, the other fighter wing using ME Bf109's on base.

Joseph and Petr found themselves sharing accommodation in a dormitory block on the far side, the operational side, of Orly Air Base. The hanger areas, and aircraft dispersal areas were crowded with a plethora of aircraft. Mostly the latest version of the ME Bf109.

They were met by a Luftwaffe orderly. An elderly Schutze who was well above normal retirement age. He met both officers at their dormitory door.

"Welcome Gentlemen, my name is Friedrich Koch. I am your orderly, " he announced, taking their bags from them.

"Leave the unpacking to me sirs. Are you familiar with the base?"

Joseph said, "We were here as trainees but on the other side of the airfield. We have just come from a tour on the Russian front and no, we are not yet familiar with this operational side."

"Well sir, " said Koch, "I have prepared a rough plan of the facilities this side of the airfield, showing the buildings and hangers you will need to be familiar with." He then handed each a sheet of paper with a roughly drawn plan of the base.

"You would normally meet your colleagues at lunch in the officers mess, " he continued. "If you want to freshen up beforehand, the bathroom is next door, and I have laid out fresh towels on you beds."

"Koch," said Joseph, " I don't want to insult you, but aren't you a little too old for the service."

"Well sir, I was in the first war, in the infantry. Managed to survive that, and afterwards went back to being a waiter in one of the large hotels in Munich. I was married but my wife died just before this war. We had no children, so I volunteered again, and here I am. I am 65 years old, but wanted to do my bit. I have nothing left to go home to. So I will make it my task to look after you two young officers and make sure you are as comfortable as circumstances allow. You can reply on me sir."

Touched by the man's passion and obvious willingness to serve, Joseph and Petr spontaneously shook Koch's hand. Who beamed at their human touch.

"Now sirs. You relax. I will get on with my work. I have a room with a small kitchen at the end of the block. There will be coffee in a minute and I will wake you each morning at reveille, or before if you are on flying duty. Please tell me your preferences. How you take your coffee. I will ensure I lay out the appropriate clothing for all occasions. If there is anything you need or want, please let me know."

The two young pilots took advantage of the time before lunch to shave and shower. Upon returning to their room, they found that Koch had laid out their uniforms, appropriate to the officers mess.

They quickly changed, watching Koch fuss over their clothing, as he put away things in drawers and the wardrobes. Taking Koch's plan, they walked to the officers mess. Major Wagner was standing at the bar with a group of senior officers. He saw the two new arrivals and detached himself from the group.

"Welcome to Jagdgeschwader 54. Our group consists of two Staffels of 12 aircraft. We fly in finger four formations, a leader and wingman, a second in command and wingman. " He nodded at Petr, "You will be my wingman, and you," nodding at Joseph will fly number two to Hauptmann Fabien Von Weiser." As he said that, Von Weiser turned at the mention of his name. Joseph gasped in recognition, then smiled.

"Fabien. We meet again, " he grinned.

"Good God, " said Von Weiser. Joseph. How are you young man. Welcome. We will be flying together again."

Major Wagner stood, stunned. "You know each other?"

"Yes," said Joseph, "Fabien taught me to fly on gliders. He was a very good instructor. We met at the Vienna Gliding Club." Turning to Von Weiser

Joseph shook his hand warmly. "How are your family?" he queried.

A cloud worked its way across Von Weiser's face. "My Father died fairly recently, but mother and my sister are well."

"So you are now the Baron Von Weiser?" questioned Joseph.

"Yes. It's come far too early for me. Unfortunately. My mother and my sister are devastated. He was only fifty six. He died of a heart attack whilst on leave from his regiment."

Major Wagner broke in, forcing bonhomie into his voice before the situation got too maudlin. "Enough of this love in. Come I will introduce you to the others in the Staffel. Then the first drink is on me." He slapped Von Weiser on the back in a brotherly way, putting his arm round his companions shoulders, an act which restored Von Weiser's mood, and allowed him to square himself shrug his shoulders and compartmentalize his grief.

He then took them to the bar, and introduced the newcomers to the other staffel members. Over drinks, they shared their personal stories. Wagner turned out to be Austrian, his family home being in Saltzburg.

After a convivial lunch where Joseph and Petr were quizzed about their backgrounds and experience, they began to feel accepted in their new environment. It helped that Von Weiser and Joseph knew each other, and this greased the wheels of settlement, especially when it was suggested jokingly by some wag that Wagner and Mozart should fly together to become the "Musicians Flight", Wagner smiled. He had already made his selection of wingman. It was Petr Muller. He now felt committed and thought it unlucky to change. "He declared, "I haven't got a musical bone in my body. I'm tone deaf. I will do well with Leutnant Muller, thank you very much." They all laughed at his dry humour.

At the end of lunch, Major Wagner announced, that he and Von Weiser would fly with the new boys that afternoon, on a familiarization flight, so they could get to know their new machines, and the men they would be flying with.

The afternoon found the two newcomers with their mentors inspecting the ME Bf109s, lined up outside the hanger where they had undergone a pre-flight check.

"Wagner said, "These are the Bf 109 F-4 model. An upgrade from what you have been used to. We will take you up now, for a familiarization sortie. Nothing too strenuous, so let's go."

Joseph climbed into his new machine, and looked around the cockpit. Most things were familiar. The armament was the same, and the dials just the same. He was confident he would soon get familiar with his new machine.

Wagner signaled start up, and Joseph heard him on the radio asked for permission to take off. They started taxing toward the runway, when suddenly the air raid sirens sounded. Over the radio he heard the control room order immediately takeoff. They were under attack.

Joseph followed his flight leader pushing his throttle through the gate, formation forgotten, as they gathered speed down the runway, explosions started at the far end of the airfield ,behind them. Debris, earth, smoke and shrapnel chased their accelerated progress, a bomb fell just off the runway to his left, showering his aircraft with clods of earth and debris, causing his machine to lurch right, which he quickly controlled, until miraculously his machine threw itself into the air, gathering speed. Joseph pulled the wheels up and the aircraft leapt forward as the drag reduced. He followed his leader, as they broke left away from the bombing pattern which seemed to have followed them. Joseph was then able to see a large formation of Lancaster bombers passing overhead, speeding away from the airfield, having dropped their load on the base. Spitfires and Hurricane fighters from high above were swooping and diving on the aircraft still parked on the field. Several were hit and destroyed, the smoke and explosions took Joseph's eye as he strained to stick to the wing of his leader.

"Let's get into them," shouted Wagner. "Muller, Climb and follow me. Mozart, stick to Von Weiser like glue." Which was all very well but the diving Spitfires and Hurricanes, having strafed the airfield, were now concentrating on the formation of four ME Bf109's which had managed to take off.

Von Weiser screamed, "Mozart, break right, break right." Joseph jerked the control column to the right, as a stream of tracer passed his left wing. He climbed in booster mode, and weaved left and right, tracer following him, as the Spitfire on his tail tried to counter his moves.

He lost sight of his leader in the mayhem of survival, twisting and turning his machine. He felt the thud of hits on the tip of his left wing, as he made another violent turn, but managed to avoid the deadly arc of fire from behind. Suddenly he heard a large explosion from behind. In his mirror he saw the Spitfire disintegrate in the air, the pieces scattering to the wind, and his flight leader was again in front and to his left.

"That was close, " came the calm voice of Wagner. "Now let's get after the bombers. The fighters are going, they must be short of fuel this far out from base."

Not seeing his flight leader, Von Weiser, Joseph asked, "Did anyone else get off the ground?".

"I haven't seen anyone. It looks like you and me," voiced Wagner with an audible sigh. "I don't know what has happened to Von Weiser and Muller. I know they got off. They were with us at the beginning. Where they are now, I have now idea. Close up on me, for the time being you are my wingman." Joseph hoped his friend Petr and Fabien Von Weiser had got safely into the air.

They closed with the tail of the bomber formation. Three of which were streaming smoke from engines, and lagging behind the main formation.

They climbed above the formation, and dived into the attack. Joseph followed his leader who selected one of the damaged aircraft below him. A short but effective burst of cannon fire turned the aircraft into an inferno. Bodies tumbled from the stricken aircraft, the bloom of deploying parachutes showing as they fell to earth.

Joseph selected the next damaged aircraft in line, and followed the example of his leader. It too flamed, and its crew parachuted to the ground.

Other German fighters, from other bases were now joining the fray and Joseph saw several of the bombers fall out of formation, but the remainder of the British formation were putting up a curtain of withering fire from their Browning machine guns, scoring several hits on the attacking force.

Wagner, closely followed by Joseph pressed home another attack, and had the satisfaction of seeing hits on the outer engine nacelle of the Lancaster in front of him, the smoke getting more intense as the aircraft flew on, weaving to avoid the bullets following its progress. Joseph added his bullets to the cone of fire, and the Lancaster staggered in the air, then blew into pieces.

Suddenly Von Weiser's voice was heard. Red leader. This is blue leader. I am joining you from below and behind. I have Red two with me. We had to take avoiding action during takeoff. Ammunition gone. Joining you on your port wing."

Joseph looked to his left and saw the flight of two, Von Weiser and Petr, joining their finger four from below.

"Welcome Blue leader," said Wagner. It's been busy. Let's go home."

More and more Axis fighters joined the fray. "Let's get out of here." Wagner repeated, " We're low on fuel now. Leave it to the others. I don't think many will get home from this attack."

They peeled off, heading towards their home base. Wagner contacted his control. They were instructed to divert to Le Bourget. The runway at Orly was too badly damaged to land at present.

They landed safely, being directed to the dispersal area where they parked their aircraft. Joseph released his canopy, pulled off his sweat soaked flying helmet, and breathed a huge sigh of release. He had survived his first combat in France, and he had contributed to the downing of enemy aircraft. His shaking hands steadied, and he climbed from his machine. There were bullet holes in his left wing. It had been a close run thing.

Wagner came over, "Are you alright?"

"Yes," said Joseph, nodding toward the damage. "That was close. Thanks for looking after me."

"My pleasure. It will cost you a drink," he smiled. "Let's go to the mess. You can buy me one there."

As they sat nursing their second drink. The first having been swallowed in record time, Petr and Hauptmann Von Weiser entered the room looking suitably dirt encrusted and sweaty. There was a tear in the shoulder of Petr's flying jacket. They saw their flight companions, smiled and sat down with huge sighs of relief. Both had survived the attack, but both had landed damaged aircraft. Their excited voices calming as the adrenalin drained from their bodies. They had all survived, although Petr's aircraft would require some major surgery before it flew again.

"What happened to you," asked Joseph.

"I was hit as we took off. My canopy was holed. " He indicated the tear in his jacket. "One passed through my coat, look," he said indicating his ragged flying jacket. "I was very lucky, but survived thanks largely to Hauptmann Von Weiser here," he smiled ruefully. I ended up wingman to the wrong leader in the confusion."

"So did I, " said Joseph. "How did they get through all the way to Orly. It's a long way over occupied territory?"

"The buzz is that they carried out a major multi-target attack on Dieppe and Rouen, with a large fighter escort, and some came on to Orly in a diversionary attack. Our fighter screen had been fighting them until they were short of fuel and had to refuel and rearm, which allowed their aircraft to get to Orly, taking us by surprise. We were lucky to get off the ground. Had it not been for the fact that we were already in our aircraft to take you both up for a familiarization flight, then we would probably been destroyed on the ground, " said Wagner. "We were very lucky." He shrugged soberly, then said in a more cheerful voice, "Let's have another drink and see if we can cadge lunch out of our hosts, " he said deliberately loud enough for the barman to hear.

"One thing I will say," he added, "Our people from the coastal bases, having had time to refuel and rearm, will give them a hard time all the way home.

I doubt if many of them will get to their home base."

This had a sobering effect on the group, as they thought of the courage of their enemies, fighting their way deep into France and taking on the formidable defenses which the Axis forces had installed in occupied France. As airmen themselves they knew the hazards such operations would endure, and they could feel some empathy for fellow fliers,

The following day, having dined well, and slept in strange barrack rooms, they bid farewell to Le Bouget, and after a short flight returned to Orly. There was a flight of three. Petr's aircraft was undergoing more extensive repair, and he was being driven back to Orly by road.

As they circled the airfield, they could see the cratering of the main runway had been hastily repaired, but there were wrecked aircraft, lorries and fuel bowsers, littered on taxiways and the grass. Some hangers had ceased to exist. They circled slowly, taking in the scene below. They landed with care, and taxied slowly to their dispersal area, taking in the scenes of devastation, passing wreckage still smoldering, and working parties frantically clearing the debris, under the demanding instruction of several Stabfeldwebels.

Orders came for the group to report to the headquarters building, where they stood outside the station commander's office awaiting his invitation to enter. Joseph did not want to be there. He was guilty of unwittingly cuckolding his commander, and had done his best to avoid all contact thus far.

General Eberthart Von Ritter stood as they entered his office, looking intently at each of them. Joseph felt himself colouring uncomfortably, and hoped Von Ritter would not notice his discomfiture. Petr was lucky he thought, he had not yet arrived back on base and would miss this interview.

"What happened to you, " he said, nodding toward Major Wagner.

Wagner reported in chronological detail, praising the actions of the members of his flight, and of the damage they had managed to inflict on the enemy bombers.

Von Ritter, his mood somber, listened intently.

"Well done, all of you. It was fortunate that you were in take off mode when it happened. I have taken the matter up with the high command. We should have been warned about such a major enemy operation. As it was, the surprise was almost complete, although we lost a good few aircraft in the raid, I have heard they lost considerably more, both coming into and getting out of France. I don't think they will try it again. Anyway we have orders to up our operations, and the high command will be planning reprisals. I am sure we will be heavily involved. Well done, all of you, there may be medals coming your way. Dismissed."

As they left the headquarters a staff car discharged Petr. Seeing them he hurried over to them.

"What's going on?" he asked.

Joseph said, "I'll tell you later."

Later they gathered in the mess, in clean more formal uniforms. It was lunch time, and attendance was down considerably. It was then they learned that the base had lost 11 aircraft. 8 pilots killed and 15 wounded personnel. There was a somber atmosphere as they dined, and they learned they were one flight of four which managed to take off, and another flight had lost three of its pilots in the attack as they tried to leave the ground. All the other losses were on stationary aircraft, vehicles and personnel on the ground.

At the week's end the base was fully operational once more. Replacement pilots were on their way. Joseph and Petr, with their flight leaders were now fully conversant with the surrounding countryside, and had settled into their new squadron successfully. Their duty was mainly the defense of Paris, but there was a rumour that they would shortly become involved in providing fighter escort to bombing raids over England.

The Battle of Britain was well over and any thought the Fuhrer had of invading England was in the past. His intention now was to keep the English busy so that they would not interfere with his planned expansion into Russia and the rest of Europe. Hitler planned the invasion of the Caucasus in an attempt to gain control of the oil rich territory. His armies were using raw materials such as oil at an alarming rate, and his solution was to capture the oil fields of the region, to fulfill his ambitions of European domination.

Shortly after the base had returned to normal operations, Joseph had a message from his father, who was still head surgeon at the main hospital in Paris. He took time between operations to go meet his him. They sat is a Parisienne café, in a discreet booth at the back of the room. Once the waiter had served them coffee and departed out of earshot, Doctor Mozart looked around to see he wasn't being overheard and said, "Joseph, I wanted to see you because I am being sent from Paris to Belgrade. You know our Army invaded Yugoslavia in forty one. Well the situation there has always been fraught with danger. The Yugoslavs have always resisted, no matter how much they have been repressed by our forces, and the amount of casualties is now growing. I have been ordered to the main hospital in Belgrade, and promoted to Generalmajor to take charge of all medical units in and around the city, and the forward aid stations on the front line, wherever that may be. I will be going home for two weeks, from next week, and then travel to Belgrade to take up my post. It's not something I wished for but orders are orders.   I will tell your Mother I have seen you, and that you are well. She worries about you, you know, as I do. But we are at war, much as I abhor violence, and as much as it is against the oath I took as a medical man, I cannot avoid my duty no more than you can, but remember we are Austrian, not Nazis. I know your real feelings about Herr Hitler and how he has changed the German people, including some Austrians, and his unremittent ambitions to rule Europe, but he has not changed me. I know you hate the persecutions which have taken place and which are still going on, but I would urge you to do your duty, and keep very quiet about your real feelings. It would be very dangerous to express any view contrary to the Nazi dogma. If you are to survive the war, then you have to put your personal feelings aside, and play your part in what we both consider an unnecessary war. I would urge you to follow my example. Keep your head down, do your duty, fight when you have to, it's that or be killed in action, and do not express dissention. When the war is over perhaps we can live our lives as Austrians once again, but I fear that we will suffer as a people both during and after this war ends. It must end. Let us pray for that day."

This long speech by his father was a rarity. Never had Joseph heard his father express his feelings so passionately, or so openly to him. That his Father's feelings accorded with his own, only reinforced his love for him and his independence of thought, but Joseph was fully aware that if these feelings were expressed in public his father would be in dire danger. Joseph had been brought up to be independent of thought, so was aware any thoughts similar to those of his father, should be well concealed from others, even his close friends and colleagues.

His father spoke again, "I hope you are keeping in contact with your Mother. She does worry about you. Write to her regularly. I know she is busy at the hospital, but she thinks about you every day."

"I write as often as I can, I know she worries, so it's good she has a busy life of her own." said Joseph.

From the café, the pair went to a nearby restaurant. A favourite of his Father's, where they enjoyed a convivial farewell meal. Joseph would not be seeing his father for some considerable time from now on, and an emotional farewell took place on the pavement as Joseph climbed aboard his borrowed motor cycle, to return to his base. He had much to contemplate.

Chapter Fifteen

Major Wagner, Hauptmann Von Weiser, Leutnant Petr Muller and Leutnant Joseph Mozart stood to attention in the base Commander's office at Orly Luftwaffe Base, as General Von Ritter formally addressed them.

"Your actions in defending this air base three weeks ago, has been noted by the Fuhrer. Your actions on that day confirmed your dedication to your duty in defending our airfield against overwhelming odds. That you all survived, was a miracle in itself. Your bravery has brought you just rewards. You, Major Wagner will be awarded the Knights Cross of the Iron Cross, as will you Hauptmann Von Weiser. You both," he said pointing at Joseph and Petr, "Will be awarded the Iron Cross- 2nd Class."

He paused, smiled and said, "That is not all. Hauptmann Von Weiser, you will be promoted to Major, and you two," pointing at Joseph and Petr, will be promoted Oberleutenant. There will be a ceremony on base next week for the presentation to be made to you all, and for the promotions to be announced. Well done." He then shook hands with them all, nodding his approval.

He then added, "The ceremony will be with full panoply, and my wife will be joining us. I would deem it a favour if you would allow her to make the presentations. She has always been an admirer of our brave Luftwaffe pilots It will be good for morale."

"We would be honoured," said Major Wagner with a smile of acceptance.

Joseph looked stunned, as did Petr. Von Ritter's wife was coming on base and would not only be present at the ceremony, she would be presenting the medals to the recipients. Joseph's heart sunk. He hadn't told her of his posting to Orly when he left Berlin, she would certainly recognize him as her Berlin paramour. He experienced a sinking feeling in the pit of his stomach. As they left the commander's office, Joseph looked at Petr whose face also betrayed his feelings of impending doom.

Major Wagner called the four together. "It's all very well getting promotion and medals, but we have work to do. There is a briefing this afternoon for an operation. It's a big one, and we are going to be part of it. We meet at 1400hrs in the briefing room. Be there."

At 1350hrs there was a hubbub of voices coming from the briefing room, as Joseph and Petr entered. They took their seats, and at 1400hrs precisely the door banged open, and in marched General Von Ritter, followed by a cadre of flight commanders including Major Wagner and the newly promoted Major Von Weiser. As they marched in the ensemble stood to attention, and the babble of voices silenced.

The General stood, legs apart, hands on hips, looking over his command, pausing for effect.

"We have a very important mission to undertake tomorrow at dawn. All permission to leave base is now withdrawn until further notice. No telephone calls off base will be allowed for security reasons. This will be a mission to destroy a very important target, and our task will be to accompany the bombers to the target area, and defend them from the enemy. I cannot stress how important this mission will be, and I can tell you the high command consider it one of the most important missions of the war so far. I will leave you in the hands of your flight commanders and our Intelligence Officer Hauptmann Mattias Bruckner, who will explain the details of the target, and why it is so important to the Reich that we destroy it."

He then strode from the room, as the ensemble rose to attention until he had gone.

Bruckner stood, paused for effect until there was silence. "Please sit, and pay attention. " He uncovered a large map of the east coast of England.

"This is your target for tomorrow. Bomb Groups, comprising units from various fields will assemble east of Bruge at 5000 metres. There will be a two pronged attack. Target one will be here," and he pointed on the map, to a small island on the east coast of England. We have intelligence that the site is used for the experimentation of a new engine. Our intelligence leads us to believe that a new engine concept invented by the British before the war, is being developed and tested on this site. If the British perfect it and bring it into general use then it could revolutionize war in the air. We are developing an engine along the same lines, and wish to be first to use it in an operational aircraft, so it is imperative that we destroy their research and test facility so we win the race. The second target will be the oil terminals on the north shore of the Thames here," and he pointed to an area west of Canvey Island. We believe a two pronged attack where our forces split at the beginning of the Thames estuary, has more chances of success in what we know is a heavily defended area. It will also mean that their fighter cover will have to be in two places at once. Fighters from this airfield will take off 3 hours before dawn, and refuel at Oostende-Middelkirke airfield in Belgium. The field is located 6.5km from Oostende and 3.25km East North East of the village of Middelkirke. A refueling unit has been sent ahead of this operation, and will refuel all your aircraft before crossing to England. In this way we will ensure longer fighter cover over the target area. Be warned gentlemen, this is a high risk operation. You will be heading into one of the most heavily defended regions of England, and where they have the most airfields and fighter cover. It is anticipated, by choosing a two site target, the defending forces will be halved in each target area. This target must be completely destroyed. It is essential to our war effort. Any questions?"

A pilot stood and said, "What if we don't manage to destroy the target."

Bruckner said, "In that case, we will have to rethink our strategy. You may pick up copies of the navigational coordinates from the back of the room. Good luck Gentlemen. Heil Hitler!" He saluted the Nazi salute and walked from the room, which erupted with a rising crescendo of voices, all expressing astonishment at the choice of target area. All the pilots were aware of how heavily defended the target area would be, and all realized the probability of success was limited to say the least. It wasn't a suicide mission, but it was close to one, and all the pilots knew there would be heavy casualties.

Joseph and Petr slept fitfully that night, each turning over the details of the coming mission in their heads. They would have to be on top form to survive such a mission, and both realized that very well.

Four hours before dawn their orderly woke them with steaming cups of black coffee. The aroma usually roused them to full energy within a short time, but this morning the overcast weather was matched by their desultory mood.

The pilots met again in the ready room. Major's Von Weiser and Wagner singled them out.

"We are Eagle Staffel. Blue one and Two and Green One and two. On this occasion I will have Joseph as my Blue Two. It seems fate that Wagner and Mozart should fly together since the raid on Orly," said Wagner. Major Von Weiser with Petr will be

Green One and Two. We take off, head NNE, and form up at 3000 metres. It's just over 300km to Oostende, and there is no head wind, so we should land within the hour. We re-fuel, and take-off from there is scheduled for dawn at 0600hrs. We will then climb to 6000 metres. We are acting as high cover for the bombers, and we are accompanying the bomb group going for the island, which is known as Foulness Island, near the small village of Shoeburyness. We will be operating over the Thames Estuary and we all know what that means. There are gun forts In the waters of the estuary, there is an army garrison there, housing at least one artillery regiment. There are also guns on the coast, both on the south and north shores, and of course there are many British Airfields in the area with short flying time from their bases to the target area. You can be sure that we are in for the ride of our lives, so stick close to our wings, and remember, over the combat area do not fly straight and level for more than a few seconds. Our lives depend upon it. If you have to ditch, then head back to the Belgian coast. The Kriegsmarine have gathered a chain of E boats to rescue any downed pilots, and they are on the radio frequency shown in your notes. So, let's go, and good luck."

They took off and after an hour were in the glide path to land at Oostende-Mickelkerke airfield. As soon as they taxied to a halt a fuel bowser came alongside, and began the process of pumping additional fuel into the tanks. The pilots were ushered into a hut where coffee and thick German sausage sandwiches were handed out by catering staff. Twenty minutes before dawn saw the pilots of "Eagle Staffel" in their machines, studying the flight plan given out to each of them. They were to escort Bomb Group "Thor", targeting Foulness Island, designated a proof and experimental establishment. Bomb Group "Odin" were targeting oil storage depots further up the Thames estuary.

At the order, Eagle staffel took off, and soon rendezvoused with Bomber Group "Thor". They headed out over the North Sea on a looped route, heading north east toward Lowestoft. As the Suffolk coast came into view the group veered south west heading for the Thames Estuary. They got within 10 miles of the coast when the first Spitfires came at the bombers from the west. Half of Eagle Staffel dived towards the attacking Spitfires, and the air became a whirlwind of diving, banking and circling aircraft. The dawn sky lit up with the firefly effect of tracer. The bombers maintained their formation and pressed on, adding to the curtain of fire criss-crossing the sky.

Wagner's voice came over the radio. "Hold position Eagle flight. There's more to come. This is just the start." As he said this more Spitfires and Hurricanes appeared in the east, at 6000 metres, diving straight down on the bomber formation.

"Here we go," shouted Wagner. "Eagles, follow me, " and he dipped his wing to the left, with Joseph following his leader. "Blue Two, we are taking the hurricanes on the left," he shouted, and he increased the angle of dive. The two ME Bf109's, with guns blazing, smashed through the formation of Hurricanes, which immediately scattered in all directions. Joseph saw his leader target a pair of Hurricanes, who seeing the danger they were in dived away, avoiding his cone of fire. Joseph followed and one of the hurricanes crossed his gun sight and he gave it a two second burst which stitched a pattern of holes across its engine cowling, and on into the wing root. The Hurricane emitted back smoke, and fell away from the conflict. Joseph was too engrossed in sticking to his leader to see what happened to the Hurricane, but his leader shouted, "Well done." Then screamed," Break left" Joseph jerked the control column hard left, as a line of tracer flew over his canopy. He looped right, until he felt vice like pressure on his chest, and then fell off his loop, to his right. A Hurricane fighter flashed past him, and he managed to squeeze off another burst, but it missed as the British Pilot weaved left and right away from him.

The tightness in Joseph's chest ceased as he levelled off, looking for his leader.

"Blue two to Blue leader. Where are you."

"Right behind you laddie." Said Wagner. Let's get after the Bombers."

In clear air, they stationed their aircraft 1000 metres above the bomber formation once again, until suddenly another flight, this time of Spitfires, appeared above and in front of the formation. There were diving in attack mode.

"Blue two, follow me again," came the instruction from his leader, peeling off left as he did so.

Joseph followed him down, as the Spitfire formation, with guns blazing, went for the middle of the bomber pack.

Wagner centred his machine on a Spitfire, which was blazing away at a bomber. He fired a burst of cannon fire, and Joseph saw him score hits on the wing of the British machine, which made it spiral away towards the ground. A web of tracer suddenly hit Joseph's right wing and he automatically jerked the controls left and dived towards sea. More tracer followed him and he felt the craft shudder as more hits were scored on his machine. The dive became frantic as he weaved left and right, pulling up a mere 25 metres above the waves until he felt himself greying out with the G force pushing him into his seat. His arms felt heavy and it was hard to move them. The Spitfire had followed him down. The pilot must have been new, and inexperienced, because so intent was he in claiming Joseph as his victim, he dived straight into the sea. The air battle became a maelstrom of deadly fire, as the bombers, with their fighter escorts flew over land on their bomb run. Aircraft were blown out of the sky by a mixture of combating aircraft and heavy ground fire, which got heavier as the German bombers dropped their loads. Some crashed without delivering their bombs the size of their explosion enhanced by their retained bomb load. Some managed to weave away from the target area, wounded and smoking, dropping their bombs anywhere to avoid being shot down. Others crashed after dropping their bombs, most of which missed their intended target. The aerial battle was total chaos. The fighters, there to protect the bombers, were fighting for their lives pursued by wave after wave of Spitfires and Hurricanes. It seemed to Joseph he was entering the halls of hell. All around him were explosions. He had no idea where Blue One was, he had lost all contact as he was fighting for his life.

Joseph fired a two second burst at a Hurricane which passed across his gun sight. He saw bullets weave a pattern across its cockpit, but it disappeared from his sight as he weaved away from a tracer pattern which passed his right wing. He dived left by instinct, pushing the throttle through the gate the engine and supercharger screaming in protest. He was now out of ammunition, and his fuel gauge showed that he had just enough fuel to make it back to base. He pulled his aircraft out of the dive just before hitting the water, and turned for home. He could add no more to the conflict. He called and repeated the call for his blue leader. All he could hear was the fading sound of shouts of warning to other aircraft still engaged, but fleeing homeward. Then all went quiet. He gained height, now conserving his fuel, and soon he saw the Belgian coast come into view, the morning sun glinting on the water, showing the dark line of the coast in relief.

Joseph called the control tower at Oostende-Michelkerke, and finally got a reply. He was running on fumes. He was given permission to land, and as he passed the perimeter fence his engine stopped. With wheels down, he glided onto the concrete of the runway, and as he ran to a stop he veered his machine onto the grass. He had no more fuel to taxi to the hangers. He opened his canopy, slowly pulled off his sweat soaked flying helmet, and sat there shaking with relief. He was exhausted. Fighting the constant G forces had sapped his energy. His heart rate slowly returned to normal and he was as tired as he had ever been in his life. Now he knew what hell was like. A place of fire, brimstone, death and destruction. Tears of relief coursed down his face, uncontrolled and unhidden.

Slowly he recovered his equilibrium, he wiped his face with his silken scarf, the sweat drying on his face in the morning breeze wafting across the airfield. He had made it home.

A vehicle drove up, and two figures got out. Joseph looked down on two grinning faces. There was

Petr, disheveled and smiling, and beside him was a smiling Von Weiser.

"What took you so long," asked Von Weiser. "We got back about half an hour ago. Have you seen anything of Major Wagner?"

"No, I lost him in the dog fights. They were swarming all over us. There was so much radio chatter, I couldn't raise him. I hope he's okay," Joseph said, concerned for his mentor.

Joseph thought back to the conflict over England. He had last had contact with Wagner just before he had seen him down a Spitfire over the Thames Estuary. He had lost contact then and subsequently really had been fighting for his life, too preoccupied to re-establish any form of contact.

Joseph climbed from his machine as other aircraft returned to the airfield. He walked around his aircraft to inspect the damage and saw holes in his wing. It had been a close call and a miracle the controls remained intact. Together with his companions, he climbed into the lorry and was driven to debriefing. No one had any knowledge of Wagner's fate. The pilots took the offered coffee and food, and after debriefing by Hauptmann

Bruckner, they were shown to unfamiliar barrack rooms, where Joseph collapsed, totally exhausted, fully clothed onto a bed. Despite the worry over the fate of his flight leader, he slept as deeply as he had ever done.

The following morning, still in his flying gear, he woke, bleary eyed, and still tired beyond measure. His first thoughts were of the fate of Major Wagner. What had happened to him? Was he at fault for losing him in the heat of battle? Was he dead, wounded, did he bale out and was he alive but a prisoner of war? All these questions ran through Joseph's head and his guilt made him feel ashamed for not knowing his leader's fate.

Joseph met the two others of his flight for breakfast, but all he wanted was coffee. He could not face food. His worry would not let him eat. The others consoled him, but he was inconsolable.

Wearily, the trio made their way to their now freshly fueled, repaired and rearmed aircraft. On Von Weiser's orders, they flew off heading South West returning to Orly. It was a somber trio who reported in and returned to their barracks. They had lost their leader, their friend, their mentor.

Later that evening, having rested, showered, and put on clean clothes, they headed for the mess. They ordered drinks, standing at the Bar.

Fabien Von Weiser, in solemn and grief- stricken voice, said, "Gentlemen. A toast. To a fine comrade, a fine teacher, and most of all to a loyal friend. Please raise your glasses. To Major Reinhart Wagner."

"I'll drink to that," said a voice from the doorway.

The trio turned as one at the familiar voice. There stood an unkempt, wrinkled, dirty and damp, but smiling Wagner, with a big grin on his face.

The atmosphere in the mess changed immediately. There was much back slapping and congratulations. There were cheers from all those present. Joseph placed a large stein of beer with schnapps chaser into his leader's hands, and when the cheering stopped he said, "What happened to you? I lost you in the battle."

"I went for a swim," grinned Wagner. "I was hit, and my engine flamed and packed up. I headed back towards Belgium, and was lucky. I passed over an E boat as I came down. They must have seen the flames. My machine floated for enough time for me to get out and get into the dingy. It was quite choppy and I was lucky. I got a soaking, but the E boat crew rescued me, and they took me, and several others they rescued to Calais. The buggers stripped me and gave me a blanket. My flying suit got put over the E Boat engine, so it stinks of diesel, but at least it dried off. I found out I'm a terrible sailor. Those boats go up and down, and sideways in any sort of chop. I spent most of my time heaving my heart up. I was never so glad to get back on dry land, except, when we got to port, I slipped off the ladder at the quayside, and got wet again. The buggers took me to the railway station, and I had to catch two trains to be here. I'm still damp, but oh so glad to be on terra firma again, and I am alive."

Von Weiser said, " I'll drink to that," as he raised his glass in a toast to his colleague returned from the dead. "From what I hear. The operation was a disaster. We lost a lot of aircraft and achieved very little. I understand that the target is still intact, and they were right at the briefing. We were heading into a hornet's nest. That part of England must be the most heavily defended anywhere. There were Spitfires and Hurricanes everywhere. I doubt that many of the bombers even found the target, let alone hit it. It was mayhem. God help us if we have to do it again. I hope the High Command think that it was worth the butcher's bill." Von Weiser did not realize how prophetic his words would be.

Chapter Sixteen

The parade stood to attention, as the band played the Deutschlandleid. The Nazi flag prominent at the head of the front rank. The four aviators stood to attention in front of the raised platform, until the last notes of the anthem faded out.

A bristling and proud General Eberhart Von Ritter stood stiffly to attention until the last patriotic notes died, and then he stepped forward, to a microphone at the front of the platform, clearing his throat as he did so.

He paused for effect, looked around him enjoying the respectful silence of anticipation as a thespian would play his audience. His wife, resplendent in a designer dress of the latest Paris fashion, with matching wide brimmed hat, stood slightly behind her husband, a bemused smile on her face, as she surveyed the four officers standing before the platform. She showed not the slightest sign of recognition, her expression innocent and impassive, as she ran her eyes along the row of men before her, pausing longer on Joseph and Petr, conveying a subliminal message of recognition in her glance. Their obvious agitation at her presence spoke loud volumes to her, but was unnoticed by the others present who were wrapped up in the panoply of the occasion.

"You are paraded here today on the orders of our beloved Fuhrer," shouted Von Ritter, preening with duty and patriotism, "To recognize the valour of the four officers you see before you. Under heavy fire, during an enemy raid on our airfield, these officers managed to take off and fight the invaders. Downing two aircraft and seriously damaging others, as they strafed and bombed our airfield. They acted without fear or thought for their own safety, and fought the invaders off. Their actions showed the highest bravery and highest dedication to duty in the face of overwhelming odds, and the Fuhrer has instructed me to promote and award them decorations to mark their heroism. My wife, the Baroness Von Ritter has agreed to present the awards on behalf of our High Command, and with the awards comes the deserved promotions."

He then nodded to his wife who stepped down from the platform, accompanied by an aide carry a cushion on which the awards lay.

"Step forward Major Reinhart Wagner," bellowed Von Ritter.

Wagner did as instructed. One pace forward. The Baroness placed the Knights Cross of the Iron Cross on a ribbon around his neck, whispering, "Congratulations, Major. You are a brave man. Well done." Wagner saluted and smartly stepped back in line.

"Major Von Weiser, step forward", shouted Von Ritter.

Von Weiser did as instructed and he was awarded the same medal with similar comments from the Baroness.

"Von Weiser is also promoted from Hauptmann to Major." Von Weiser saluted and stepped back in line.

"Step forward Leutnant Mozart and Leutnant Muller. Both promoted Oberleuntnant"

Once they stepped forward, the Baroness, with a knowing and lascivious smile, stepped forward and hung the Iron Cross, 2nd Class, around their necks.

"We meet again," she whispered to Joseph, sotto voce, with a slight pout of her lips, and a mischievous smile. "I hope you both enjoyed your time in Berlin." She teased. They both reddened in embarrassment, as she smiled graciously at their obvious discomfiture.

She then demurely stepped back, unaffected by the encounter, and the two embarrassed pilots returned to their places in the line, with inaudible sighs of relief. Hopefully their secret would remain just that, a secret.

General Von Ritter shouted for cheers, "Seig Heil! Seig Heil! Seig Heil" " echoed the parade. The four men basking in the glow of the accolade. He then ordered a march past for the heroes. At the General's cue the band struck up the Horst Wessel, and the General, together with the four heroes of the hour, took the salute as the ranks marched smartly past the rostrum, in time to the music saluting as they did so. At the conclusion of the parade, the heroes of the hour were invited to the Officers Mess for drinks and a formal meal with the General and his lady.

Joseph stood at the bar, champagne in hand, sipping gently as he glanced over his glass at the beauty of the Baroness, who, sipping her own champagne, was devouring him discreetly with her eyes. Joseph didn't know where to look. His embarrassment total.

He turned to Petr. "Phew!" he declared, "I'm glad that's over. I was dreading her coming. She keeps looking at me. What do I do now?" he pleaded.

"Nothing," said Petr. "Act normal. She doesn't seem phased at all. Just go with the flow and enjoy the party."

"That easy for you to say. You didn't have a liaison with the CO's wife. If he knew, it would be me for the chop, not a medal. It would be back to the Russian front.

"Act normally," said Petr. "She doesn't seem bothered, so why should you. Anyway, she taught you a lot in a short time in Berlin, didn't she?" laughing a soft but dirty laugh.

Joseph threw Petr a cautionary look, wishing his friend would be more discreet.

General Von Ritter, followed by his wife, worked his way round the room, stopping and talking to his subordinates. He was a good politician, doing the rounds. He approached the four heroes and, still exuding bonhomie, loudly pronounced they should sit either side of him and his wife at dinner. Ever the politician, it being a good political move to bask in the vicarious glow of those awarded the honours.

Joseph groaned inwardly. Another two hours of making small talk to and in the presence of his former secret lover. The General noticed his discomfiture, and put it down to a natural adolescent shyness, in his book a trait of the young they should grow out of in time. Many young men had found themselves struck dumb in the presence of his beautiful aristocratic wife. Why should these young men be any different to others she had enchanted.

Joseph found himself seated next to the Baroness, and was not looking forward to the next two hours. He would be obliged to indulge in small talk with the Baroness which could be overheard by the General who was seated the other side of her. She however, he discovered, was a consummate actress, the situation did not seem to faze her at all. In fact she seemed to revel in his discomfiture. She simpered, smiled a beatific smile, and asked him innocuous questions about his family, his life and his flying, not put off at all by his hesitant monosyllabic answers. At the same time, she slipped her shoes off under the table and slowly, very, very slowly, rubbed her silk stockinged foot up and down his leg. Joseph stiffened at the touch, but kept his features in a rictus of false attention to her conversation, whilst his whole body reacted to the surreptitious sexual encounter, making him break out into hot sweats beneath his close fitting, high collared dress uniform. He was managing to control his reaction to a degree, until he felt her hand stroking the inside of his left thigh under the table. He glanced across at the General in panic, who fortunately was engaged in conversation with Major Wagner on his other side, so he sat, rigid with fear and frustration, as the arousing sexual contact continued. He didn't know what to do, until he suddenly went into a spasm of coughing, where he was able to double over and feign a morsel of food stuck in his windpipe. Napkin to his mouth, he doubled over, continuing to feign a choking spasm until it drew the attention of the General, at which point she withdrew her foot and hand. He then emerged from his crouch. Red faced, he took a drink to calm himself.

The General, sympathetically asked, "Are you alright, Mozart?"

Pretending to still choke, Joseph stammered, "I am now thank you General. Food went down the wrong way," taking another drink to calm himself. The General chuckled.

He resumed his seat and was grateful the sexual stimulation on his leg and thigh had ceased. He was greatly relieved when the dinner finally ended, and there had been no repetition of the footwork. The ensemble stood as the General and the Baroness stood to leave.

She turned to Joseph, offered her hand to him, which he kissed with as much embarrassed grace as he could muster.

She said, "Well done Oberleutnant. You were very brave," its double meaning clear. She smiled a smile that would melt rocks, and whispered out of the hearing of her husband, "If you get to Berlin again. Look me up."

The General and the Baroness then swept imperiously out of the room.

Joseph let out a long sigh of relief. Petr clapped him on the back. "Does she want to see you again?" he whispered.

"Yes," said Joseph. "But at this moment I would rather fight a whole squadron of Spitfires than go through that again."

Petr laughed. "What happened," he said knowingly.

Joseph told him, and Petr could hardly contain his mirth at his friend's ordeal by the femme fatale.

"Let's get to the bar," he suggested. "A drink will calm your nerves."

The next morning, after breakfast Major Wagner announced they all been granted a weeks leave. Joseph started to make immediate plans to go home to Vienna. He spoke to the others at breakfast and they were all heading to their various homes. Petr would have the longest journey but he managed to get a flight to his local airfield in Hamburg. Joseph was planning to travel by train from Paris to Vienna, when Major Von Weiser sought him out.

"I will be returning home to Schloss Weiser for my leave. I have a friend in the Air transport division on this airfield, and he is going to Neuleiberg Air Base near Munich. He leaves in about an hour. He is willing to take us. If you want to come, we leave in about an hour. I have telephoned my sister, Annaliese. We own a pre-war Fieseler Fi 156 Storch at home, which I have used. She is a qualified pilot and is willing to fly to Munich-Riem airport to meet us, and she will fly us home to my Schloss. From there it is a short journey for you to get home, and we can arrange transport for you. Do you want to come home with me?"

Joseph jumped at the chance and very soon he was sitting in a Junkers JU52 Triplane, with Von Weiser, for the journey to Munich.

"My sister has a pilot's license she learned to fly in the Storch. All we have to do is get from the air base to the civil airfield at Munich and she will fly us home."

Two hours later they landed at the air base, and Von Weiser arranged for a lift to the Munich-Riem airport. The military transport deposited them outside the terminal building, and on entering, Von Weiser looked for his sister.

"There she is, " he declared, waving frantically at a 19 year old ravishingly beautiful, blonde haired young lady, dressed in flying gear which enhanced, rather than detracted from her lithe figure. She was stunning.

"Analiese, " he shouted, and she turned, and her face lit up at the sight of her only brother. She waved, and walked towards the two men, a warm smile spreading across her face. They embraced warmly as brother and sisters do, she then looked at Joseph, curiosity showing on her face.

"Analiese. Let me introduce you to my flying companion. This is Oberleutnant Joseph Mozart from Vienna. He is in my flight, and has saved my life on numerous occasions."

Joseph looked embarrassed at the exaggerated compliment, and said, "It's more the other way round. I wouldn't still be here, but for him."

Analiese smiled, looking directly into Joseph's eyes, and he was instantly captivated. She wore no makeup, she didn't need to. She was the most beautiful woman Joseph had ever seen. He was enmeshed at once. Her flowing blonde hair framed her tanned face, her startling pale blue eyes appraised Joseph. Joseph became aware of her scrutiny but did not quite understand the instant effect Analiese was having upon him. He suddenly felt shy and hesitant in her presence.

Analiese on her part secretly liked what she saw in Joseph, feeling an instant attraction. He was tall, muscular and good looking, with an honest face. Her curiosity was peaked. She secretly took to him immediately. She wanted to find out more about him.

"Any friend of my brother's, is a friend of mine," she said, shaking Joseph's proffered hand. "Come,

I am parked just airside of the terminal building. I have already filed a flight plan. We can take off as soon as you are both aboard."

She led them through a door marked "Flight Crew Only" and after answering cursory questions from an enraptured airport official, led them to the tarmac taxiway, where sat the pre-War Storch on its ungainly undercarriage legs.

Once they were settled inside the aircraft, with permission from the control room, she taxied to the main runway. The Storch leapt into the air after a very short take off run. After piloting an ME Bf109, Joseph found the Storch very slow, and fairly cramped for three people, but the journey would be short. Two hours later they were circling the grass landing strip of Schloss Weiser, with its pastures and wooded areas. The baroque building situated magnificently in its pastoral surroundings. She taxied to a barn like structure, shutting off the engine, as the aircraft slide inside. Joseph saw Von Weiser's glider in the same building, neglected and now covered by a dusty tarpaulin. It had obviously not been used since the outbreak of the war.

They walked out of the barn, to be met by an elderly man, dressed in black.

"Welcome home Baron, " said the man.

"Thank you Bauer," said Von Weiser. "It's good to be home. This is my flying companion and friend Oberleutnant Joseph Mozart. He lives in Vienna. We will take him home. Bauer has been our manservant for as long as I can remember, he explained."

Bauer gave a half bow to Joseph.

"How is Mother?" inquired Von Weiser.

"Engaged with the wounded and sick, as usual Baron." Said Bauer

The arrivals then got into waiting Merecedes-Benz, and Bauer drove them to the Schloss. Joseph sat in the back and was very aware of the presence and beauty of Analiese, who sat beside him.

"Our Mother is always involved in some good works or other. She volunteers to care for the sick, and we have some wounded soldiers in the east wing whom she cares for. She has allowed the Reich to use our home as a rehabilitation centre for the military. We have resident Nurses and Doctors living in our annex, and the ballroom has been set out as a hospital ward. She organizes everyone."

"My Father is a Surgeon, " said Joseph. He was in the first world war, and has been recalled for this war. He was running a hospital in Paris, but has recently been promoted to Surgeon Generalmajor in Belgrade. My Mother works in Vienna General Hospital as Matron, she was a nurse when she met my father. "

Analiese looked appraisingly at Joseph. He felt her scrutiny, and it made him feel uncomfortable. He had been drawn to her as soon as he saw her, and now, sitting beside her in the back of the car, he felt a pang of want. No other woman had had that effect on him. He wanted to know her better.

The car drew up in front of the main entrance to the Schloss. Standing at the top of the steps was an elegant woman, an older version of Analiese, dressed in a black silken dress. It was obviously Von Weiser's mother.

Von Weiser ran up the steps and hugged his Mother for a long moment, suffering her kisses and embrace. Detaching himself from his mother's arms, he turned.

"Let me introduce you," said Von Weiser. "This is my mother the Baroness Sophia Von Weiser. Mother this is a member of my Squadron and good friend, Oberleutnant Joseph Mozart. We gave him a lift. His home is in Vienna."

The Baroness held out her hand to Joseph, who took it and gently gripped her small hand. She had long and slim pianists fingers. She exuded elegance and sophistication. When she spoke, her voice was low and sultry with an air of natural authority.

"Welcome to Schloss Weiser, Oberleutnant." She said. "You must stay for dinner. I insist. I would hear all about you, and what you have been doing with my son. He tells me nothing. Do come in."

They settled in the library. A cosy room, with a fire burning brightly in the imposing marble fireplace, three walls covered in book filled shelves. Baroness Von Weiser, declining the services of her man Bauer, offered and served drinks to her family and guest. She was an extremely effusive and attentive hostess, and spent the next hour or so gently teasing details of Joseph's life, current circumstances, and future ambitions. She was a people person, an effusive hostess of that there was no doubt, and within a very short time she had extracted Joseph's life story from him, and his family antecedents. The dinner that followed was a very convivial affair, and Joseph was made to feel very much at home. That he had the approval of the Baroness became very apparent. Fabien Von Weiser was much amused by his mother's gentle interrogation of Joseph. He had seen this behavior from her before. Was it normal matriarchal behavior? He did not know for sure, but it seemed that every guest of marriageable age was subjected to the same form of questioning. Had she guessed that Joseph was struck by the beauty and desirability of Analiese, and was this her way of vetting suitable young men?

At the end of the meal Fabien Von Weiser said, "Well, I expect you want to get home to see your Mother, Joseph. I will drive you."

"I'll come," said Analiese. Her mother noticed her eagerness, and smiled a knowing smile of approval, knowing with certainty that her daughter was interested.

It was getting late as the Mecedes-Benz, with Fabien behind the wheel, drew up in the driveway outside the Mozart house, which was in darkness. Joseph hoped that it was the blackout curtains, and not that his mother had gone to bed already. He knocked on the door to warn his mother, before opening the door with his key. The light from the hallway silhouetted him, and his mother, her recognition instant, rushed forward and clung to her son, sobbing with joy at the reunion, even though she had been pre-warned of his arrival.

Joseph waved to his friends to come inside and meet his Mother. As Fabien and Analiese walked up the steps to the door, his mother looked at Joseph, with slightly raised but very questioning eyebrows.

"Mother. I would like you to meet my Staffel Leader and very good friend Baron Fabien Von Weiser, and his sister Analiese. We managed to get a lift to Munich from the Luftwaffe, and Analiese brought her aircraft to Munich to meet us. So, you see, I am home a day earlier than I thought I would be, thanks to their kindness." His Mother formally shook hands.

"Baron," she said, "Thank you for looking after my son, and for bringing him home to me."

"Call me Fabien, Frau Mozart," offered Fabien. "May I introduce my sister Analiese, she came along for the ride."

Joseph's mother shook their hands warmly. "Come in, come in." She said, to Fabien, whilst appraising Analiese in the only way a mother can appraise a candidate for her son's affections. "I want to hear all about you and your adventures. I am sorry my husband is not here to greet you. He is in Belgrade running a hospital and various aide posts near the front line of the fighting there."

They sat in the comfortable Mozart sitting room. Joseph poured cognac and they sat chatting in front of a glowing fire. The conversation was almost a duplicate of the one Joseph had had early at Schloss Weiser. It appeared that matriarch's in general were gentle but subtle inquisitors of new friends when it came to the welfare and future of their offspring. The scene in the Mozart house was almost a repeat of Joseph's earlier inquisition except it was centred on the Von Weiser's. Joseph thought his mother would get on very well with the Baroness Von Weiser, they were of a similar ilk.

After an hour, Fabien said, "well, we had better be going home, it's getting late, and we all have had a long journey. There is always tomorrow."

He stood, shook hands with Joseph and said, "I will be in touch." He turned to Frau Mozart, "It has been a pleasure to meet you." He then dipped into a short bow and brushed his lips to her proffered hand. "Thank you for your hospitality."

Joseph saw them to the door, shook Analiese's hand, holding it longer than a normal handshake, whilst looking deeply into her eyes. She smiled, her face taking on a warm glow, matching Joseph's expression.

"You are most welcome. We will be in touch. Perhaps we will meet again whilst you are on leave?" Her allure leaving him hungry for more time in her presence.

He stammered, his face reddening. "Thanks. That would be nice. Thank you again for the lift."

When they had gone, Joseph's mother sat down with her son, quizzing him on his adventures, and especially his contact with the Von Weiser's. She was wise enough to realize that her son was smitten. He might not know it yet, but his mother sensed it.

Chapter Seventeen

Joseph woke late, in his own bed and stretched, wallowing in the luxury of a comfortable mattress and a warm and cozy down duvet. He lay there lazily contemplating rising, when he heard movement outside his room, and a discreet knock on the door, before it opened to reveal his mother, holding a breakfast tray, with eggs, cheeses and toast, and the all pervading and delicious smell of freshly ground coffee.

"Good morning darling," said his mother brightly, "I though you would never wake up. It's gone 10am, and the sun is shining, and I have to go to work at the hospital soon. What will you do with yourself today while I'm gone?"

She placed the tray beside him on his bed, the aromas firing up his taste buds. He then realized he was hungry.

He sat up, crunching on a piece of toast, thinking of what he wanted to do whilst on leave.

"I think I will go round to the Baumgarten's and see if Walter's about. I don't think he will be, but I should make contact with them. Walter is my oldest friend after all."

"I will try to make arrangements with the hospital to take some time off this week to be with you, " said his mother. "It would be nice to see more of you for the short time you are here."

After a leisurely breakfast, a long bath, and a change into little used civilian clothes, Joseph left the house and walked the short distance to Walter's house.

His mother was in, and she greeted Joseph like a long lost son, insisted on making him fresh coffee and wanting to hear all his news. She then told him of what she knew about Walter, who was with his squadron and on active duty with them. She had no latest information about his movements but updated him from Walter's letters home. She promised to write to her son saying she had seen Joseph, and also promised that should he contact her during Joseph's leave, she would pass on contact details.

During their conversations she warned her son's, and Walter's nemesis, Ernst Bruen, the old school bully, was now an Hauptmann in the Schutzstaffel (S.S), having transferred from the S.A. He now had even more authority and his reputation had not improved. He was still a bully, but now he could wield his authority with the backing of the state.

He was still based in Vienna, and his reputation as a Nazi Party Zealot, and localized bully, caused people to shun him. He was reputed to revel in his cruel reputation, and seemed to enjoy causing misery and fear among the local population. His treatment of the Jewish population of Vienna, was nothing short of vicious and appalling. He was now one of the most hated and feared men in Vienna, pursuing what he saw as his patriotic duty to the Fatherland and the Nazi cause. He and his squad of SS thugs pursued, what they considered as their duty, with vigour and enthusiasm. His father supported his son in every way, and as a consequence, most of the people who knew the family, shunned them. They had become local pariah's.

"If you see him, walk away. He's a nasty piece of work," was her advice.

Joseph wished Frau Baumgarten well, and left her house heading for his old school. He wanted to catch up with his old headmaster, whom he liked and who had mentored Joseph during his school years.

Doctor Frederick von Schmidt greeted Joseph warmly. He was now looking much older than Joseph remembered. They chatted over old times, and of Joseph's time in London on the educational exchange scheme. Of course, due to the war, Dr Schmidt had lost contact with his long time friend at the Westminster School, William Camden, whom Joseph remembered fondly. The war had seen to that.

Joseph was invited to walk round the school, which was still an active institution despite the conflict, the tour bringing back warm memories. It was noticeable that there were no seventeen or eighteen year old students present. They were, apparently, all in the armed forces. The school Hitler Youth organization was fully attended and thriving, much to the headmaster's obvious displeasure as it continued to feed recruits to the Wehrmacht.

Leaving the school, he walked towards his home, when on the other side of the street, he saw a squad of black uniformed storm troopers. They were beating a man in front of a shop, calling him names, shouting and kicking him. Joseph recognized their leader, it was Bruen, his nemesis. He appeared to be enjoying meting out punishment on the street, whilst passers-by hurried away in fear, joining in the violence, until apparently sated, he stood back and glared around him, defying interference.

Joseph stopped, stunned by what he had seen. He was spotted by Bruen, who with a wicked grin of recognition, walked arrogantly over to a stupefied Joseph.

"Ah. Joseph bloody Mozart, " he leered. We meet again. "Shirking are you, when you should be fighting for the Fatherland. Been thrown out of the Luftwaffe, have you? Conscientious objector?" he sneered. "Well, if you are, we have ways of dealing with you."

"I'll have you know, " said Joseph with some authority in his voice, " I am a Oberleutnant in the Luftwaffe, on leave from active service. I have been on the Russian front, and on raids over England, and I am now on a few days leave from my Squadron, based in France, before returning to active duty."

"We'll see about that," sneered Bruen. "I will check, and if you are lying we will meet again soon. So watch your step," he threatened, pointing a swagger stick in Joseph's face.

He strode off with a swagger, the rest of his squad of bully boys, dragging the now comatose man they had been beating, with them. Where they were heading, Joseph did not know, but what he did know was the poor man they held in custody had a bleak future.

The encounter with Bruen left a very bad taste in Joseph's mouth, as he thoughtfully wandered homeward. His day, and return home, completely spoiled.

His gloomy mood, however, did not last long, because as he neared his home he saw the Von Weiser Mercedes-Benz in the drive outside his house, and getting out of the vehicle were Fabien and Analiese von Weiser.

As he approached, Von Weiser spotted him. "Ah, Joseph. I'm glad we caught you. My mother has decided to hold a party to celebrate my homecoming. She wanted me to invite you, and your mother."

Joseph smiled, and looked at Analiese. "You will come won't you, please?" She urged.

"Come inside, " he invited, we will have coffee and cake if I can find some."

They entered the house and he took them to the sitting room. A cozy room, with deep armchairs and settees, and chintz curtains at the window. He then went to the kitchen and made coffee, finding cake in the pantry, all of which he brought into the sitting room on a tray.

"We have no servant now. He went to war and we have not replaced him. With father and me away, and mother working at the hospital, it's busy times, so there is not really a need for a servant. So we make do without. We do have a cook, but she only works in the mornings, and when she is needed, such as if we have a dinner party. It's not like before the war started. We had staff all the time," he explained, as he poured coffee. "When will the party take place?" he asked.

"Well Mother is planning it on Saturday. Two days time. Please come," said Analiese with a pleading smile which made her irresistible.

How could Joseph reject her invitation? She was beautiful, intelligent and in his eyes his perfect woman. He wanted to know her better. There was no doubt he was smitten. Of course he would go, but he needed to speak to his mother to see if she would be available.

"It's very good of your mother to invite us, I will certainly be there. I will ask Mother when she gets home and let you know. I'm sure she would be delighted if she is not working. Anyway," he said, "What are you doing here. You could have telephoned the invitation."

Analiese said, "I wanted to go shopping. Fabien agreed to accompany me, If you are doing nothing you could come with us."

Joseph agreed at once. They drove into the centre of town, parking near the Rathaus. The two men trailed along with Analiese, as she went into several dress shops, and perfumeries. After two hours of relentless shopping, the two men, carrying numerous bags, took her to the Café Centrale, a huge 19th century gothic building, with high and impressively beamed ceilings, one of Vienna's most select coffee houses. They sat, enjoying the rest, the ambiance, and the coffee with their famous pastries.

It was at the coffee house that Joseph discovered that Analiese had attended Vienna's Fine Arts Academy. She was there at the time of the Anschluss, when some of the students were expelled by the Nazi regime. She was lucky, being the daughter of a Baron who had fought in the first world war, she was allowed to remain and finish her course. She qualified with a Batchelor degree in Fine Art. She told Joseph, she had wanted to work for a museum or gallery, but the war had intervened. He learned she was a qualified pilot, having been first a glider pilot, tutored by her brother, then qualified on normal aircraft, at which point both she and her brother had persuaded their father to purchase a light aircraft. They purchased the Storch, and she had been flying it since. With her fine art ambitions on hold because of the war, she was currently seeking employment. She wanted to fly, but realized flying was not considered proper for a woman at this time, so she would have to overcome ingrained prejudices to achieve her ambition. She lived in hope. Albeit a forlorn one.

The Von Weiser's drove Joseph home, and his mother, who had finished her work for the day greeted them at the door. Joseph told her of the invitation, and she accepted at once.

As the Von Weiser's left, Joseph felt a pang of longing. As they waved goodbye his mother gave him a knowing look. That was the look your father gave me whenever we parted, she thought. My son is in love. He might not know it yet, but he certainly is. She seems a nice girl, she thought. I am longing to meet her Mother.

Joseph spent the two days between the Von Weiser's visit, and the day of the party, luxuriating in the comfort of his home. His mother continued with her work, and in the evenings Joseph insisted in taking his mother out to dinner. She urged him to wear his uniform. Most of the male population were in some branch of the services at this time, and it had become the norm to wear uniform. In any event, Joseph had the idea that his mother wanted to show her son off in the best light, in uniform, wearing his Iron Cross. They went to their favourite restaurant Weiner Rathauskeller, and enjoyed the ambiance and even though it was war time, the food was good. The Mozart's saw several family friends and acquaintances during their excursions, and he felt his mother had deliberately put him on display, proudly showing him off in public, a role he found uncomfortable, but one which he endured for the sake of his overly protective and proud mother.

The day of the Von Weiser's party arrived. Joseph, driving his Father's 1938 Lagonda V12 sleek black saloon, arrived promptly at Schloss Weiser, at 12midday. He wore his uniform with medal array. His mother, dressed in black silk, with pearls, hair coiffeured to perfection. On entry to the Schloss they were greeted warmly, as close friends, by Major Fabien Von Weiser, his sister Analiese, and the Baroness. They could hear music in the background as they entered.

"Welcome to our home, " said the Baroness. This is just a small party to celebrate the homecoming of my son Fabien. As you know the Schloss is also being used as a rehabilitation centre for the wounded. So I have invited some of the medical and estate staff to celebrate with us. You will probably know some of the medical people with your background. The music you hear is a local string quartet, and in honour of your visit I have asked them to play some Mozart, a rare treat in these hard times."

Joseph looked around, his mother waved and greeted some of the medical staff, knowing them through her profession. They were approached by a distinguished looking gentleman, dressed in a black jacket, striped trousers, with a high winged collar sporting a spotted bow tie, and wearing a monocle, who was smiling and holding out his hand toward Frau Mozart.

"Emma my dear. How good to see you again. How is Max. I heard he was in Paris."

"Joachim. It's good to see you again. Max has been transferred to Belgrade. He is running a large military hospital there and a few emergency medical facilities near the front line. He is now a Generalmajor but still carrying out some of the more complicated operations. You know Max. He will never stop practicing his skills."

The Baroness intervened in their conversation, "You know Professor Kaufmann?" She asked.

"Of course. He is an old family friend. He and my husband often worked together before the war. He is an eminent Orthopaedic Surgeon and a long time friend, said Emma Mozart,"What are you doing here?" she asked of Professor Kaufmann.

"I came to assist in the rehabilitation of the wounded. Sophia, here," indicating Baroness Von Weiser," asked me some time ago when she set up the medical centre here. I visit and help out when I can. She is thought of an as angel by the patients. Giving her time, money and putting her effort into their welfare. This will embarrass her, but she has become a latter day Florence Nightingale," he said with a smile at the Baroness.

"Oh, you old flatterer," admonished the Baroness, turning to Emma Mozart. "Don't take any notice of

Joachim. I only do what anyone in my position would do for our poor wounded. Since my husband died and Fabien became the Baron, Analiese and I have little to do. The estate runs itself, although because of the war we are short of labour. It's not easy to run a 10,000 acre estate and its farms, but we need the crops. That is all managed, so what else would I do to keep busy. There was a need and we filled it. Joachim gives us his time, as do the others on the staff, and the wounded are grateful for the attention. At least they have clean clothes and beds, and the staff are very caring."

The afternoon proceeded well and the partygoers ate, and drank well. A hubbub of voices could be heard over the string quartet playing in the background, and everyone was having a good time, a break from the constant threat that war provoked.

Analiese approached Joseph. "Are you having a good time?" she asked.

Joseph looked at her and said, "Yes. It's very pleasant. It's good of you and your family to invite us. It's also good to see my Mother having a good time. She seems to be forging a friendship with your Mother. She is charming and a wonderful hostess."

"It's what mother is good at. She seems to like your Mother very much. They have much in common. It would be good if they became friends."

"I think that is self evident, " said Joseph. " Look at them. Chatting away like long lost friends."

Analiese said, "Come with me. I will show you round the house and the estate if you would like."

"Lead on." Said Joseph. "I am yours to command," and found that secretly he was in her thrall.

They toured the Schloss, with its antique furniture and paintings, and went outside to the pasture which doubled as a landing strip. In the barn Analiese showed him her brother's glider, which Joseph remembered seeing from the air when Von Weiser was teaching him to become a glider pilot, and she proudly showed him over their Storch three seater monoplane. She was proud her family owned the machine, she was even prouder that she held a pilots license, and was able to fly. Joseph also learned of her interest in fine art, and that she wanted, when the war was over, to find work in the art world. Perhaps a museum or gallery. But that was for the future, in peacetime.

Joseph found, during his tour he was able to talk easily with Analiese. They talked of the way the German Nation had risen again with the National Socialist movement bringing Hitler to power, and how it had affected them as patriotic Austrians. They talked of how the Anschluss had effected their lives. He found his views, accorded with hers, but both realized it would be dangerous for these thoughts to be publicly expressed.

On the tour he studied her. She was beautiful, and totally unaware, he thought, of the effect she was having on him. Analiese on her part was aware of a frisson of feeling between her and Joseph. It was if she had known Joseph all her life. It became obvious they shared many common interests, and their relationship, if allowed to blossom, had the potential to develop into something more. He hoped and prayed it would. She, on her part, had an instinct their relationship would certainly develop into something more, but there was a war on and there was no time for them at present. Joseph was committed to fight for the Reich, even though she suspected he was not, nor would ever be a committed Nazi. She was glad, and said so, that Joseph and her brother were serving together. They could look after each other, and perhaps live through the conflict. It was her ardent hope both would survive, and return home to peace.

They slowly walked back to the Schloss, to find the party was near its end. Joseph found his mother still in conversation with the Baroness and Professor Kaufmann, whilst Fabien was still circulating, playing the convivial host.

As they entered the room Fabien saw Joseph with his sister.

"There you both are," he said, with a questioning expression and smile on his face. "What have you two been up to?"

Joseph's face reddened. "Nothing really. Analiese was showing me the Schloss, and then your glider and the Storch. I remember seeing your glider from the air when you were teaching me, but it was interesting seeing it on the ground. I've never flown that type before."

"Well, when you come back, and I hope you will come back," he said looking at his sister for her approval. "Perhaps we can fly her. I suspect it will have to be in peacetime though. I can't see us sharing the air with warplanes. They might think we are raiding, if they see us up on their radar, " and he laughed.

"I see what you mean," said Joseph. "We might get shot down," and he joined his colleague in laughter.

On the way home Joseph asked his mother how she had enjoyed herself.

"Very much so." She said, "They made us very welcome, and I felt at home. It was as if I had known Sophia, for that is what she insisted on me calling her, for ages. I would say she will become one of my friends. When you and Fabien go back to war, we have arranged to meet every now and then for coffee and a chat. I liked her and her family very much. You have a good friend there in Fabien." She looked askance at her son and said, "What do you think of Analiese?"

Joseph coloured a little, looking wistful, and said, "She is beautiful. I really liked her."

"Well?" said his mother knowingly.

"Well Mother," he said determinedly. "There's a war on. I have to go back to my Staffel. I must keep my mind on my job. If it were peacetime, then anything could happen, but I have to keep my mind clear. So stop looking at me like that. I know what you are thinking. You can't use your womanly wiles on me."

The last day of his leave he spent at home, getting ready for his trip back to the war, staying with his mother. The following day he drove his father's car to Schloss Weiser, his mother accompanying him. They were again greeted like long lost friends. His mother was invited by Baroness Von Weiser to stay for lunch, whilst the two men said their goodbyes to their parents. Analiese prepared the Storch for the trip to Munich, took them aboard and took off. She circled the Schloss, seeing her Mother and Frau Mozart standing on the front steps, she waggled her wings in farewell, saw their mothers waving, and they then headed away to Munich.

They took a taxi from Munich airport to the main station. There was no onward flight to take them on this occasion and Analiese accompanied them.

They boarded the train for Paris, placing their luggage in a first class compartment. Their uniforms giving them a passport to VIP treatment by the station staff, and servility from the staff on the train. Steam hissed from the train, and the whistle sounded, as the group stood on the platform by the open door.

"Goodbye sister." Said Fabien. "Look after yourself and if you get the job jnvolving aircraft please be very careful."

She hugged her brother, and he kissed her cheeks in the continental fashion. Unexpectedly, she turned to Joseph, who held out his hand to shake hers, and ignoring his outstretched hand, she hugged him and kissed him. Amazed at her own temerity, she coloured in sudden embarrassment. Fabien laughed. Joseph gasped, as she stepped back into the rising steam from the engine.

The cry went out, "All aboard," and with the waving a flag and a whistle from the conductor, the train started suddenly forward, wheels spinning, until they gripped the rails. The two men jumped through the open door, slamming it as they boarded. They both looked out of the open window.

Analiese stood forlornly on the platform, wreathed in steam, her hand to her face, weeping quietly, and waving. As they lost sight of her Fabien looked at Joseph, a broad smile on his face and a quizzing eyebrow raised.

"Well?" he declared, looking directly at Joseph.

"Joseph stammered, "She took me by surprise." Colouring at the unasked question.

"I see, " mused Fabien. "Mmmm" he mumbled, knowingly.

"We better get into our carriage before someone sits in our place." said Joseph, glad of the distraction from the implied questions he could see forming on his friend's lips.

They sat in silence for the first part of their long and tedious journey, both had much to contemplate. They changed trains at Nuremberg and Strasbourg, and 10 hours later pulled into the Gare de Nord in Paris. It was now evening. They then boarded a local train to Orly, and took a taxi from the station to their airbase, arriving, tired and hungry at 8p.m. They were in time to report in, dump their luggage in their rooms and take an evening meal in the officer's mess, where he reunited with Petr Muller. It had been a long day. Joseph had much to contemplate, but Petr wanted to know what had happened to Joseph on his leave, and he wanted to tell him of his own leave, so they talked until the early hours. Petr could see his friend had returned smitten, and was amused that the cause of it was the sister of Joseph's flight commander. His own experiences on leave were not nearly so interesting.

Chapter Eighteen

The whole Geschwader (Wing) which included Joseph's Staffel (Squadron) was assembled in the briefing room, together with pilots and navigators of various bomber staffels. The room was crowded, and the noise from the excited crowd was a rising cacophony, until the door banged open, and a Stabsfeldwebel shouted. "Attention!"

The room froze, the sound ceasing, as General Eberhart von Ritter, accompanied by his entourage, marched into the room. Everyone stood to attention. The General marched to the platform at the end of the room, his boots sounding heavily on the wooden floor in the anticipatory nervous silence. He stamped his way up the steps, and then stood, looking at his audience, building up the tension, until he suddenly bellowed, "Sit."

Once the scraping of chairs and movement noise had abated, he looked over his audience, building the anticipation like an actor on the stage. He was a good orator and knew how to play an audience.

"You are gathered here because we now have the full results of the raid on Foulness Experimental Establishment and the oil refinery we carried out two weeks ago. The results we hoped for have not been achieved. Reconnaissance has shown us the intended target is still intact and the place is still able to function. Reichsmarschall Goering has ordered we carry out another raid, and this time the target must be destroyed. He was unhappy with our previous result. The new raid will be known as Operation Donnor (Thunder). I will now hand you over to Hauptmann Brucker for briefing." He then sat down at the back of the platform to listen to the briefing.

The photographs of the raid on Foulness and the Oil Refineries in the Thames Estuary were on display, on a board at the side of the stage and officers of the Luftwaffe Intelligence Branch were there to discuss the raid and its outcome.

Hauptmann Brucker held the floor, showing the photographs on a screen behind him. He pointed out the damage done to the target, which was slight, considering the number of aircraft involved, the mission being only semi-successful.

Slides shown from a projector revealed any damage done had been quickly repaired and reconnaissance photographs, projected on screen showed the site to still be fully operational.

"This facility is still a priority target. We know it is heavily defended, and that the RAF have bases close by to allow them to defend their territory with numbers, but the Reichsmarschall has instructed us to devise a plan to return to the target and destroy the facility. Therefore we have to go again."

There was a collective groan throughout the room. The flight crews who had been on the first raid knew exactly what they would be facing again, and knew their losses would perhaps be even greater.

"We have doubled the number of aircraft involved on this occasion, and instead of raiding the oil refinery at the same time, we will carry out a diversionary raid on the port of Harwich. Part of the Harwich group will precede the main attack force and deal with the coastal radar system the British call Chain Holm. The British will know you are coming and be able to track you, until Chain Holm is dealt with. Eliminating their radar is priority, and will allow the main attacks to succeed."

He paused again for effect, then continued, "Aircraft have been drawn from two Geschwader's giving us combinations of Donier Do17, Heinkel He111, Junkers Ju 88, and Junkers Ju 87's. These will be accompanied by fighter Geschwader's giving cover by Me Bf109's, and Fw 190's whose duty it will be to protect the bombers. Again there will be a chain of E boats covering the escape route back to the Belgian coast. This time the attack must be pressed home to total destruction of the target."

He explained the details of the operation, which allowed for the fighters to use Oostende-Middelkirke airfield in Belgium to refuel. Which would ensure that all the fighters had full tanks in order to provide the required top cover for the bombers and provide more time over the target area. He re-emphasized there was an artillery barracks near the target area, gun forts in that part of the Thames estuary, and the target area was heavily defended by its own anti-aircraft guns. Added to which, the east of England had a large number of airbases within easy flying time of the target, so heavy resistance was expected. It was expected since the first raid, defenses in the area would have been reinforced. Never the less, the Fuhrer insisted the target be eliminated. He reiterated it was most important to prevent the allies gaining superiority in the race to develop a jet engined aircraft.

This remark created a mutter of incredulity from the assembled air crews, silenced by a shout from the Stabsfeldwebel.

As Brucker finished his briefing the meteorologist gave his assessment of expected weather conditions, and the communications officer gave call signs and radio frequencies. He reminded them that the operation was named Operation Donnor. Success over the target would be reported as "Blitzen" (lightning)

The bomb group targeting Foulness would be call sign, "Gladiator." The fighter group accompanying them was nominated as ""Centurian".

The bomb group targeting Harwich Port would be designated "Poseidon" and their accompanying fighter screen was designated "Trident".

As the briefing for pilots came to an end, General Von Ritter stood, and called for silence once again.

"As you now must realize this is one of the most important targets of the war so far. If the allies develop a jet aircraft before the Reich, then the consequences would be catastrophic for Germany. Our intelligence is creditable. No one will be allowed to leave base tonight, and no one will have access to a telephone, except through me. Take off will be one hour before dawn. Good luck to you all, give the Reich the result the Fuhrer wants. Heil Hitler!" He then produced a Nazi salute, and walked from the platform through a hushed crowd to the door.

As the door closed behind him, the room erupted. Everyone talking at the same time. The aircrew's could not believe they were being ordered to return to the same target in such a short space of time. It was sure to be more heavily defended a second time.

Major Wager stood, shouting for silence. When the room was hushed again he said, "Fighter pilots will man their machines in two hours from now. We take off for Oostende-Middelkirke, where we will spend the night. Ground crews are there ahead of you to top up your machines, and ensure they are in top mechanical order. We take off from Oostende an hour before dawn, rendezvousing with the bomber force over the Belgian coast at 5000 metres. At this height you will be on oxygen. Targets will be given to the navigators, who will remain for a separate briefing on targets, locations, compass bearing and call signs. Good luck to you all. I will see you at dispersal in two hours." He then left the room, followed by all the fighter pilots. The bomber pilots remained with their navigators to take notes and ensure target identification.

Two hours later Joseph sat in his ME Bf109 on the taxiway at Orly, behind his leader, Major Wagner. Behind him was Major Von Weiser, and his wingman Petr Muller. Their engines warm, they were given the green light for take off.

An hour later they were circling the Oostende-Middelkirke airfield, awaiting instructions to land. Once given they followed their leaders, swooping down and landing in line astern. Joseph followed his leader to dispersal, where ground crew, boosted by reinforcements from Orly, descended on each machine, and began pre-flight checks. The pilots themselves headed for the mess to a hot meal, after which they were shown to dormitory accommodation for rest before the operation. He was sharing with Petr again.

Joseph slept fitfully, running thoughts of Analiese through his mind, experiencing a strange yearning to be in her presence again. He pictured her beautiful face, and passed his hand over his lips remembering the unexpected kiss on Munich station. He savoured the thoughts, and drifted off in a contented but apprehensive sleep.

At 4am his dreams were rudely interrupted by an orderly shaking him awake, proffering him a steaming cup of coffee. He rose and washed and shaved, whilst gently sipping from the piping hot cup. Petr was his usual sluggardly self, rubbing his eyes, yawning, and scratching his stubbly cheeks. Goaded by Joseph, Petr gradually came awake, and once they had both used the ablutions, they were ready for a meal and takeoff.

Meal over, they had a final briefing from their respective flight commanders, and one hour before dawn saw them gathered in Staffel order at 5000 metres above the Belgian coast, circling to rendezvous with the bomber force. Within the Orly Staffel, their finger four formation, comprised of Major Wagner, with wingman Joseph Mozart as Red One and two, and Major Von Weiser, with wingman Petr Muller, as Blue One and Two.

The formation of fighters circled 1000 metres above the assembled bombers, and at the instruction of the Bomber Flight Commander they set of on a course for the east of England. The plan was, when 20 kilometres from the English shore, one third of the bomber force, with a third of the fighters covering, would target Harwich Docks and port, with a splinter group ahead of the main group, dealing with the known Chain Holm radar installations on the east coast of England. The other two thirds would head for their real target of Foulness Experimental Establishment. Joseph's flight would be coverage for the latter prong of the attack force.

All went well for a period of time, correct navigational changes were made until the split point. As the bomber force targeting Harwich Port and Chain Holm, split from the main force, came the first contact with British defenses. Two ships below the split point opened up with anti-aircraft fire and one of the bomber force was struck. Flames came from one of its engines, and emitting black smoke it turned back towards the Belgian coast.

A short time later, a squadron of Spitfires appeared in the dawn light and began attacking the bombers which had turned towards Foulness. Joseph saw in the distance a fire fight taking place on the formation of bombers heading toward Harwich. His impression was only momentary, as suddenly the sky was filled with approaching British Hurricanes, which were diving on the attack force.

The Oberstleutnant leading the flight, of which Joseph was a part, ordered the fighters to defend the bombers. Major Wagner's voice came over the radio.

"We attack. Follow me," as he dived towards the oncoming Hurricane Force.

The next few moments for Joseph became a maelstrom of tracer bullets, of G force turns, weaving, climbing and firing as targets presented themselves. The sky was lit up with tracer, and flak explosions from coastal guns. Several aircraft were hit. Two bombers fell out of formation, smoking and diving toward the sea. One Hurricane, hit and in flames followed.

Joseph clung to his flight leader as closely as he was able, following his gut wrenching twist and turns, as he lined up targets trying to get at the bomber formation below. In the chaos he had no idea if any of his bullets had hit home. The air battle was one of fast and furious action and reaction, twists and turns, G forces to grey out and even momentarily blackout. Joseph glimpsed a Hurricane cross his path allowing him a two second burst of machine gun fire, and saw his bullets shred its tailplane. He did not follow its escape path as it dived away from the conflict, but stuck to his task as wingman to Red One and protector of the bomber force.

Just as suddenly as they appeared, the sky cleared of British fighters. The bomber force, depleted by two, maintained formation and ploughed on toward their target, which was now only 5 kilometres away.

The fighter force regrouped 1000 metres above the bombers, positioned to counter another attack, which was not long in coming. More Spitfires and Hurricane formations honed in on the attacking bombers, diving in from an even greater height than Joseph's formation. They were intent on the bombers and again Major Wagner ordered the attack. Guns on platforms in the estuary opened up, making the sky ahead black with exploding shells, and an inferno of fire. Joseph heard and sometimes felt the woosh of high velocity shells from the forts as near misses screamed past his aircraft, causing it to wobble frantically in the heavily disturbed air. The compression of the detonations pressing his aircraft down and sideways causing him to fight the controls for a few seconds.

Again Joseph pushed his control column forward, his machine screaming as the engine revolutions pushed through the red. Led by Red One, and again sticking as closely to his leader as possible, the finger four formation of Red and Blue flights, dived through the middle of the attacking Hurricanes. Tracer again marked their swift progress, and Joseph was only able to fire a one second burst as they split the enemy formation. Tracer bullets passed Joseph's right wing, but some of the bullets from an attacking Hurricane, punctured holes in his wing. He violently swung to his left as Petr screamed, "Red Two, break left.", and the attacking Hurricane zoomed past Joseph, close enough for him to see the pilot fighting his controls. Joseph managed a two second burst which stitched across the airframe of the Hurricane just behind the cockpit. He must have hit an aileron or control cable, because the Hurricane started to spin towards the sea. He saw it splash in the water close to a sandy beach.

Recovering, Joseph looked for his leader. "Right behind you," came the reassuring voice of Wagner, as his aircraft drew alongside and accelerated past Joseph to take the lead again.

They were now over the island of Foulness and they could see the now depleted bomber formation dropping their bomb loads. Many fell short of the target, others overshot. Very few actually got near. The pilots had no opportunity to steady their bomb runs as they were too busy avoiding waves of attacking aircraft and high volume anti-aircraft fire. Joseph's Staffel was doing its best, but wave after wave of British fighters were joining the fray. Condensation trails marked the sky. Dirty clouds of explosives marked the ground and the sea shore around the island. Newly arrived Spitfires and Hurricanes joined the battle. Shore batteries added to the cacophony, the air alive with whizzing shrapnel and explosions . Joseph felt impacts on his canopy, some starring the Perspex and clouding his all round vision.

More tracer followed Joseph as he moved in to attack a lone Spitfire which was attacking a Junkers JU 88 bomber. The bomber was on fire, and Joseph saw its crew jump from the stricken aircraft. It crashed into the sea just short of the island. Cones of fire were now coming from gun emplacements circling the target area, and there were explosions all around his aircraft and the rattle of more shrapnel hitting his machine, where he had no idea.

Tracer shot past Joseph, and he weaved right and dived towards the sea. The tracer came nearer and he felt multiple hits on his fuselage, then he felt a numbing pain in his left leg just above the knee.

Blood seeped into his flying boots. He saw a Spitfire in his rear view mirror, as he weaved away, a wave of pain coursed through his body. He pushed his hand over the wound in his thigh to stem the blood flow, and as he did so, bullets from the Spitfire smashed into his engine, which immediately emitted black smoke. His aircraft was doomed. He was too low to bail out.

Joseph, sweat running into his eyes, and pain coursing through him from the wound in his leg, looked for a place to land his stricken aircraft. In front of him was a line of a defense boom, close to a sandy beach and beyond was water, which appeared flat and calm. His engine stopped, he was now a high speed glider. He dived slightly to gain speed. He had to clear the fast approaching anti-ship defense boom which was sticking 10 metres out of the water. It was now right in front of him and with a huge effort he pulled the stick back to clear the boom by feet. He now had to land on water. Ignoring the undercarriage controls, he swept over the boom, and flattened out to ease his aircraft onto the water.

His aircraft, skimmed the water, like a stone skimming a pond, then hit with force. The water was only one foot deep, the outgoing tide would expose the extensive mudflats beneath shortly. His aircraft was tearing itself apart in the shallow water as it bottomed on the mud. Debris, water, mud, and oil splashed up and over his machine from the impetuous of his aircraft as it ploughed through the shallows, forming a bow wave as it slewed to a jarring stop, 100 metres from shore the muck and debris splashing over his cockpit, blanking out any forward vision. The pain from his leg increased at the impact, the shin of his wounded leg smashing into the control column, and he found he could not move. He felt a wave of nausea and fainted. Luckily there was no fire, the water had doused any flames coming from the engine.

Joseph came to, feeling sick. He looked around. All the aircraft had gone. There was smoke in front of him at various locations on shore where bombs had fallen and other aircraft had crashed. The ack ack guns had ceased firing. A lone Spitfire was circling overhead and when the pilot saw him move in the cockpit, he waggled his wings and flew off over the nearby beach disappearing inland. He struggled out of his harness, gasping as waves of pain engulfed his body, but could not get enough purchase to climb out of the cockpit. He was weakening through loss of blood, but through his misted goggles he saw a strange machine driving toward him. It looked like an open lorry, but was shaped like a boat. He could see armed army personnel on board. It was creaming through the shallow water towards him. He had never seen such a strange vehicle. It drew alongside his machine, and soldiers armed with rifles jumped out into the shallows, appearing to walk on the water. They pointed their guns at Joseph and indicated he should open his canopy. He unclipped it and with a heave it opened to the elements. Fresh cold air washed over his face and he took several deep breaths, controlling his nausea.

"Hande Hoch!" Shouted a soldier, waving his .303 rifle at Joseph's face.

Joseph said in English, "I can't get out. I am wounded in the leg. I surrender," and he then fainted again.

When he recovered consciousness, he found himself on the deck of the strange machine, and the soldiers were in the process of fitting a field dressing over his wound.

"You speak English," said the soldier tying the bandage in place.

"Yes," said Joseph. "I went to school in England before the war."

The soldier said, "My name is Harry Shipley. It looks like you have been shot in the left thigh, and I think that your leg is broken below the knee. It's lucky you fainted, because we were able to get you out of the aircraft while you were unconscious. The tide has now gone out and your plane is sitting on the mud. You were lucky, it looks like you were shot to pieces. Now lie still, and we will get you ashore to hospital. You are lucky, our barracks is just over there," he said nodding toward shore, "and we have a military hospital there. Now let's get going."

Joseph looked around him, "What kind of machine is this. I've never seen one before."

"It's called a Duck, that's DUKW, " said the soldier. "You're lucky. We have one on trial from the Americans, and this is it. It can travel on land and water. You're the first one we've rescued in it, and it's the first time we've used it. We'll soon have you ashore."

They headed for the beach, and Joseph found that the machine drove straight up the beach, through an opening in the barbed wire defenses, onto a road and very soon they were inside an army barracks, drawing much attention from squads of curious soldiers inside the barracks who had never seen such a vehicle before or a Luftwaffe pilot.

Soldiers brought a gurney to the strange machine and Joseph was lifted, crying out in pain as they did so, onto the gurney. He was then wheeled into what must be a military hospital. White coated medical staff took over, and stripped him of his blood soaked flying clothes. He felt a needle enter his arm, and suddenly he was at peace. He felt no pain and his drifted off into a dreamless sleep.

Chapter Nineteen

The attack force of Operation Donnor had been badly mauled by a combination of heavy flak, coming at the aircraft on their approach from three directions, the land, the barracks and the gun platforms in the estuary. Added to this incessant barrage were the swarms of defensive fighters from nearby airfields, who were able to take off, fight and harass, land, refuel, rearm, and return to attack the Swarm of enemy bombers and fighters. Not only were they attacked on their approach to the target, the British fighters guided by the Chain Holm radar installations along that part of the coast, but also over the targets and all the way back to the apparent safety of the Belgian air space.

The British fighters were able, because of Chain Holm, to ambush the Germans well out over the North Sea, and hunt the enemy squadrons, as wolves hunt deer. Nibbling and running, nibbling and running. A tactic which spilt the German formations as they took frantic evasive action, destroying their concerted effectiveness. With more time in the air and easy access to refueling and rearmament, the British defending forces had the advantage.

To be truly effective the bombers had to stay in formation, and carpet bomb their target, whilst the German fighters had to stay within range of the bombers, to protect and defend their charges against the British attackers. The British did not have to win, Joseph realized, all they had to do was prevent the raiders from hitting their targets to win the day.

The ferocious dogfights between the Spitfires, Hurricanes and the German fighters caused fuel critical ME Bf109's and the other German fighters to run their engines on high revolutions and boosters, which greatly limited their time and effectiveness over the target area. The survivors of the German fighters swarms had to curtail their action because they would be left with barely enough fuel to get home, leaving the bombers undefended and vulnerable to attack by the home defenders. Those that did manage to turn for home, were pursued by a dogged and determined home force.

The German losses were the greatest of any mission of the war so far. The enemy bombers were shot out of the sky in what amounted to a turkey shoot. The sky was filled with black clouds of explosions and shrapnel from the intense ground fire . It was not all one sided however. Many of the British fighter force were damaged or destroyed, but the advantage was with the British pilots over their home territory. Those who managed to bail out, would land on home ground. Those wounded, would be treated in their own medical facilities and many would live to fight again.

The German pilots had no such luxury. If they crashed in England and lived, they would be prisoners of war, and lost to the Reich. If their aircraft were damaged they had a long way to return to home base, over inhospitable waters, pursued by a determined enemy, and some would not be able to complete the journey.

Major Fabien von Weiser was out of ammunition. He had shot down two British Hurricane fighters in the melee. He saw their pilot's parachute to the safety of the ground, Petr, his wingman was still with him, but he had been hit and his engine was losing oil, leaving a trail of black smoke, as he fought the controls to keep the aircraft airborne.

Petr heard the calm voice of Von Weiser, easing his panic, "Gain height Petr. I am with you. If your engine gives out with height you might be able to glide in."

"Acknowledged," said Petr, carrying out his instructions, his goggles steamed with sweat.

"I am out of ammunition," said Von Weiser, "but I will stay with you as long as I can. Remember the compass bearing which the E boats are on. Take that bearing and stick to it for as long as possible."

Petr looked around, there were no other aircraft now in sight. He maintained a height of 5000 metres, but his engine started losing power, and his aircraft gradually began to lose the height he had fought for. The black oil and smoke from his engine increased.

"My engine is giving out, " said Petr. His leader acknowledged.

"Keep going, " came Von Weiser's voice. We're 25 kilometers from the Belgian coast, and you're on the correct compass bearing. Oostende – Middelkirke is about 15 minutes away. You can make it."

Petr's temperature gauge was now pushing through the red. He reported this to his leader.

"Keep going, " came the advice. "Only 20 kilometres now."

Suddenly, with a cough and grinding sound, the engine stopped. Petr, as calmly as he could reported this to his leader.

"We are now at 3500 metres, losing about 1000 metres every 3 minutes. I suggest that you dive for 500 metres, to build speed up, and then climb as far as you can. Bunny hopping might give you more distance. I will stay with you, and get on the radio on the other frequency to see if there is an E boat about for you."

After a pause, the voice of Von Weiser came back. "There is an E boat ten kilometres from the coast. They tell me they have picked up three crews so far. Two bomber crews and one fighter pilot. I will stay with you, although I must tell you that my fuel is getting low. When you get near the water, make sure your wheels are up, and glide onto the surface as you have been trained. I will direct the E boat to your position, and hold over you as long as I can. Good luck."

Petr was now at 1000 metres, and dropping fast. He studied the waves, and saw a slight chop on the water. He knew he would not make it to land. His only hope was landing on the water, getting out quickly and into his dingy. He tightened his straps, the surface of the water was coming fast. He just had time to say to his leader, "I hope to see you back a base," he shouted just before he skimmed the surface. His aircraft dug into the water with a smash, water poured over his canopy momentarily blinding him, as he slammed to a sudden stop, his head jerking forward despite the restraints. He hit his nose on the control column. He felt it crack and blood spurted. He was slightly dazed, but instinct took over. He threw open the canopy, pulled out the dingy from beneath his seat, unstrapped and threw himself, clutching the dingy, into the sea.

It was cold, very cold. He pulled the toggle on the gas cylinder and the dingy inflated. He struggled in, fear giving him additional strength despite his now soaked clothing weighing him down. As he did so Von Weiser passed over his head, waggling his wings. He then circled, twice, before, with another wing waggled, he disappeared towards the Belgian coast.

Petr lay, soaked, cold and shivering, in the bottom of the dingy. Seawater slopping over him, further soaking his clothing. The wave motion, after a few minutes, made him nauseous and he was violently sick over the side. The wind was cold. In one way he was lucky the wind was in the north west and would be pushing him towards either the Belgian or French coasts. He looked around. Could see nothing. After a time, shivering from the cold, he began to despair. Then he heard an aircraft overhead. His spirits lifted until he saw a JU88 with its tailfin shredded and one of its engines smoking, heading toward the Belgian coast. It passed low overhead and he heard the spluttering of the engine as the pilot fought to keep his machine in the air. It passed from his sight, and he was alone again.

He felt dreadful. The motion of the dingy kept him nauseous. At that moment he would have cheerful wished for death, but such thoughts were interrupted by the sound of an engine. The light on his floatation vest was flashing, and suddenly large above him, was the welcome shape of a German E Boat. He was rescued. He had never been so glad to see a fellow human being in all his life. He was grappled by a boathook, and brought alongside, where strong hands lifted him aboard. He was frozen. A blanket was thrown around him and a big mug of steaming coffee thrust into his hand by a welcoming sailor. He drank. The taste of brandy pervaded the coffee as he swallowed, feeling a warming glow as the drink went down. He was taken below, into the warm, finding himself among eight other rescued airmen.

One of the German sailors said, "A bomber with an engine on fire passed over us a little while ago. We are now going to look for it. It can't be far away, it was low and must have crash landed."

The E Boat creamed away in the direction of the homeward bound bomber, and there on the horizon they saw the outline of a tailfin just disappearing below the waves. There were two yellow dingies in the water, with four German airmen in them. All four were brought aboard. Two were bleeding badly from wounds and the sailors busied themselves applying field dressings and giving morphine to the injured. The E boat sped onward toward the Belgian coast, which quickly came into view. The airmen were landed at the port of Zeebrugge, where waiting ambulances took the injured away. The uninjured were guided to an office on the quayside, where they were able to warm themselves in front of a glowing pot bellied stove. They were given alcohol laced cocoa to drink, and warm blankets. Petr had made it back. He would live to fight again. He had staunched the bleeding from his broken nose, but bruising had spread across his face which was swelling and showing a nice shade of roseate.

The raid on the port of Harwich was as big a disaster as the raid on Foulness. As the German force closed with their target, guns from Languard Point at Felixstowe on the north side of the harbour opened up, together with the guns on the south side of the estuary at Beacon Hill point. They caught the oncoming force in a deadly cross fire. Two flak ships, moored at the confluence of the River Orwell and the River Stour also joined the fight. The combined firepower against the intruders was powerful and accurate. There were two ships in the harbour, they added to the fire power, making the sky over the harbour laced with shot and shell. Aircraft were hit, some crashed into the sea, others crashed on the nearby peninsulas of Shotley and Felixstowe and some in the mud of Bathside Bay. The real crunch came when the British fighter force of Spitfires and Hurricanes appeared, pecking at the outer edges of the German formations, and dogfighting with the escorting German fighters.

Only a few of the bombers got close enough to release their bombs on the port facilities and the oil refinery off Parkeston Quay. The accuracy was appalling, many of the bombers releasing their loads before turning away in panic for home. Several of the bombs cratered the golf course adjacent to the oil refinery. No doubt to form ponds and bunkers, when landscaped at a later time.

This raid was a failure. What possessed the German High Command to plan it, even as diversionary raid, on such a well defended target, spoke of desperation within the Nazi regime.

The British fighters pursued the enemy far out over the North sea on their return journey, and many aircraft would never make it back to their home base. The day had been a catastrophe, a disaster of planning, timing and execution. The Luftwaffe had been given an almost impossible task, and although some damage had been done, and some losses suffered by the British forces, their losses were nothing against the losses the Luftwaffe suffered.

Out of a bomber force of 100 bombers targeting Foulness Island, 27 were lost. Over 89 aircrew were either killed, wounded or captured. The 40 escorting fighters lost 11 destroyed, 7 crash landed either on land or in the sea. 21 pilots and crew being rescued at sea, some critically wounded.

Whatever secrets Foulness hid from its enemies and its own people, remained a secret. The base remained functional, its operation only marginally effected by the raid. That there had been two raids in three weeks on the same facility only increased local speculation about what was going on there. Its purpose remaining a mystery. Rumours only increasing its mystique.

The Harwich port attack force of 50 bombers, lost 9 destroyed, 5 crashed on land and 3 at sea. The 20 escorting fighters lost 6 destroyed, and 3 crash landed in the sea. 15 pilots and crew were rescued at sea, and 8 pilots and crew were taken prisoner.

Major Von Weiser landed at Oostende-Middelkirke airfield. His ammunition expended, and nearly out of fuel. The attendant ground crews rearmed and refueld his aircraft, and together with the remains of his Staffel, he took off again returning to base at Orly.

Later in the briefing room, he was interviewed by a Luftwaffe Hauptmann of the Intelligence Corps. The other returning pilots were also interviewed in turn.

Von Weiser walked into the mess room where he was served a meal of German sausage and sauerkraut with coffee. He picked at his meal in a desultory way, totally depressed at the outcome of the raid. Missing were his friends Major Wagner and Joseph Mozart, and he didn't know the fate of Petr Muller, although he had seen him in his dingy in the North sea, with an E boat fairly near heading towards where he had crash landed.

Other returning pilots came in, and the atmosphere in the room was depressive. Many others were missing. The butchers bill was heavy. Von Weiser reflected on the raid believing it to be ill conceived and badly planned. He secretly, although he would never say what he felt, blamed the High Command and in particular Hermann Goering, whose brainchild the raid had been.

The following day Von Weiser was cheered to see his wingman, Petr Muller, walk through the door in a bedraggled state. He as alive, and grinned as he saw his leader. His face puffy and swollen, and his nose crooked and sore. They shook hands warmly, Von Weiser saying, "Welcome home Petr. Did you have a good swim?"

"I was sick. So sick. I never want to be a sailor," he moaned. "It was awful."

"What about the raid, " queried Von Weiser.

"That was awful too." Responded Petr. "Did anyone see what happened to Joseph and Major Wagner. "

"I have asked the other pilots, and one thinks he saw Joseph crash land in the sea just off the coast near Foulness Island. I haven't any information about Reinhart Wagner. No one, so far, has any sight of him or knows what happened to him. We have a debrief to go to this afternoon. Be in the briefing room at 1400hrs. The Base Commander wants us there."

Later that morning a Junkers Trimotor JU 52 landed at Orly. An honour guard had hastily formed and the base Commander, General Eberhart Von Ritter, stood to attention, at the head of his staff, as the door opened. He saluted as out stepped a grim faced Reichsmarschall Hermann Goering himself, resplendent in his tailored light grey uniform. Behind him came a small cadre of SS Officers headed by an Oberst in his black and sinister uniform, accompanied by an unknown Luftwaffe General in full uniform.

The party got into a column of staff cars and disappeared toward the headquarters building.

Once inside the building, General Von Ritter and the Rechsmarschall disappeared into the General's office. A tirade of shouting was heard by the staff in the outer office, which went on for a full five minutes.

Goering then opened the door and invited the SS Colonel in. The door closed, and more shouting was heard. A red faced Reichsmarschall then came out, followed by an ashen faced General Von Ritter, escorted by the SS Oberst. Two other SS officers formed up on the General, and he was marched outside to a waiting staff car. In silence, he got in the back of the car, flanked by the two SS Officers, and the SS Oberst got in the front with the driver. The car drove away at speed with its passengers, and was last seen speeding through the gates towards the road to Paris.

The Luftwaffe General who had arrived with Goering was called into the office with the Reichsmarschall, and after a short time, Goering, now all smiles and bonhomie, announced to the staff that General Darius Ahren was the new base commander with immediate effect.

At 1400hrs the pilots and associated staff, were assembled in the briefing room. The room hushed as the door banged open, and in walked

Reichsmarschall Hermann Goering, followed by the new base commander General Darius Ahren. Everyone stood to attention as the party clumped its way to the platform at the head of the room.

Goering stood, feet apart, stocky legs bearing his considerable weight. He surveyed the room, heightening the growing tension.

"Sit," he shouted.

Chairs scraped the floor as the pilots and associated staff sat in silence awaiting the expected wrath of the Reichsmarschall. He sudden beamed a warm false smile. Turning his head to encompass the whole audience.

"The raid on Foulness and Harwich Port was a disaster of planning and concept." He said in a harsh clear voice. "It was badly planned," he repeated, "with little chance of success, and despite the bravery of all you pilots and crew, it failed." He then paused for effect, looking round the audience, cowering them to his will.

"Those responsible for the planning of this disaster have been dealt with. Your commander has been replaced, and I wish to introduce you to your new base commander General Darius Ashren. He will take over immediately. Operation Donnor is now a thing of the past. Put it behind you. The Fuhrer was not pleased, but he believes that his Luftwaffe are the best in the world, and through your efforts the Reich will succeed. I will leave you with your new commander. Heil Hitler, " he shouted, raising his arm in the Nazi salute. "Heil Hitler" he repeated, until he achieved the required response from his audience, and he then stomped from the room, as the ensemble stood to attention.

When he left, the room erupted into a cacophony. Amazed at the sudden departure of their base commander under SS escort. An obvious sign of disfavour.

General Darius Ahren stood. His adjutant called for quiet. When this was achieved the general spoke.

"Gentlemen. This base will resume normal flying duties in two days time. Before that I want to see all flight commanders in my office at 0900hrs tomorrow. We, together, will recover from this disaster. Now take time off until I post flying duties for you all. There will be replacement aircraft and pilots coming in the next two days. Welcome them into our ranks. This is a new beginning, and we will succeed."

Someone, unidentified, in the audience shouted, "What happened to General Von Ritter.

"General Ahren looked around for the culprit, still unidentified, and said in a quiet voice. "He has been reallocated duties on the Russian front."

He then marched from the room, as the ensemble stood again to attention.

Chapter Twenty

Joseph awoke to find he was in a side room on his own, with a uniformed medical orderly sitting beside him. As he turned his head, the man said, "You're awake," stating the obvious. He then pressed a button beside the bed and very shortly a white coated Doctor arrived.

"Good, " said the Doctor, "You are awake. Do you understand English?" He queried.

Joseph repeated that he had been to school in England and could understand and speak the language.

The Doctor, satisfied he was understood, explained. "My name is Doctor Edgar Wheatley. You have been shot in the left thigh, and you have a broken left leg below the knee. We have put you on a drip." Joseph then noticed he had a needle in his right arm connected to a tube to a bottle on a stand. Seeing his look, "It is to help with the pain and blood loss." Continued the Doctor. "However, we have not been able to remove the bullet, and we have no facilities for setting your leg and plastering it here. We have arranged for you to be transferred to a local hospital, provided your airforce hasn't bombed it. Where you will be treated. You will be escorted because old son, you are now a prisoner of war," he said with an ironic smile.

Thirty minutes later he was wheeled to an army ambulance, and driven to Southend General Hospital, a large red brick, Victorian looking establishment on the outskirts of the town. The hospital was busy with casualties from the bombing raid, and Joseph was quickly taken to a private room away from any hostilities from the wounded and grieving civilians. It was feared there might be reprisal action. As it was, he already overheard mutterings of "Bloody Jerries. Why are we treating him before our own, and bloody Nazis bastards, think they rule the world. We'll show 'em."

A while later another Doctor entered the room. He was obviously hostile but his hippocratic oath prevented retribution. "You will be taken to x-ray, and then when we have treated the wounded from your raid, we will treat you. Meantime you are on a morphine drip which will allow you to sleep."

Some hours later, a semi-comatose Joseph was wheeled from the room to x-ray and from there taken to an anti-room waiting surgery. A white coated and masked figure appeared at his side. He felt another prick in his arm and he drifted off, giving in to the welcome anesthetic.

Several hours later he woke. His left leg was in plaster from the knee down, and he had a large bandage round a throbbing left thigh. Standing at the foot of his bed, with light behind him, giving a sort of ethereal glow, stood a uniformed RAF Officer, showing the rank markings of a Squadron Leader.

"It's Joseph, isn't it? Joseph Mozart?"

Joseph squinted, the light confusing his recognition.

"I'm sorry. Do you know me?" said Joseph.

The officer moved away from the light, and a dawn of recognition crossed Joseph face.

"It cannot be. Surely. It's James Cavendish. Good God. Where did you spring from?"

"Well, old boy, you are here because of me. I shot you down. I did not know it was you until I entered this room. I only came to look at the wreckage of your aircraft, and get a trophy from it. Then I was told the pilot was here, so I came to see who I had shot down out of curiosity, only to discover it was an old friend I had shot up. You have changed some, grown up, like we all have, but I studied you when you were asleep, and then recognized you. So you are a pilot like me. Eh!" said Cavendish. "Well it was on the cards. We both enjoyed gliding, and it was obvious we both wanted to fly. What a strange coincidence. As I said, I thought I would come and see my enemy face to face. I didn't realize he would be a friend."

"I can't believe it. You of all people shooting me down. I have many questions. How are you, how long have you been in the RAF. You have done well, a Squadron Leader so young."

"Whoa. Slow down. I will sit a while and tell you all and then you can tell me your story. I'm not after secrets. There will be no thumb screws. You are injured and will be here a while until they transfer you to a prisoner of war camp I suppose. Oh, by the way, I must tell you. I am in contact with an old friend of yours, Robert Kronfeld. He escaped the Nazi's and came to England as you know. He is a Squadron Leader in the RAF. They won't let him carry out combat missions, but he's doing a great job as a test pilot. He is living near Oxford and comes to visit now and again. I will tell him your situation next time I see him. I am based at Hornchurch at the moment. I fly Spitfires."

The two old friends spent two hours catching up and Joseph discovered that Cavendish was now the 5th Earl of Luce. His father having passed away at the beginning of the war. He had inherited the Luce estates in Dumfries and Galloway in Scotland, but his duty in the RAF, in war time, took precedence over family ties.

Once Cavendish left, a uniformed soldier was stationed outside Joseph's room. As he lay there, he felt a sudden wave of home sickness, loneliness and isolation. He was lucky to be alive, he knew, and he wondered how his fellow pilots had fared in the attack, which he now realized was doomed to failure from its beginning. The Thames Estuary was too heavily guarded, and their target was heavily defended from the ground, sea and air. That the British knew that the Luftwaffe were raiding in large numbers, would have been known before the Geschwader's had left the Belgian coast, through their Chain Holm radar defense system. This coupled with the fact that the east of England proliferated in airfields, with many squadrons of defensive fighters just a short flight away, virtually made this a suicide mission. That he had survived amazed Joseph, and despite his wounds, he realized he was fortunate. He was also amazed that it was Cavendish who wounded him and shot him down. There are coincidences in life, and this was the biggest so far in Joseph's. With these thoughts in mind he drifted off to sleep, the drugs taking their effect.

When he awoke, a new Doctor came in his room to check on his patient.

"I hear your father is a surgeon and you are Austrian rather than German, and that you speak English having learned it at school over here. Don't worry Squadron Leader Cavendish told us all about you. He was an old school friend I understand and is quite concerned about you. He wants you treated civilly."

"Yes," said Joseph. "I had to return home and cut my exchange short because of the Anschluss. It took us all by surprise. It changed a lot of things in my country. Many did not want to go to war, but Hitler changed all that. My mother is a Matron at a hospital in Vienna, and my Father was seconded into the Army Medical Corps, and is running a hospital in Belgrade. But I suppose I shouldn't be telling you all this, as I am an enemy."

The Doctor laughed. "In here you are a patient. We endeavor to cure our patients, and once you are able to walk again, you will be transferred to a prisoner of war camp. I'm afraid for you, the war is over. If it helps you are not the only one. There are others who crashed and were captured. We have patched up a few."

This made Joseph wonder about Petr and Major Wagner and Fabien Von Weiser. I hope they survived, thought Joseph. They will be back at base by now. If either Petr or Fabien survived will they tell Analiese or his mother that he had crashed in England. Would they realize he was alive and now a prisoner.

Some days later, Joseph was dozing in his room. The wound in his thigh was healing, the scabbing itched and irritated. He was also irritated by the plaster cast which encased his left leg from knee to ankle.

A man in the uniform of a Squadron Leader in the RAF entered the room. Joseph looked up, immediately recognizing Robert Kronfeld, his hero and gliding world champion, and a fellow Austrian.

"Hello Joseph, " said Kronfeld. "How are they treating you?"

"Well, thank you," said Joseph in amazement. How did you get here? Cavendish told me you were in Oxford."

"I live there, yes. He told me about you and as I am testing a new type of aircraft, I thought I would come and visit. I flew into Southend airport and got a lift here to visit you. I haven't got long, before I have to go back."

Joseph was amazed at seeing his hero once again and grateful for the company of a fellow countryman. They discussed the war, and its effect on Austrians. They discussed Hitler's persecution policies. Kronfeld was one person Joseph thought he could confide in. He told him of the Anschluss, and how it had effected Austria. How the Nazi's had brutalized people who didn't fit the Aryan profile Hitler had set, and how the regime had banned all youth organizations after the introduction of the Hitler Youth.

"I had to join the Hitler Youth just to get to university, " said Joseph. "If you didn't join up, you couldn't get to university and I want to be an architect and Structural Engineer when the war is over. As it is, I only completed two years of my three year course before I was marched to the recruiting office to join up. Because I was a qualified glider pilot they put me in for pilot training in the Luftwaffe. I am not, and never will be a true Nazi. I am Austrian, " he declared with feeling.

Kronfeld told Joseph he had escaped Germany because of the persecution of the Jews, he being Jewish, and he had been able to bring his widowed father out with him. They both now lived in the Oxford area, and he was an RAF Test pilot, but not allowed, because of his faith and background, to go on overseas operations. He was using his considerable flying skills to improve the performance of British aircraft. Doing his bit, as he called it.

He left saying, "I will try to see you again. Good luck. Perhaps after the war we can go gliding again." They shook hands and he waved farewell as he walked out of the room.

At his departure Joseph felt a strange loneliness and feeling of loss. He knew then, that for him, his war was over.

From that moment, Joseph noticed the treatment and contact with the hospital staff improved immensely. Cavendish and Kronfeld obviously had influence.

Chapter Twenty One

A week later, having been laying in his hospital bed for a few days, and graduating to a chair beside the bed, two soldiers walked into his room. They gave him his clothing back, now dry and ironed, and a new pair of trousers, split at the bottom of the left leg to allow room for his plaster cast.

"My name is Bombadier William Stone, Royal Artillery, Shoebury Barracks." Said the Bombadier. "We have come to escort you to a prisoner of war camp. Where you will be held until the end of hostilities."

An orderly came into the room and assisted Joseph to dress, and a wheelchair was produced. The orderly helped him sit in the chair and he was wheeled to a lift, taken to the ground floor, through outer doors to a waiting army lorry. The soldiers help him climb into the back of the lorry. The rear canvass was pulled down and the lorry drove away from the hospital.

After a short journey, the lorry stopped outside the Police Station at Rochford. One of the escorting soldiers got out and came back a short time later with two more German prisoners of war, who climbed in the back of the lorry, one with his arm in a sling, and the other limping badly, accompanied by another two soldiers, one of whom was Captain Bernard Camp, Army Intelligence Corps. He had been put in with the prisoners to overhear what they might say to each other. He spoke, unbeknown to them, fluent German.

Joseph looked up but did not recognize either of the men. As the lorry drove away from the Police Station Joseph introduced himself to the two new prisoners, and found that they were both Leutnant's and pilots who had been shot down on Operation Donnor.

One of the new Leutnant's said, "I don't know what sort of establishment Foulness Island is, but to have us raid it twice in two weeks, it must be a pretty significant target. They were obviously ready for us."

Joseph held his finger to his lips to stop the Leutnant speaking about operational matters, and then steered the conversation to his own experiences of being shot down and taken prisoner, which prompted similar stories from the other two pilots.

Three hours later the lorry stopped. The soldiers led by the Captain, pulled back the canvass and got out. They had arrived at their camp. The wounded Luftwaffe Officers were helped down from the lorry, and ushered into a wooden building which was obviously the Commanding Officer's headquarters.

Joseph looked around. He saw a double barbed wire fence, surrounding lines of Nissan Huts. He saw watch towers, with armed soldiers on each, and he saw a small cadre of RAF Officers standing on a veranda in front of the Headquarters.

An elderly officer bearing the insignia of a Wing Commander stepped forward.

"I understand that one of you speaks English?" He said.

Joseph said, "I do sir."

"Well please translate what I say to the others," and he paused. " Let me introduce myself, I am Wing Commander Hugo Randall, I was a pilot in the first world war, and rejoined to do my bit. This is POW 125 RAF Flixton, in Suffolk, England of course. It is a camp for Luftwaffe Officers, run by the RAF. We hold approximately 300 Luftwaffe personnel. The camp guards are from the RAF, and all are armed. Each watch tower has at least two sentries at all times and is fitted with a Bren Gun covering the compound. You will be assigned accommodation, but I see that all three of you are wounded, and you will therefore spent at least your first night with us, in the medical wing. Once you have recovered from your wounds, you will be allocated a berth in one of the huts. If you behave, and are recovered from your wounds, and if you earn our trust, you may be invited to join outside working parties. Many of our prisoners do, it keeps them fit and active and they like the fresh air. We mainly supply work parties for local farms. You will be fed three meals a day. Breakfast, Luncheon and Dinner, The food is brought from the Mess to your huts by an appointed trustee, and we run some keep fit programs and hobby courses to keep you mentally active, but more of that later. These are my officers," indicating one elderly Squadron Leader and two Flight Leiutenants behind him, "You will get to know us all in time."

He then indicated to a flight sergeant standing behind the prisoners. "Flight, please take these officers to the infirmary. I will see them there later. He then turned away and entered his HQ building.

The Flight Sergeant, with a medical orderly led the prisoners to a Nissan Hut, which was fitted out as a medical centre. Many of the beds were occupied by wounded air crew. Joseph was led to a bed at the far end of the room and laid down.

"The doctor will see you shortly," said the orderly and he left to attend to other duties.

A short time later, a Captain in the Medical Corps entered the room. He approached Joseph, saying, "I am Doctor Maurice Key, RAF medical branch, and I am in charge of this infirmary." He then read the accompanying notes on Joseph's condition, and examined the wound on his leg, leaving the orderly to re-dress it.

"It looks to be healing nicely. You should be up and about within two weeks, and fit enough to leave the infirmary. I will examine your wounds every few days, and when I declare you fit, which might take about six weeks in all. When I take the plaster off then you can volunteer for outside work. I see from your notes that you were a university student before joining up, and you are an Austrian, not German. It says in the notes you went to school in England and speak our language. It also says you know and are friends with two RAF Squadron Leaders."

"Yes," said Joseph. I went to school in England with one of them. We were friends, and the other , who taught me gliding, escaped Germany and is now in the RAF. I count them both as friends, despite the war."

The Doctor looked at Joseph for a long moment. "You may find there are a few committed Nazi's here. Most of the prisoners are normal people, but these few are National Socialist fanatics. We know who they are, be careful of them. They are trouble."

"Thank you for your advice, " said Joseph. "I suppose I am what you might call a reluctant protagonist. But I am Austrian, I love my country and I will do my duty by it. I hope you understand?"

"That's interesting, " said Doctor Key, making notes. "You must be hungry. Lunch will be brought to you shortly, now lie down and rest, Once the healing has taken place we will put you in the care of our physiotherapist." He laughed and said, "He's a sadist by the way," and walked off chuckling.

The days were long for Joseph, who slowly healed. He finally had the leg plaster removed, and found scratching a new pleasure in life. He was then referred to the physiotherapist. He found that the

Doctor had been right about physiotherapy. He was a trained torturer. He made Joseph exercise, pushing him to exhaustion and beyond his pain threshold and he also gave him an exercise routine to follow on a daily basis. The effect was within six more weeks, Joseph had the leg plaster removed, his wound had healed nicely, and he was walking freely, with only a slight limp.

Much improved Joseph was called to the Commandant's office, and then allocated a berth in hut fifteen. He limped through the front door of the hut, to see it sparsely occupied. He saw one of the Leutnant's he had travelled to the camp with sitting on a bed.

"Where is everyone, " queried Joseph.

The Leutnant said, "Most are on work parties. It's voluntary, but a lot work on the farms around here. I expect when you are fit enough they will make the same offer to you. Let me introduce myself. I am Leutnant Paul Schaffer. I was shot down on Operation Donnor like you. I have now been declared fit, and if they offer me work, I will do it. It will pass the time and keep me healthy."

Joseph introduced himself. "I was shot down too. I was shot in the left leg and broke the same leg when I crashed. They picked me up on the mud flats in the strangest vehicle I have ever seen. They say it's called a Duck, and it will travel on land and water."

Joseph was shown a spare bed and locker, and spent a little time settling in. Some hours later the door opened, and eight other men walked in. They were grimy, suntanned and healthy looking. They had all been working on various farms in the neighbourhood. Joseph studied the men as they entered the hut, as they studied him, the newcomer. The last one in caused Joseph to gasp in amazement. He instantly recognized his flight leader, Major Reinhart Wagner. He sprang to his feet,. A wide grin on his face, and in a moment of ecstatic joy hugged his flight leader and danced him round the room. Embarrassed at his unusual demonstration, he ruefully stepped back from his leader and said, "Sorry about that. It's just so good to see you and know that you are alive, and looking so well. Wagner and Mozart, back together again. Who could believe it, " laughing at seeing his friend again.

"What happened to you," asked Wagner. The last I saw of you, you had a Spitfire on your tail, and you were all over the sky trying to shake him off. I tried to come to your aid, but two of them got on my tail. They shot me up and I had to bail out. I got captured by the army, and was brought here. I was lucky, apart from a few scratches and bruises, wasn't injured. I landed in a farm field and three blokes with pitchforks surrounded me. They pinched my parachute. They obviously wanted the silk. My aircraft crashed about three fields away. I saw the smoke and heard it explode. Then what they call the Home Guard came, and took me to the Police, and the army came and collected me. I've been here since. Now I work on a farm for the exercise five days a week."

What happened to you?"

Joseph told him his tale, with the others in the hut listening to what he had to say. Two others in the hut had been captured from the Foulness raid, and one was on the diversionary raid on Harwich Harbour. Joseph was told that there were several other fighter pilots and bomber pilots in other huts who had been on the raids. It had been a disaster for the Luftwaffe. All the pilots had an opinion of the planning and execution and all agreed, to put it mildly, it had been a colossal cock up the odds of being successful with the British air defenses available were minimal.

On a brighter note, Wagner told him of life in the POW camp. It was run by elderly RAF Officers, or Officers recovering from wounds, and there was a certain respect between flyers, even though they were on opposite sides. There were certain German officers in the camp who were committed National Socialists, and out and out Nazi's. He was warned that these would be pointed out to him, and were to be avoid at all costs. They were the fanatics and as a consequence the camp trouble makers.

"What of the farm," asked Joseph. "I would like to get out in the fresh air, and working on a farm is honest labour and would fill the time?"

"Where I go, it's an arable farm, about 500 acres, owned by a family named Ward. It has some sheep and cattle, and cows for milking. The milking is done by a squad of what they call Land Girls. They have a Womans Land Army, and supply woman to do all of the jobs around the farm. The milking, the lambing, gathering in the crops. They wear a sort of uniform of overalls, and a green jumper. Some are very pretty, but we are not allowed to fraternize with them. They work on separate areas the farm. We see them from time to time, but so far we haven't been able to get near them. The family own the farm, and they have two sons, and a daughter. The sons are in the Army, so the old man Ward runs the farm, with his daughter. We don't see much of her except at lunchtime. She and her Mother bring food out to us in the fields. She's very pretty, but mother keeps wary eye on her. They usually give us cider to drink. It's made from apples and is very good. The life is not so bad, and as you say, it's fresh air and welcome exercise, rather than struck in this camp all day. Looking at you, with your broken leg and wound, it will be a little while before you can do farm work, but we can always do with extra help, so perhaps when you are fit again, you can come farming with us."

Joseph, thoughtfully said, "Yes. I would like that. I am better now, the worst part lately was the plaster on my leg. It itched like mad at times. Now the plaster is off, I am having physiotherapy so I should soon be up for the work."

They talked more of their Staffel, and speculated on who had got home after the raid and who might not have done. The shared information provided a sketchy picture of events, none of which was really good news. Joseph told Wagner of his leave, where he had met Von Weiser's family as they lived near his family home, and how they had been invited to a party at their Schloss. He also mentioned Von Weiser's sister, Analiese. Wagner, being an astute reader of human nature picked up the signs that Analiese had certainly stirred Joseph's emotions. He queried this relationship by the merest inclination of his eyebrow. Joseph saw the expression and felt himself colouring up, which made Wagner say, "I see!" In such a way that suggested he knew exactly what Joseph was thinking about Analiese.

Joseph covered up by whispering confidentially, "Anyway, it's academic now. We are prisoners of war. For us, I believe, the war is over, and I for one am reconciled to that fact, I have friends here in England. Funnily enough I was shot down by an old English school friend, he came to see me in hospital, and I don't know if you remember me telling you of Robert Kronfeld, the champion glider pilot. He came to see me. He taught me gliding at one time, and he is now an RAF Officer. He is Jewish and saw trouble coming and fled to England before the war. I have always liked and admired him, and Cavendish, that's the name of the Squadron Leader who shot me down, was a mentor and friend at school in England. His father died and he is now the Earl of Luce in Scotland. They live in a castle like Von Weiser."

Wagner said, "So you have friends in high places here. That could be useful. Perhaps they will tell us how the war is going."

"Judging from the result of the raid on Foulness and Harwich, I would say not very well, " opinioned Joseph.

Wagner shrugged. "You could be right. Anyway, let's get some food. It should be here in a few minutes. We have a duty officer, rotating on a weekly basis, who collects the food from the kitchens. It's usually something like potato soup, and something hot. It's not very much, but it's enough to get by. We keep getting told that there is a war on, and food is rationed. We do better on the farm, at least that fills our bellies."

Joseph brought his issue of eating utensils to the centre table, sitting with the other POW's, and was served potato soup, which he had in a tin mug, and an indiscriminate mash of vegetables and bully beef, in a sort of brown gravy. Not very palatable or interesting but it kept hunger pangs at bay. There was no waste.

Joseph discovered every morning there was a parade, where numbers of inmates were counted. There had been no attempts at escape thus far. It was well known that Britain was an island, and had fought German Forces to a standoff where invasion plans had been scuppered. The whole population was on a war footing, and they would stand out as the enemy on the outside of the camp.

Joseph slept fitfully that night. His wooden bunk, with wooden slats was hard, as was the thin, straw filled mattress. The army blankets were rough to the tough, and the pillows were covered in a rough canvass. Sleeping in such conditions would take a mite of getting used to.

He underwent his first parade. Standing in the cold light an hour after dawn. Shivering in his RAF issue greatcoat, bearing a large white "POW" on the back. The camp Commanding Officer attended the parade, making a speech of welcome to the newcomers. It was just like a first day at school.

They then returned to their huts for a morning meal of almost unpalatable porridge, after which they assembled outside once again. Names were called out, and parties of officers left in trucks to go to various farms, leaving very few personnel within the camp. It was noticeable that there was a small group of what Joseph learned , were the committed Nazi's. They seemed to hang around together, sharing their extreme political views, no doubt boring each other with political dogma and hatred. They were the most watched, and the most disliked in the camp by the guards. Fortunately the group was small in number largely shunned by most of the prison population who although patriotic, were never going to be committed to such an extreme political cause. The vast majority of prisoners saw themselves as victims, caught up in a war which they did not want or did not cause.

Joseph was called, as were several others, for sick parade. They were marched to the medical centre. Another Nissan Hut within the compound, where they were seen again by Squadron Leader Key of the RAF Medical Branch. He gave Joseph and all-over medical examination, and looked at his wounded thigh, and plaster cast.

"The wound is healing nicely. I would say that you would be fit again in about two weeks, if you continue to exercise then we can see about recommending you for some useful work. Perhaps on a farm or factory. Which would you prefer?"

Joseph said, "Farm work I think. The healthy outdoor life is more appealing than a factory."

When the time is right I will make that recommendation, " said the doctor. "Meanwhile, exercise when and where you can, and get some strength back in that leg. I understand there is a fitness instructor among your number and he runs classes. I should find out who he is and join his class, meantime keep up with the exercises I gave you."

Joseph was heartened by the news his injuries were healing and he immediately asked to join the fitness classes. Leuntnant Rudolf Finck was the fitness guru, and he set Joseph a different set of low level exercises, which would strengthen his dormant limbs. Joseph found these exercises difficult at first, but after a few days, his fitness began returning. At the end of two weeks came the great day. The camp doctor called for him and he pronounced Joseph fit enough to work. The crowning glory came when the Doctor produced a pair of trousers and proper POW overalls, without a slit in the leg, which he gave to Joseph. "Now go and register for farm work, if that is what you want," said the Doctor.

Joseph walked out of the medical centre, and reported to the main camp office. The adjutant there, an elderly Flight Lieutenant, looked at his schedules, and at the list of those assigned to various farms I the area.

"I think you can go with Major Wagner and the others from your hut to Maylands Farm, Ilketshall St Andrews. It's a mixed arable and dairy farm, with some sheep, and cattle. Some 10000 acres, run by George Ward and his family. He is a member of the Home Guard. He has some staff from the Woman's Land Army there. They live in quarters in and around the farm. His sons are in the army and away fighting, and he has one daughter. You will not be allowed to fraternize with the females there. You will be working in separate areas. The farmer will assign you your duties and work schedule. You will work from 0800hrs to 1800hrs, five days a week, with a break for lunch which will be provided for you by the farmer and his family. You will be provided with work overalls and wet weather gear. Major Wagner will be responsible for the behavior of your party. There are certain of our inmates who are not allowed to do outside work. These you will know about because they are not allowed out of the camp. Do a good job and your life will improve. The food on the farm, I am told, is superior to that in the camp. You will start next Monday. Any questions?"

"I am happy to work on the farm, but I was wondering if it is at all possible to notify my family that I am alive, even though I am a POW. They will obviously be extremely worried not knowing."

"Take this card, " said the Flight Lieutenant. "You will be allowed to write that you were shot down and crashed. That you are alive and well and a POW. The card will be censored by one of our German speaking officers. You will not be allowed to say where you were shot down, but you can reassure your family you are uninjured. The card will be forwarded to your family via the Red Cross, who operate the system of notification both for the Germans and us. You will not be allowed to say where you are held. Fill it out and bring the card back to me and I will see that it goes out through channels."

"Thank you, " said Joseph. My mother will be relieved to hear I am alive and well," hoping at the same time that she would pass the news on to Von Weiser and his beautiful sister.

Chapter Twenty Two

At 0730hrs the following Monday, after parade and breakfast, Joseph found himself in a party, led by Major Wagner, wearing his newly issued overalls and carrying his wellington boots and wet weather gear. They marched to the main gate of the compound, and were counted onto a lorry, with two armed guards, and driven to Maylands Farm, where they were met by the farmer himself.

Joseph was the only newcomer to the work party, and Major Wagner in his halting English attempted to introduce Joseph to the Farmer. Joseph took over the introduction as he spoke fluent English.

"My name is Joseph Mozart, " he said to the Farmer. "I am a pilot and was shot down over the coast. I was wounded in the leg, but now I am well enough to work."

"Good," said the farmer, "My name is George Ward. This is Maylands Farm of some 10000 acres, and we run cattle, sheep, and a dairy herd as well as arable crops. My wife does the cooking, assisted by my daughter, so you will be fed here during the day, usually eating in the fields unless the weather is bad, in which case you will eat in the barn. The farm is divided by a road. You prisoners will work this side of the road, and I have a few of the Woman's Land Army working on other parts of the farm. There will be no fraternization. Understand?"

Joseph nodded.

"We will bring the drinks and food to you in the work areas. There are milk churns around the fields and we keep fresh drinking water in them. So you need not go thirsty whilst you are working. We will bring the food out to you in the tractor or using horse and trailer, and each time there will be a head count. If you go missing, then the whole party will be returned to camp until the missing person is found. If you do go missing, you will not be allowed to work here again. Understand?"

Joseph nodded again.

"Right," said Mr Ward. "Major Wagner will show you your duties. Work well and we will get on. Don't let me or the others down." He then chuckled, "This is the first time I've known a Mozart and Wagner work together."

Joseph shrugged at the jest he had heard many times from others who knew them both. The joke to both was now a little thin.

Joseph was set to work hoeing between rows of young potatoes. Row upon row, in a 10 acre field. The work was repetitive and boring, but it was in the fresh air and out of the camp.

At 1230hrs a carthorse, pulling a cart came onto the field. The horse was being driven by a sun tanned young lady of about 20, with long dark hair, tied at the back into a pony tail. She was medium height, well built, and despite the lack of makeup, she had a natural earthy beauty, her movements suggesting rude health. Sitting alongside her was an older woman, who from her looks, was the mother of the girl doing the driving. She was middle aged, with a hint of grey in her hair, but she had obviously been as good looking as her daughter when she was younger. They stopped at the edge of the field, and started to unpack a wicker basket.

Major Wagner called a halt to the work party, and walked over to the trailer, the other prisoners following him.

"Good day Frau Ward, Fraulin Martha," said Wagner in his halting English. "It is time for break, yes?"

"Yes, " said Mrs Ward. "I have brought cheese, pickles, new baked bread, butter and cake. There are apples and pears. Please have your men help themselves."

"Let me introduce our newest recruit, " said Wagner, beckoning Joseph forward. "This is Leutnant Joseph Mozart. He was in my flight and was wounded in the leg. He crashed and broke his leg so he has been recovering. He is now part of our work party."

Indicating Joseph. He said, "Joseph this is Frau Ward and her daughter Martha."

Joseph stood to attention, slightly bowed and with a smile said in perfect English, "I am very pleased to meet you. You have a lovely farm." He noticed as he introduced himself a flicker of interest from Martha, and a challenge in her eyes.

"You speak English," said Martha?"

"Yes, " said Joseph " I spent a year at school in London on an exchange from my school in Vienna, until the Anschluss. Then I had to go back."

"So you are Austrian," said Martha, showing more interest.

Her mother, noticing the daughter's attention to the handsome young aviator, quickly intervened. "Please take one of the food parcels and sit and eat. We will bring you cider. Tea and coffee are in short supply, with the war and all. We make cider, so I hope you will drink that instead. Be careful, you will only get a half pint, it's home made and powerful."

Joseph sipped the proffered cider. It was slightly sharp and he could tell it was fairly alcoholic, but it was delicious and he could feel a warm glow as it went down. A powerful brew indeed.

As he sat eating his delicious home made cheese, with home made pickles, and warm bread, he felt Martha's eyes upon him. He looked up and caught a frisson of interest in her eyes, before she glanced quickly away. He ate his apple, as he sat in the sun, taking in the tranquility of the rural scene, until he heard a roar of aero engines and a flight of Spitfires appeared on the horizon, obviously to the trained eye, in a landing pattern.

He said in German to Major Wagner, "There is an airfield nearby?"Wagner said, "Yes. RAF Flixton. It's an operational Spitfire base. I have seen them taking off and landing quite often."

With lunch over, the ladies gathered the empty tankards and detritus of the meal. They climbed back on the cart and drove off towards the farm buildings in the distance. Martha looking back, saw Joseph following their departure and she smiled at him, until admonished by her mother,

The men from the camp returned to their work, as the cart disappeared toward the Farmhouse.

Mrs. Ward looked at her daughter, with a questioning expression.

"I saw you making eyes at that young prisoner. Don't think I don't know what's in your mind young lady. Forget it. He's a German and they are the enemy."

"He's not German, he's Austrian," said Martha defensively, pouting. "He's nice looking."

"Look," said her mother. "He is a prisoner of war. He may be Austrian, and very polite, but he is still an enemy pilot, and he's been shooting at our men. There's no future in it. So forget him. There's a war on, and he is here to help us grow food for our country. Be warned," she emphasized with feeling.

At the end of the day, an RAF lorry turned up at the farm and collected the work party from the POW

Camp. The accompanying officer counted his charges as they boarded the vehicle. The family were there to see them off, and Joseph could feel Martha's eyes on him as the lorry departed.

The same routine was followed over the ensuing days and weeks, with the same prisoners working on the same farms. The crops grew as the weeks went by, and the summer came with warm sunny days. It was an idyllic country life. The work varied according to the time of year and the days working schedule. Joseph became tanned and fit, especially so, as at weekends when he was confined to camp, he joined the boxing club which the prisoners had started, resuming a passion for the sport he had since his school and university days. He was now a middle weight, and took part in some bouts organized for the entertainment of the other prisoners and the RAF guards, becoming the camp champion at his weight.

Although confined, the prisoners were treated well and with respect by the RAF personnel assigned to guard them. Their meals were basic, and not very substantial, they were definitely fed better, with tastier food, on the farm at lunchtime.

As the summer progressed, so Joseph felt the presence and attention of Martha. She appeared to take every opportunity to seek him out. The other POW's noticed the extra attention he was getting, especially when she took every opportunity to be in his presence.

Over the weeks she learned a lot about Joseph's background, and his family. She was fascinated by details of how and where he grew up, and how he had graduated into the Luftwaffe. She also extracted the details over the ensuing weeks about his crash on the Essex coast, Although she tried to conceal her interest from the other POW's and her parents, it was noticeable that she was drawn to Joseph, and with all the attention he was receiving, he was gradually being enmeshed like a fly caught in a spiders web. She was attractive, in a robust healthy way. Her long hair shimmering in the summer sun, her healthy tanned face and arms, her ample eye- catching breasts. Her fitness and stamina working on the farm, all added to her growing allure, especially as she was the only female of his own age Joseph had contact with. However the ever present father and mother, prevented any progress to her obvious attraction and amorous inclinations. In the height of summer with the sun beating down on a sweating workforce, pitching sheaves onto the cart, with

Martha driving. Joseph, shirt off allowing his now tanned muscular torso to be exposed to the heat, was on the cart behind Martha, as the carthorse plodded the field, working each sheaf into place to secure the load. As he worked, Martha surreptitiously watched him, admiring muscles rippling with effort as he heaved the sheaves into place, and her pulse quickened at the sight of his lithe body as he stood swaying to balance on the straw laden cart. She was moonstruck. Joseph was aware of her attention, and he couldn't suppress a feeling of interest. He was after all a young man, in the flush of health and vigour It had been many months since he had been alone with a woman, especially one who was making her interest in him so obvious. In an earthy sort of way she was attractive, and he couldn't deny a physical interest. However, the ever present family was a dash of cold water to any amorous intentions on his part. The chaperoning effect of her parent's presence goaded Martha to even more cunning and secretive efforts to make Joseph aware of her attraction. She was smitten, but frustrated, and she knew any open show of affection toward Joseph would result in his removal from the workforce. This was the last thing she wanted or needed to happen. It was heart rending for her. The more she was denied the more frustrated she became.

They walked the horse and cart towards the farmhouse, followed by two others pitching sheaves as they went. Just in front of the yard were haystacks made previously, and the beginnings of another, started that morning. The cart was brought up against the low stack and Joseph began heaving sheaves from the cart onto the stack. The two POW's who had followed, climbed onto the stack and began positioning the sheaves as they arrived from Joseph. Mr Ward, the farmer, watched, as the men worked. His daughter disappeared into the house and came out with a jug of cool refreshing cider. They emptied the cart onto the stack, and the workers climbed down to slake their thirst with the delicious cider. Joseph then went to the horse trough and sluiced his upper body, cupping the water over his head, cooling his body and his rising ardour. He returned to the cart, water dripping from his head and torso, sunlight making his wet body shine with health. Martha was watching his every move. The sight of his naked and tanned upper body and dark hair dripping water, stirred her emotions to the point of absolute frustration. She looked for her father, and he stood close by, watching the men. His eyes mainly on Joseph, as if he could read his daughter's thoughts. She quickly recovered herself, and started the cart back to the fields, leaving her father with a questioning look on his face. As Joseph regained his place on the cart, some of the women from the Land Army entered the yard and started giggling and making open lewd remarks and nudging each other, upon seeing the half naked men, sweating in the sun. They were starved of male company, most of their men friends having joined the armed forces. Male company was a rarity and their open admiration was something which would be inappropriate in other times, but the girls, who were carrying out an essential wartime role felt the emancipation allowed them a hitherto denied freedom of expression and thought. They were not to be denied their new status.

The work day came to a close, with the new stack completed, and the POW workforce weary from their labours, gathered in the farmyard waiting for transport back to camp. They were handed another cooling drink of cider by the farmer's wife. The lorry arrived to take the POW party back to camp, and again the land girls appeared in the yard, catcalling and waving to the prisoners as they departed. Mr. Ward remained in the yard until the men departed, then turned and scowled at the girls, admonishing them for their lewd behavior, with a disapproving look, until they turned and walked off, laughing, unconcerned, to their own accommodations.

The summer of 1942 was hot. Life between the camp and the farm became a routine for the farmer and his family, the land girl workforce and the prisoners of war. Joseph was grateful for the days he spent working on the farm. It filled his day with interest, and the physical work kept his fitness at a high level. The working conditions, considering the circumstances, were good. They were treated well. He was very aware of the increasing attention he was receiving from the farmer's daughter, but the presence of her parents made him wary of being caught alone with her, as he knew it would incur the wrath of her father and have consequences. The other prisoner's knew of the special attention Joseph was getting from Martha. Some were envious and others amused by her determination.

The harvest was nearing an end. The haystacks were mostly complete. The livestock had produced their young, and the prisoners were now more proficient at their duties. Joseph found himself on the cart with Martha again, gathering and stacking the sheaves onto the final haystacks of the season. Martha was driving the cart as usual, with Joseph clinging to the load as it swayed behind the plodding horse, toward the farmyard. They stacked the final sheaves. Leaving Joseph to finish the stack, Martha disappeared into the barn. She called Joseph to join her. Curious, Joseph walked into the barn to find himself alone with her.

She clung to him, taking him by surprise. He pulled away, fearful of being found in her arms by the watchful parents.

Seeing his hesitancy, she whispered in a low lustful voice, "They've gone to market. We are alone at last." She then kissed him with a passion he had not experienced for a long time.

He came up for air, from the passionate embrace. Fearfully he looked around, torn between arousal and panic.

"The other's will know what is going on, " said Joseph. "We had better get back."

She forcefully kissed him, deeply and passionately, until his resistance melted in the fire of their mutual arousal.

He lost his equilibrium. He was a young and passionate man after all, and he gave in to the moment. Desire overcoming fear.

They lay on the straw in the back of the barn. He felt her body against his. Her hands ran over his naked torso, feeling the taught muscles of his chest. She unfastened her blouse, and Joseph gasped at the sight of her gleaming, sweat sheened breasts. He was now beyond reason. She reached for him. She guided him. He fumbled her out of her dungarees. They kissed deeply, their breathing became torrid, their tongues playing and darting. Joseph was lost, he could not stop if he wanted to and at this moment that was the last thought in his mind. They came together. It was all over too quickly. Both lay in the straw gasping at their temerity. Fear returned to Joseph's mind as logical thought started to return, his gasping breath returning gradually to a more sedate rhythm. His hot and sweaty body started to cool in the shade of the barn. The moment of high passion slowly faded, and the realization of what had occurred hit him like a dowsing of cold water. He was remorseful, felt guilt, shame, but at the same time elation. She was a good looking lusty girl, and she had been the instigator of their moment. She laid there, smiling a satisfied smile.

"I've wanted you ever since I first saw you. Don't worry. No one will know. It was wonderful and I'm glad it happened." She said,

"But your parents, " said Joseph, his fear of discovery returning.

"They will not be back for some time. It was over too quickly. I want more. We have time my love." She smiled lasciviously, her arms outstretched to entice him back to her embrace.

Joseph stood. "No. It's too risky. The others will be looking for us. We must go."

She pouted, "Come back to me." Showing a pleading expression.

"No," said Joseph, forcefully. "It cannot be. The others will talk. Your parents have been good to me." He quickly dressed himself before she could break his resistance down again, and walked outside. Relief at his decision dampening the fire in his brain.

Martha, sullenly, dressed herself and followed. "There will be other times," she whispered. "I can wait," she said with feeling.

Joseph splashed water over his heated body from the horse trough in the yard. This helped to cool the fire of passion which had coursed through his body just moments ago. If the others of the work party had noticed he might have to suffer their ribald comments and teasing, but he felt sure that they would keep what they knew to themselves even though some would envy him.

He went back to work in the fields. No one said anything to him, but he suffered one or two knowing stares from his colleagues, particularly Major Wagner, which made him feel uncomfortable. Martha on the other hand, carried on as if nothing had happened.

Mr and Mrs Ward returned later in the afternoon, towing a trailer. They had bought a ram at the local market. His task would be to father a new breed of lambs the following year. Seeing the ram unloaded, Joseph could not help but compare the destiny of the ram, to his own actions in the barn. Had he been cornered by Martha to fulfill a similar earthy function? He wondered.

On the journey back to camp Major Wagner looked at Joseph, with a knowing smile on his face. "You were a long time in the farmyard?" He whispered.

"Yes," said Joseph, "We had to sort the straw out. It was all over the place."

He hoped that this would be the end of Wagner's curiosity.

More days went by in a round of hot weather and toiling under the summer sun. Joseph went to work fearing his illicit association with Martha would be known by her parents, his colleagues or the Land Girls who, when together, were prone to calling out, whistling and making loud, often rude, comment, particularly targeting the POW's. As time passed, Joseph began to feel more comfortable as nothing was said, and Martha did not repeat her behavior. It was a false hope however, as there burned within Martha a desire to further their relationship, she was just waiting for an opportunity, such as the previous time when her parents had left her alone on the farm. She had every Intention to continue her pursuit of Joseph. She indicated this to him surreptitiously by secret smiles, gestures and longing looks, which made Joseph jumpy and nervous of discovery.

Her opportunity came when again her parents left the farm to go shopping in the nearby town of Bungay. Joseph was working in the fields, cutting cauliflowers with the other prisoners. They were putting them in sacks, and Martha, again using the horse and cart was collecting the filled bags from the fields, and stacking them in the barn. She called on Joseph to help, and he assisted in the loading of the cart and then accompanied her, with much trepidation, to the farm yard to help unload. They pulled into the barn, and immediately Martha flew into his arms. He looked around in panic, looking for who might be around, but could see no one. She kissed him, long and passionately, her tongue darting to caress his, her hands all over his body, feeling him both outside and inside his clothing. She could feel his arousal, and continued until her was past the point of no return. They laid on the straw in the barn, tearing at each other's clothing, inhibitions gone, fear of discovery gone, they made frantic and wildly physical love. Satiated, they both lay in the straw, gasping, rimed with sweat. The slow realization of what had happened again came to Joseph in a wave of both fear and some satisfaction. Never the less he dressed quickly leaving her staring at his body as he frantically fumbled buttons and belts. He sloshed water over his face, disconcerted at her apparent ease, when he was in a frantic state of remorse and panic.

Finally she smiled and slowly dressed herself, whilst he mentally urged her to restore her clothing and equilibrium to normal before anyone became suspicious of their behavior.

They finally left the barn to return to the fields, what they didn't see was Margaret Judd, one of the Woman's Land Army assigned to the farm, enter the yard as they emerged, disheveled, from the barn. Deprived of contact with the opposite sex, Margaret stared from concealment, envy and jealousy raging through her. Why should the farmer's daughter, reap all the benefits of a man in her life, especially of one so handsome, when she had no male friend in her own life. Seething, she stewed with resentment and determined when the time was right to do something about it.

Martha and Joseph, unaware they had been spotted, returned to the fields, where Martha distributed food to the workers, who sat around on the filled sacks, and on the cart whilst they ate.

Joseph attempted to appear normal, but his heart was racing. Particularly when Major Wagner looked at him in a meaningful and understanding way, with a wistful smile playing around his lips. Joseph tried to appear casual, but inside he was in torment. It had happened again, and he was really pushing his luck, but he didn't know how to get out of the situation. Martha held all the trump cards.

At the end of the day, the POW's returned with the laden cart to the farmyard. Mr Ward and his wife had returned from their shopping trip, and were talking to the group of Land Army girls in the farm yard. Margaret Judd was one of the group, and when she saw Joseph and Martha Ward with the other POW's, she again felt envy and resentment.

The RAF lorry arrived and the prisoners climbed into the back to return to camp, leaving Mr Ward talking to the head girl, surrounded by the all female group.

Unaware, she and Joseph had been seen. Martha went into the farmhouse, leaving her Father talking to the Land Army group. She saw Margaret Judd single out her father as the other girl's were leaving and they had a short conversation, at the end of which Mr Ward looked furious. He stormed into the house, his face like thunder, calling for his daughter. Shouting was heard coming from the farmhouse kitchen. Doors slammed, crying and screaming could be heard, and then all went silent.

Epilogue

After morning parade at the Flixton POW Camp, Joseph and the others walked toward the lorry to taking them to work another day on the farm.

Wing Commander Hugo Randall appeared at the gate. Gesturing to Joseph, he walked with him to the camp headquarters, leaving the other POW's to leave without him.

Once inside his office, the Wing Commander turned abruptly, stood in front of Joseph and said, "I have had an irate farmer, Mr. Ward, in my office complaining about you. He has made some very serious charges about your behavior with his daughter."

Joseph paled at the accusation.

"Is, it true that you have been having a relationship with his daughter Martha, behind Mr Ward's back?"

Joseph, confused and taken completely by surprise, took a step back.

"Stand still when I'm speaking to you." Barked the Wing Commander. "Well is it true. Don't lie to me. Have you had a relationship with his daughter, behind his back?"

"Well", said Joseph, attempting to prevaricate, "She, I mean we, have had a sort of liaison."

"Liaison, " shouted the Wing Commander, glowering furiously. "What does that mean. Have you or have you not had a relationship with Martha Ward?"

"Well, yes. In a way. I suppose."

"You suppose. In a way. What does that mean. Have you or haven't you?" Questioned the Wing Commander, raging at Joseph.

Joseph hung his head, cheeks reddening as he said, "Yes. We have had a bit of a fling. It wasn't me that started it."

"That's not very gentlemanly Leutnant. Whoever started it, it's happened. You can't go back to that farm. You were lucky the farmer didn't shoot you." He said softening, now more amused than threatening.

"Fraternization is strictly forbidden. I have no alternative but to stop you going back to that farm, and I also have to remove you forthwith from this camp. You cannot stay here. You will remain in camp until I have made the necessary arrangements. Gather your possessions. You are leaving. Today!"

Within four hours, an ashamed Joseph found himself on board a lorry, between two RAF Corporals of the RAF Police, being driven out of camp. He had not been told his destination. All he had been told was that it would be a long drive.

Three hours later the lorry pulled in through the main gate of RAF Scampton in Lincolnshire. Joseph was taken out of the lorry and placed in the guardhouse, where he slept that night. He felt isolated, lonely and missed the companionship of his previous POW friends. He spent a miserable night, in isolation, listening to the ravings of a drunken airman in the next cell, who kept him awake most of the night singing ribald and lewd songs.

A tired Joseph was fed at 0600hrs the following day then, together with his escort, he re-boarded the lorry, and they set off again. His guards, not understanding that he spoke fluent English, were talking about his misdemeanors involving the farmer's daughter. Laughing together, possibly in envy, lewdly suggesting what might have occurred. Joseph, highly embarrassed, kept silent.

Five hours later the lorry came to a halt at the main gates of RAF Kingtown, just north of Carlisle. The base was an operational elementary flying training school. Again Joseph was housed in the guardhouse overnight. This time he was lucky. There were no other inmates and he slept fitfully. He was again roused at 0600hrs and after a quick breakfast and ablutions, he was on the move again, with the same escort.

Three hours later the lorry stopped outside the gates of a POW Camp. Once the RAF Police escort had identified themselves and their charge, the lorry was allowed through the gates, where it stopped in front of a headquarters building. There was a light dusting of snow on the ground, and noticeably colder than his previous camp in Suffolk. The escorting RAF Police Officers marched a shivering Joseph into the Camp Commandant's office. Where stood, behind a desk, was an elderly RAF Squadron Leader. He was in full uniform, with bristling moustache.

Joseph stood to attention and saluted the officer. Salute returned he patiently waited whilst the Squadron Leader, read the accompanying paperwork, then eyed him slowly up and down, before saying.

"Welcome to POW Camp 103. I am Squadron leader Duncan McKay. You are now in Luce, in Dumfries and Galloway, Scotland. Our camp is situated on the Earl of Luce estate. We have 3000 prisoners of war, most are Luftwaffe Officers, but we also have a large population of Italian aviators. If you behave, we have a scheme whereby we provide workers for the Luce estate, mostly forestry, but some arable, some sheep and cattle. There are also two farms on the estate, and you can, if you behave, work on the estate, or on the farms. However, I understand that you have been moved from your previous camp because of indiscretions with the farmer's daughter. That will not be tolerated here. There will be no liaison with female civilian personnel, other than work contact. Understand?"

"Yes, sir. I understand. I speak English," said Joseph, colouring. The two RAF Policemen looked at one another. They now realized he spoke and understood English and had known what they were talking about throughout the journey.

McKay said, "I don't know what kind of pull you have here. But someone has seen to it you were transferred here by special request. Do you know why?"

"Possibly, " said Joseph. "It may be because I went to school with James Cavendish in England, and I understand he inherited the Earldom. Co-Incidentally, he was the one who shot me down."

McKernzie said, "Your record shows you were wounded."

"Yes, " said Joseph, "Cavendish shot me in the leg and I broke the same leg when I crash landed. I was lucky he could have killed me. A little higher and I would be talking in a higher voice."

McKenzie laughed, a red faced spluttering laugh, moustache bristling in amusement.

"It's a tangled web weave!" said a sage and knowing McKay. "Welcome to Luce! Here, you must behave."

Later, as he laid in his bunk, in the darkness of a cool northern night, he had a long moment of reflection on his life's path so far. Here he was, a prisoner of war, having been shot down over enemy territory, where he had friends with whom he had no feelings they were his enemy. He was fighting for a cause which he had no empathy with, only fighting because if he had not joined in the conflict he would have been labelled a traitor by his own countrymen. All he really wanted in life was to become an architect and structural engineer, to fly, live and love in peace with his fellow man, and look forward to the future. What he was currently living through was incarceration and a very uncertain future. He really was a reluctant protagonist.

Printed in Great Britain
by Amazon